Praise for *Something in the Water*

A *New York Times* bestseller
Nominee for Goodreads Choice Award: Best Debut Author
Finalist for the ITW Thriller Award for Best Debut Novel

"A psychological thriller that captivated me from page one. What unfolds makes for a wild, page-turning ride! It's the perfect beach read!"
    —REESE WITHERSPOON (Reese's Book Club pick)

"Deftly paced, elegantly chilly . . . [Catherine] Steadman brings . . . wit, timing and intelligence to this novel. . . . A proper page-turner."
    —*The New York Times*

"A darkly glittering gem."
    —*Kirkus Reviews* (starred review)

Praise for *Mr. Nobody*

"Twisty . . . a highly imaginative tale tinged with Hitchcockian tension and kinetic pacing . . . There's a good chance [Steadman's] intelligently descriptive, written-for-TV-and-film writing style grew out of her experiences in front of a camera. Her literary instincts are spot on, and the protagonists she creates feel as alive as some of the characters she's inhabited on film."

—*The Washington Post*

"Ample twists and a rollicking pace make [this] a perfectly thrilling read."

—*Vanity Fair*

"A mesmerizing psychological thriller . . . Steadman's story is wholly unique and exceedingly well executed. Suspense is peppered in all the right places, and every bread crumb dropped throughout the story returns in wildly imaginative ways."

—Associated Press

Praise for *The Disappearing Act*

"Stylish, riveting, hugely atmospheric—I couldn't put it down."
—Lucy Foley, author of *The Guest List*

"Pure catnip for the soul."

—CAROLINE KEPNES, author of the You series

"Page-turning . . . tackles the dark side of Hollywood."

—*Entertainment Weekly* (The Best Thrillers)

Praise for *The Family Game*
A *New York Times* Editors' Choice

"The Holbecks are what you might come up with if you took the Roys from *Succession* and blended them with the Murdochs, the Macbeths, and the Borgias. . . . Let the fun begin!"

—*The New York Times Book Review*

"Both sharply modern and timeless."

—FLYNN BERRY, *The Washington Post*

"Be prepared for a nail-biting roller-coaster of a ride . . . classy and ingenious."

—B. A. PARIS, *New York Times* bestselling author
of *Behind Closed Doors*

BY CATHERINE STEADMAN

Something in the Water
Mr. Nobody
The Disappearing Act
The Family Game
Look in the Mirror

LOOK
IN THE
MIRROR

LOOK
IN THE
MIRROR

A NOVEL

CATHERINE STEADMAN

BALLANTINE
BOOKS
NEW YORK

A Ballantine Books Trade Paperback Original

Copyright © 2024 by Catherine Steadman
Book club guide copyright © 2024 by Penguin Random House LLC

Published in the United States by Ballantine Books,
an imprint of Random House, a division of
Penguin Random House LLC, New York.

BALLANTINE BOOKS & colophon is a registered
trademark of Penguin Random House LLC.

LIBRARY OF CONGRESS CATALOGING-IN-PUBLICATION DATA
Names: Steadman, Catherine, author.
Title: Look in the mirror: a novel / Catherine Steadman.
Description: New York: Ballantine Books, 2024.
Identifiers: LCCN 2024020237 (print) | LCCN 2024020238 (ebook) |
ISBN 9780593725764 (trade paperback) | ISBN 9780593725740 (Hardcover) |
ISBN 9780593725757 (Ebook)
Subjects: LCGFT: Thrillers (Fiction) | Novels.
Classification: LCC PR6119.T436 L66 2024 (print) | LCC PR6119.T436 (ebook) |
DDC 823/.92—dc23/eng/20240510
LC record available at https://lccn.loc.gov/2024020237
LC ebook record available at https://lccn.loc.gov/2024020238

Printed in the United States of America on acid-free paper

randomhousebooks.com
randomhousebookclub.com

2 4 6 8 9 7 5 3 1

Book design by Elizabeth A. D. Eno

For Celeste. Don't read anything into this—I just love you.

Who is the third who walks always beside you?
I do not know whether a man or a woman
But who is that on the other side of you?

—T. S. Eliot, "The Waste Land," 1922

LOOK
IN THE
MIRROR

CHAPTER 1
NINA

The letter must have sat unopened for a month on your abandoned hall table as things carried on around it, the correspondence inside quietly waiting for me to find it.

I look down at its crisp envelope as it rests on my black-clad knee, the grain of its paper heavy, expensive, everything about it signaling that the correspondence contained within is *substantial*, *important*, and I wonder how I could have missed it.

But I have been busy with you: coroners, certificates, funerals, and memorials. The business of losing a father is a full-time, short-term contract with limited perks and a clear cutoff point. Though the admin thankfully fills the sudden gulf of hours.

The letter gathered dust in the worn leather letter holder where you always kept mail, while I tried to impose order on the inevitable chaos that a death leaves in its wake. There is chaos left behind even when the person who is gone was a meticulous genius, like you. And you *were* a genius, or as close as

I'll ever come to knowing one, the most fastidiously brilliant man I have ever known.

But the truth is, even you, with all the possible permutations of your thoughts, the clarity of your mind, were still not fully prepared to go. Of course. You were human, you couldn't possibly have thought of everything. Or perhaps you did think of everything and you left things deliberately undone in order to give me purpose. In which case you succeeded, because I have allowed events to carry my full weight along this past month. And I looked for you, and found you, in everything after they told me you were gone.

The obituaries were well researched, kind, kingmaking, even if the kingdom you presided over was a small one. A rarefied one. Your books were collected by the university as your wishes stipulated. A few friends and colleagues were moved to receive what objects and chattels you left for them. Your clothes were dry-cleaned and given to the charities of your choice, your essentials cleaned and distributed.

Death, it turns out, to those left behind, is an activity centered around the cataloging and dispersal of material objects.

I put the house on the market as per your wishes. You knew that I would not, could not, live in it. That it would always be *your* house and as much as I love you, *loved* you, you knew it is not healthy to live in a parent's shadow. And we both know you cast a long shadow.

The rituals, the process, of bereavement held me, protected me from the simple inescapable fact that it all boils down to . . . I am now alone.

I was too busy to notice the letter. And now I see—alone after the party—that perhaps I have been too busy all my life. I was too busy to find someone of my own, to make a life for myself. After all, I had you.

But now, in the silence of the freshly emptied house, I do

not have you. And I am not busy. I am whatever the opposite of busy is . . . Directionless? In search of mental employment? In search of a sign? Anything to distract me again—to avoid the yawning void—to not feel the full force of the fact that *I am where I am.*

I am a thirty-four-year-old literary academic with inherited wealth and no one to share it with. A chuckle bubbles up inside me and echoes through the empty house as I think of the Magic 8 Ball you bought me for my tenth birthday, the one I demanded. You did not want to get it for me, believing that even children should not put faith in randomness, nor look for patterns in curls of smoke. "Chaos holds no answers," you told me, a child of nine. "Look for the answers to your questions in the structure of things," you told me. "That's where meaning lies." And of course you were right, though you bought the Magic 8 Ball for me anyway after tears and the promise of more applied study. I promised to achieve and you listened.

I cannot help but imagine the forecast that long-discarded 8 Ball might give me now, if I rolled it over and asked what tomorrow holds: OUTLOOK NOT SO GOOD. My chuckle deepens—but there's no point in being morbid, is there? Another sentiment you hammered home early.

Besides, thirty-four is still young, right? You used to joke that mathematicians peaked at twenty-one while biologists peaked at seventy. There was something in it about the predictability of numbers and the unpredictability of living things.

Regardless, I have yet to peak in any sense.

I look down at the envelope again.

A sign would be good.

On it, your address, in cursive black: your name beneath my name. I turn over the thick envelope and slide a clear, memorial-service-manicured thumbnail under the seal. It crackles open satisfyingly.

More of you would be good. One more hug. One more minute. Something to sink my teeth into.

I pull out the thick-gauge paper and take in the sender's
address. An address thousands of miles from England, from
our lives. The humidity of the location written into the words
themselves, transportive and optimistic.

Clarence, Mitfield & Booth
Suite 3610-13 Harbor Quay
Tortola
British Virgin Islands

FAO Ms. Nina Lillian Hepworth,

We would like to offer our deepest condolences following
the sad news of your father, John Stanley Hepworth's,
recent passing.

We are writing to advise you that in accordance with
his Last Will and Testament, Clarence, Mitfield & Booth
have been appointed as estate executors for your late father's assets here in the Virgin Islands. We understand
that the late Mr. Hepworth's UK assets are being over-
seen by Lansdown Lowe with his foreign assets being
managed through Clarence, Mitfield & Booth.

We would like to advise you that we have successfully
collected in the estate assets, ascertained and renumer-
ated any outstanding debts prior to applying for probate,
which is now complete.

We thought you would like to know that in accordance with your father's Will you are the sole beneficiary
and have been bequeathed:

Property: A 3-bedroom Beachfront Estate, Pond Bay,
Gorda, British Virgin Islands

When I look up from rereading the letter the light outside has faded and the empty sitting room is lit only by the bare bulb in the socket above me.

My father never even visited the Caribbean.

I wanted a sign and I got one.

CHAPTER 2
NINA

Neither the letter, from Clarence, Mitfield & Booth, nor the existence of this new house make immediate sense to me.

My father was not a holiday-home sort of man. The very idea of him sitting *shirtless* in shorts on a sun bed is beyond the scope of my imagination. To say my father was a cerebral man would be an understatement. So a house, thousands of miles from the autumnal chill of London, bathed in sunlight and vivid Caribbean hues, does not sit quite right. The only reason I can imagine him ever requiring a house overseas would be if he had work out there. But he didn't. At least to my knowledge.

I briefly call his UK solicitor; they too have received the correspondence and vouch for the authenticity of the firm. Whatever this house is . . . it is real.

I dial the long international number at the base of the letter. The elongated purr of a foreign ringtone reminding me that a time difference might hamper me. But just as the thought arrives so does a crisp Caribbean voice, a woman, who promptly transfers me to another voice. This one older, male, American.

"Ms. Hepworth, we've been expecting your call. James Booth. I am currently handling your case," he tells me with such a calm, quotidian tone that I have to remind myself of the strangeness of the situation. I go on to explain that I have only just had a chance to open the letter from his firm and was surprised to read its contents. "Yes, of course," he replies unfazed, his tone hinting that this might often be the case in his line of work. "It's been a busy time for you."

He is correct: it has been. I let my eyes roam around the darkening room, my father's now blank-walled sitting room, parquet floors bared, bookshelves hollowed out. I shiver deeply.

"Yes, very busy," I conclude, then clear my throat and re-focus. "I'm just a little confused, James. About this letter. This *additional* will. We've already executed my father's will in the UK. This Caribbean property. I wasn't aware of it . . ." I trail off as I realize how unlike myself I sound. I *sound* like a daughter who barely knew her father, but that is not the case. I saw my father every single Thursday night since graduating from university, our games night: checkers, chess, crosswords. We spent almost all holidays and occasions together. I knew his schedule inside out. We spoke about everything. And yet here I am, for the first time, at a loss.

"I see. More than a little surprised then, I should imagine. Yes," James answers, remaining warm but noncommittal. "Well, hopefully we can shed some light on—"

A thought suddenly occurs and I interrupt. "Sorry to ask, but could this letter be an error, James? Is there a possibility that you might have contacted the wrong person?"

James clears his throat, caught off guard. "Ha. No, no. Although be assured you are not the first beneficiary to have uttered those immortal words. But I can assure you, Ms. Hepworth—*Nina*, if I may?"

I hum a consent to the use of my first name.

"Thank you. Yes, I can assure you, *Nina*, that your father was most definitely the owner of the property in question prior to his death. There is no question of that. But more importantly, *you* are clearly named as sole beneficiary of the estate in Mr. Hepworth's will. He was very clear about wanting you to inherit the property in its entirety. I can email you a copy of his list of wishes if that would be helpful at this juncture?"

"Um, yes, that would be. Yes," I manage after a moment. The idea of reading anything new that my father has written is suddenly too desperate a need to articulate without fully exposing my grief.

"I will ask Melissa to send that across. Just be aware, Nina, that it is only a legal document so fairly dry in terms of content."

The list of wishes is not a letter, or an explanation.

James has obviously been through the ebbs and flows of this process a hundred times. I take considerable comfort in being part of such a vast and timeless congregation in James's mind.

It takes me a moment to regroup.

"So, the property was definitely my father's. Can I ask when or how he acquired it, James?"

"I'd be very happy to go through everything with you in person, if you're available later in the week?"

Thoughts scrambled, I ask, "Oh, do you have a London office then?"

James chuckles. "Unfortunately, not. No, we would fly you out here to the British Virgin Islands to take receivership.

Whenever fits in with your schedule—provisions were made *within* the will itself to cover all fees and expenses involved in the transition of ownership. First-class airfare and transfers have been covered, so I can action your travel arrangements whenever works for you?"

I believe, at this point in the conversation and for the first time in my adult life, my mouth falls open. By the sounds of it my father had another life. A life that included first-class air travel and second homes. His UK assets were already sizable, as reflected in the inheritance I received a few days ago, but this sounds like another matter entirely.

"Nina?" James asks after a moment of silence.

"Yes, sorry, it's just quite a lot of new information to take in." Slowly a new question forms, a crude, blunt one that I do not know how to phrase well. "Sorry, James, but this property, this estate, is it substantial? I mean, how much—" I trail off, hoping not to need to add more. And thankfully James saves my blushes.

"It is a *generous* property, yes, in one of the most exclusive areas of the BVI. But we can get into numbers and the rest as and when we meet."

A generous property. My father was rich. Very, very rich. And I had no idea. The thought snags—because, how did he get that rich?

"But do you know when my father might have bought or used the house, James? It's just, I can't quite square away when he would have gone out there," I ask.

"Well, we can certainly look into these things for you and get into the weeds when you're over. When would you be available to fly?" he asks, his tone pragmatic.

I look around my father's empty sitting room once more. There is no more to be done here and the university has already granted me a sabbatical, my lectures covered, my students aware. Time off "for grief." It seems everyone in my life, except me, obviously, has foreseen that once the music finally stopped, I would need time to scrape myself off the floor.

Mistaking my pause for reticence, which it may well have been, James pushes on.

"Of course, if you would rather not come out in person we can supply e-contracts and assist in placing the property directly on the market for you? If that would be something—"

"Are his things still there?" I interject, the question flying from me before I can couch it in politeness.

"His *things*?" James asks, seeking clarification.

"Yes, does he have possessions out there. Personal items? Is the house left as it was?"

I hear understanding drop into James's voice. "Yes. The house is vacant but lived in. There are the standard personal effects present, I believe. Yes. Pictures, books, personal items." He sounds sad now. I have made James sad; I've managed to depress a will executor.

But that doesn't matter, because the prospect of what I might find out there, in that house, still undiscovered, lifts me out of my void. The idea that I might find more of my father out there, the possibility that our story might not yet be over, is a salve.

A fizzle of excitement crackles to life inside me. I thought I knew everything about my father, but this house has shown me that, clearly, there is more to know. More of him out there, halfway across the world, and wasn't it just like him to leave something behind for me to ponder, to provide me with a series of questions that demand answers? A puzzle, clues to follow, more to solve. Hope glows afresh inside me, but with it a sharp splinter of fear, because a truth has been kept from me and I cannot imagine why. Good things are rarely kept secret, which means I might find something I don't like in all this. It is always dangerous to look too hard into the lives of those you love and respect more than anything.

It occurs to me that I could just instruct James to begin the process of putting this bizarre property on the market without my involvement. I could request they ship his personal items back to me. Though out of context would any of it make sense? Perhaps it doesn't need to? I could just let my father lie, rest . . . in peace. I could plop the enormous sale value from this *generous* property into my bank, then go back to work at the university and never think about money, or this mystery house, ever again.

But would I never think of it again; or would I always think of it? Of what it meant . . . I would never know. And that would drive me mad, not knowing.

I have never been the kind of person to turn away from an unanswered question. The cat cannot be shooed back into the bag and Pandora's box cannot be repacked. My father would have known that, and knowing that, he deliberately left me the house.

By doing so he is trying to tell me one last thing, about him; he has left me one last challenge, a puzzle to solve. And if anyone could set something in motion from beyond the grave it would be him.

"When is the soonest I can fly out?" I ask.

IN THE DAYS BEFORE I depart, I do what research I can. I scour online for any reference to my father's work abroad but I find nothing. No mention of a holiday home, no clues to be followed.

The initial excitement I felt at this new discovery about my father begins to darken as the question of how he funded the purchase of this property rises in my mind like a specter. What additional work did he undertake to secure this massive asset, and how could he have compartmentalized his life to such a degree that I, his only living relative, could know nothing about it?

I tentatively question a few of his friends: men and women in their late seventies, snowy eyebrows raised in youthful surprise that John had any connection out there. *He never spoke of a second home. How wonderful for him. What's it like?*

I do not tell them the extent of what I imagine it will be like, this *generous* property. To tell them that would be to lead them in the direction of my own thoughts—that a man like my father, a man with a career like my father's, should not have had that much money. Should not have had a secret house.

One of his long-term co-workers, Maeve Rittman, a force of nature now in her late sixties and still lecturing at the university, told me something that lodged in my mind.

When I asked her if she could spare an hour or so to talk about Dad, she invited me to tea at Brown's in Mayfair. I don't doubt she must have thought the meeting purely about my need for comfort post-bereavement, but regardless, she was happy to oblige. That was the kind of man my father was, you see, the kind you care about to the extent your goodwill bleeds to anyone else they might know or like.

At least, that was how others saw him. As the child of a great man, things are often more complicated: he loved me, but I was never not aware that he feared finding his own faults in me. Though what his faults might have been I could not tell you. But I knew enough to know they haunted him. He could not abide thoughtlessness, carelessness, letting standards slip.

In the years we had together, in all the puzzles we solved and games we played, and in all the life we lived, I found myself fearing both losing to and winning over him.

If I lost, I risked his disappointment; if I won, I feared de-

stroying the foundations of our relationship. Though of course
he gave no such indication that this would ever be the case if I
did win.

But that is academic. I never really won against him. I did
not have that extra spark that seemed embedded in him from
birth. I could never win without his encouragement, his direction, his nudging, his sometimes cold pulling away. And when
I won, I would burst with pride and he would say he had always known it was there—and we were both happy enough
with that, I believe. I was a trier, and that was enough.

I don't doubt Maeve likes me because I'm John's daughter.
An undeniable pedigree before I ever even uttered a word. He
loved me, so I am lovable.

I have always felt at home with Maeve. But no doubt everyone feels that with Maeve, funny, beautiful, and as close to genius as it might be possible to be, though with the good grace
to keep it to herself most of the time.

She smiled at me over the rim of her teacup, her garnet
lipstick expertly applied, her eyes still twinkling as they always had.

"I'm glad you asked me to do this," she said after a sip.
"You're a long way off this yet but there comes a time in your
life when people start to go. Die. And of course you attend the
events, but it's never enough, there is still so much left unsaid.
Memories to be turned over, inspected. If you can find someone willing to listen to your memories, so much the better.
And trust me, dear Nina, you lovely girl, I have a lot of memories of your father."

And she did. Mostly stories about the pranks they played
on each other as PhD students at Cambridge. They had been
researching in different departments: *she* clinical neuroscience
and *he* applied mathematics and theoretical physics, and they
might never have met had it not been for their mutual love of

bog-standard pub quizzing. Their ragtag quiz team going on to rinse every pub in Cambridge and the surrounding areas out of their accumulated jackpots to hilarious effect.

I found myself childishly hoping as Maeve spoke that this mysterious house on the other side of the world might be entirely funded by pub quiz winnings. That spry, edgy young man she spoke of was so different from the calm, staid man I spent my life with. The stories made me laugh and then they made me sad. I cried a bit. She responded in kind and I was at least spared the embarrassment of being the only one in the piano-tinkling tearoom with damp eyes and a blotchy face.

The questions around the existence of this house introduced a more existential concern, I told her: That if I discovered more, I might lose the old idea of who my father was. That I might find out something out there that destroyed my memory of him and I might, in a sense, lose him again with even more permanence.

With the arrival of a fresh pot of tea and more scones, her tone shifted.

"I know you want me to give you something, some *reassurance* or even perhaps a seismic disclosure about who your father was. But he was a private man, Nina. We shared so much but I never got *in*, if you understand my meaning. He was a closed circuit. He never remarried after your mother. There was a lot of sadness there. He battled it, I think, but one would never know. As far as I can tell he never even tried to find someone else. He was married to his work and his diversions and, in a way, to you."

Maeve broke off, seeming to suddenly see my predicament for what it was and adding, "He was a good man, though. Perhaps he cut off a side of his life to preserve the rest; we do what we must. But don't ever doubt that he was a good man. Secrets or no. No one is perfect, you just need to know that he loved you immensely—he made a life out of it."

Then Maeve reached a delicately boned hand across the table and squeezed my forearm with surprising strength.

"Whatever you find out there: he will have had his reasons. If there is one thing I *do* know about your father, it's that he never did anything without at least one very good reason. If he left you the house, he wanted you to go there."

CHAPTER 3
MARIA

The door slid open with a hydraulic smoothness.

So weird, Maria thought, after three days of trying, nothing and then this. The woman had told her the rules when she arrived at the house. There were always rules for clients like this. The bigger the property, the shinier the surfaces, the quieter the rooms: *the stranger the clients*—it was a truth universally acknowledged, though Maria hadn't gotten the measure of this client at all as she hadn't even met him, or his children, yet.

She had been hired for two weeks to cover the client's usual nanny's annual leave. She had done enough of these now to know what that entailed, and these short jobs were always the easiest. Be quiet, cheerful, fun, but incredibly reliable, *yes* to everything, *no* to nothing, in a nutshell: the dream. Well, everyone else's dream. But the money was always, always good. The best.

The rules of this particular job were simple: Wear the

clothes provided, impeccably made soft white polo shirts and chic linen shorts; be amenable; and when not immediately required, make yourself comfortable in the house. Make yourself comfortable. *What a joke*, Maria thought. *No one wants to see the hired help comfortable.*

Of course, Maria hadn't dreamt as a child of being the hired help. She started doing short contracts between her first-year terms at Cornell Medical School, each contract easily paying off her course fees. She had no particular ambition to become a nanny, but she was savvy as well as intelligent, and it turned out she was good with kids, or at least they listened to her, and the astronomical amount she could make as a *live-in* nanny to the super-rich had made it a simple choice.

Then as the course's study schedule began to leak into her "free time," it got harder to do both. Holidays between terms had ceased to exist. So she had to make a clear-minded decision: an unsentimental, rational decision. Training to be a doctor required money, money required a job, a job required time. She had needed to quickly reassess her career trajectory. The truth was that Maria could make more as an attractive, highly educated, polite young child-minder to the super-rich than she could as an overworked junior doctor back in New York City.

And with the hefty nannying wage packets she had been hoarding over the last few years, rent-free, overhead-free, she'd be able to pick up her med course again in, say, five years and be able to pay for it all outright—hell, she'd even be able to buy her own apartment in Manhattan near the hospital in order to study there comfortably if she wanted.

And this new contract, her largest and most life-altering paycheck yet, would push her closer than ever to the figure she knew she needed to be safe, to be comfortable. After a lifetime of hustle, she would soon be secure.

Even if Maria hadn't memorized the payment breakdown on the new contract, she would have been able to guess this placement was a good one just from the list of requirements that came with it.

The house rules on this job stated that she could use all the property's facilities: pools, spa, sauna, steam room, grounds, as well as the two-hundred-foot private beach. The only stipulations being that she would need to: keep things tidy, not leave the house unless in the company of the client or the children, and not interrupt any of the client's phone calls or speak to other visitors. Though why the hell anyone would think she would want to talk to any of the client's friends Maria had no idea.

The woman who had shown Maria around the house—her chignon too tight, her smile too warm—had also explained how the biometric door lock system worked on the property. That had worried Maria at first. High security often meant shady clients, clients with a reason to be paranoid. She'd had one such experience on a yacht off the coast of Monaco the year before. The number of room searches and security briefings had been enough to put her off working for a certain type of client for life. But the woman who had shown her around this house explained that this client, a single father of two, was just fond of tech. And as the property, with its glass corners and steep staircases was most definitely not toddler-friendly, he had made the decision that only adults should be able to activate the doors between various safety hazards. A child-proofing of sorts.

A Silicon Valley guy, Maria inferred, and relaxed. Tech guys were the easiest to work for. The easiest pleased. They knew what they wanted, had no problem telling you, sometimes with eye-watering bluntness, and then often completely ghosted you so you could get on with it.

The woman had placed Maria's hand on the spotless glass

panel and entered her information into the palm-scanner. Maria would be able to go anywhere in the house freely, except, she was told, the locked room at the end of the lower ground-floor passage. *A private office*, Maria surmised. She could go anywhere but there—*so far, so Bluebeard's castle*, Maria thought with an internal smirk. The idea she would care to nose around a tech guy's office was somehow reassuringly ridiculous.

In a vague way Maria wondered if somehow this privacy was meant to increase her curiosity, if that was the point? She had experienced a few *tests* in previous jobs. The rich were predictably terrified of being stolen from or cheated in some way. The room downstairs could well be just that, some weird trust exercise. Not beyond the bounds of believability, she'd had stranger: nanny cams, jewelry left out, clients who thought they were paying for *more* than child care! All of human life was here. It's best to be on your toes with clients; when the rewards were this high, the risks often were too. And at the back of her mind, she had considered the possibility that this job might not actually be, as sold, *covering* for their permanent nanny, but rather that she is being actively trialed for the permanent position.

The woman with the too-tight chignon went on to explain that while Maria could go anywhere within the grounds, she wouldn't actually be able to leave the property through any of the perimeter exits unless accompanied. That was the bit Maria hadn't liked.

The woman went on to clarify that Maria could leave with the client and the children, on excursions, lunch dates, et cetera, but if Maria wanted to leave alone, she would need to terminate her two-week contract. To do that she would have to call the chignon woman on her direct line; the woman would inform security, who would then escort Maria from the property. It sounded undignified, Maria thought, but then wasn't it all undignified? What she did and what these rich people couldn't do themselves—equally undignified.

But dignity didn't pay for Maria's lifestyle, and this job did.

So, Maria had squared away that she wouldn't leave the property, as requested. But she hadn't been born yesterday. She'd been doing this long enough to have her own assurances in terms of "client risk." If anything here was even slightly off, a lot of people at the agency knew where she was.

After the woman left Maria remained on her best behavior for a full forty-eight hours.

She unpacked her personal items in the smallest room, showered in her own marble wet room, and slipped into her expensive, if anonymous prescribed uniform. Then she found and gathered what few child-friendly books she could find around the minimalist house. The children's books seemed to focus on broad pop-culture Central American figures and themes: Frida Kahlo, Botero, Pérez. Figures from her long-left-behind Central American culture to a degree that made her wonder if her heritage had been a deciding factor in her hiring. Perhaps the client also had Colombian ancestry, she figured. After all, the rich could cherry-pick who looked after their children. And if they paid this well and the perks were good—she didn't know why they shouldn't pick whoever they wanted.

She just hoped the client didn't expect her to speak fluent Spanish, because she didn't. She'd left too young, her parents hadn't spoken it around her, and her high school had only taught French as a second language.

She lay the bright adventure books out on a soft blanket with gathered cushions and pillows: her thinking being that the children might arrive tired from the journey when they finally appeared, so they could snuggle and listen to stories while she surreptitiously took the measure of their father. But after a few hours of no-show from father and children Maria slipped off her anonymous uniform tennis shoes, lay down herself on the blanket, and let the warm Caribbean sunlight pool at her feet.

She jolted awake two hours later as the integrated air-conditioning kicked up a gear, its hum intensifying in frequency. But still, no one had arrived.

When evening approached, Maria made her way to the fully stocked pantry to cobble together one of her sure-fire children's hits, bacon-y mac & cheese. The property had been prepped with everything before her arrival, the level of organization a thing of beauty, cans stacked labels-out, jars filled with cookies, pasta, cereals, everything in its place and ready. There were no children's bowls or cutlery in the cupboards, she noted, but that was easily worked around; it wasn't particularly unusual in the families she'd worked with for the children to use what the adults used. That and the lack of toys and other accoutrements told Maria that these children, like others she had looked after, must have their entire worlds shipped around in suitcases between global residences. Maria placed the warm, comforting meal on the table at the hour requested in her manual. One adult portion and two children's portions, but time passed and no one came. Finally she placed the meals in the warming oven and ate her own out on the darkening twinkle-lit terrace, the sound of tree frogs croaking and distant waves crashing her only company.

It was a kind of bliss there. She closed her eyes and told herself to make the most of this quiet before the inevitable storm of children. And when she opened her eyes to the gleaming of the pool lights in the growing darkness, she let herself imagine for a moment that this was her life. Out here, with all of this. This life.

After another hour she removed the meals from the warming oven and packed them away in the fridge, just in case. But the evening ebbed by and when she was absolutely sure no one was coming, she tidied the kitchen and slipped silently into her room for the night.

The next morning, her alarm did not sound, and she groggily woke, instead, to the loud cries of a seabird calling from the clifftop surrounds. Still no one had arrived.

Assuming the client had probably been held up, Maria decided to call the woman with the too-tight chignon. Her suspicions were confirmed.

The woman promised to follow up with more news soon. In the meantime, she told Maria to *enjoy* the facilities. Maria, wary of doing anything as extreme as that, instead allowed herself the possibility of a nervous swim and sauna in an attempt to clear her jet-lagged head. The flight from her last family in Paris had been a real kick in the circadian rhythm.

On the way to the indoor pool, she passed the locked lower ground-floor door, a door identical to all the other doors in the house except that this one's biometric lock glowed blue instead of green like the others.

Maria considered the room, the warning she received about it. She hadn't thought she'd be curious at all, but now she was. *Where the hell was this family? What was the holdup?* Lingering by the forbidden door Maria vaguely considered pressing the glowing door panel. She contemplated entering the room, perhaps seeing what kind of job might get you a house like this, but then she came to her senses, let out an audible chuckle, and headed to the pool. She wasn't going to take the bait that soon, if indeed it was even bait.

As she swam Maria weaved a narrative around the room and concluded that if the client's late arrival and the out-of-bounds room were a form of trust test, these clients would need to try harder than that. Maria had worked incredibly hard to get into Cornell, and even harder to make sure she could secure these premium high-paying private staff contracts— she knew how to delay gratification like no one she had ever met, and in Maria's heart she was pretty sure she could put up with anything longer than most if she knew it would ulti- mately benefit her. If this new employer was testing her, if they were hoping to uncover someone with no self-control: *More fool them.* Maria stepped out of the pool a few inches taller. She didn't rate most of her personal qualities but she did rate that.

Throughout the day she ran through the scheduled events in the client's manual, regardless of having no audience, as she waited for the client to arrive—keen to ensure that she would not be caught out should the family suddenly appear. An art station was cobbled together from what she could find about the property, and later some adult pool floats inflated and made ready poolside. A jug of homemade lemonade with huge clunk- ing ice chunks was laid out beside three frosted glasses on the kitchen counter. It was always better to be overprepared, to anticipate needs. Maria had worked out fairly early on as a nanny that the tips and gifts from families at this client level often superseded the original negotiated fees. And she was well aware that clients turning up to find her *not ready* would not garner her a fat high-denomination stuffed envelope at the end of the two weeks or another Patek Philippe, with a poten- tial resale value of over $200,000. Best to exceed expectations, always.

The next morning she lay out a strawberries, yogurt, and orange juice breakfast, and waited. She vaguely wondered what would happen when the supplies in the fridge ran low, if another member of staff or a catering firm would arrive laden with produce at some point—but she did not linger on this thought. Households like these ran like clockwork, even if their owners didn't.

The breakfast lay untouched. And once she had finally decanted everything back into the fridge, she decided to call the woman with the too-tight chignon again.

The clients would definitely not be arriving that day. She was encouraged once more to make the most of the facilities.

Maria did as she was told, now safe in the knowledge that she wouldn't be imminently required. She applied sun lotion liberally by the outdoor pool then stretched out on a plush lounger in the sun, a book in hand, her toes dragging lightly into the cool outdoor pool water.

Later she explored the grounds, showered, cooked herself an elaborate lunch, and by the evening even allowed herself the small bottle of wine left for her as a welcome gift along with her manual.

But by day three, when the client had still not arrived, Maria had developed concerns, or rather niggling questions, about their now increasingly strange absence.

Would she still be paid? Maria asked the woman over the phone as much. The woman seemed surprised to find out the client had still not arrived. She herself seemed unsure about why this was happening, but reassured Maria that she would be paid regardless.

Maria was good at reading people. The woman's tone confirmed, at least, that this late arrival was not part of some greater plan.

Recognizing what was and was not part of a client's plan had become a very useful adaptive quality.

But this client's absence didn't seem to be part of anyone's plan.

Perhaps he was old or sick. Perhaps something had happened to him or one of the children on their way out?

The thought of those eventualities hovered, for a few minutes, in Maria's mind, but the truth was it really didn't matter what the hell had happened to them. She didn't know them, she'd never met them. Either they would arrive eventually or they wouldn't. The truth was she'd lucked out in paradise, for the time being; she was now, it seemed, on a paid vacation.

And that's when Maria's best behavior began to slip.

She relaxed. She let her uniform crease as she lay on the deep cool sofas and read. She dived into the pool, used the floats, ate at the pool edge. She even allowed herself a double bill in the crisp air-conditioned darkness of the home cinema room as she shoveled freshly popped corn into her mouth. In the womblike blackness she let herself imagine again that this was her life.

A swim. A sauna. A steam. A shower.

Then exploring the rest of the house, the other rooms, the art, the books, the hints left behind by her absent employer.

She thought again of who the client might be. If he might actually be ill. No client of hers had ever not turned up.

And so, the insidious question of *who* the missing client was would not leave her alone. In the minimalist white library, she went as far as googling the house's address on the desktop before deleting the search history. No celebrity lived here, no titan of commerce, or if they did, that information was not available online.

Maria thought again about the house rules. She thought about the room downstairs. The locked room. The room she definitely wasn't allowed to go in. *What was in there?*

If it was a home office, as she had been told, it might hold the answer to whose house she was in. All she would need to do is go down there and take a look.

She shook off the notion as unprofessional and predictable.

But the notion would not release its grip and finally Maria went back downstairs.

The door lock glowed blue. She placed her palm on it and then a low tone sounded: a denial tone. *Access denied.*

Maria was oddly relieved. The illusion of choice had been removed from the equation. She didn't have to worry about going, or not going, into that room anymore.

Instead she went for a walk down to the private beach and swam naked in the secluded cove to feel the world on her skin—and as she did, she struggled to remember the last time she had felt so calm. Again she mused on what her life might look like if she lived here—if there were no client at all.

Salty, she returned to the house and got ready for dinner.

Halfway through her meal the house's phone burst to life, ringing shrilly. Maria almost choking on her steak, a small chunk of it leaping from her coughing mouth across the swirling marble of the kitchen island. She rose as if suddenly interrupted by guests, smoothed down her hair self-consciously, and lifted the receiver.

It was the woman with the too-tight chignon. She had tried but failed to reach the client. She would keep trying, but she cautioned Maria it might be that the client would not be joining Maria at all. Though Maria would still be paid regardless.

That fact should have reassured Maria, however, when she put the phone down, she felt instead . . . what? Nervous. Though she couldn't imagine why.

She thought of the door downstairs again and shivered, her imagination again taking flight. *Were there ever any children? Was there even a client?*

The only person Maria had met was the woman with the chignon. And why wasn't she allowed to go in that room downstairs?

She knew her thoughts were childish, ridiculous, but without any other diversion she reveled in them for a moment, the drama of them, the horror of them, just to feel something. Before bed she tried the locked door again. But it was locked. She wouldn't have been able to enter even if she wanted to.

In the middle of the night Maria woke to the lights in her room mechanically flashing on and off. Some kind of electrical fault, she inferred. She rose.

Tentatively, ready to reach for a vase or andiron as a weapon, Maria made her way to the living room phone and called the woman with the too-tight chignon to tell her about the fault.

The woman promised to send someone to fix the electrical problem first thing in the morning.

Could Maria manage with the lighting malfunction until then? Was the issue affecting other rooms in the house?

Maria checked. It was just her bedroom.

Maria offered to change rooms for the night and wait until the next morning for the problem to be fixed. Maria put down the phone with a mild excitement of knowing she would see another human being the next day.

As she walked back toward the largest bedroom, she heard an automated tone come from downstairs. An *access granted* tone. She took a peek down the stairwell. The sound was coming from the locked door. The electrical fault had affected other areas of the house. The door panel glowed green; Bluebeard's room was no longer locked. Maria could enter if she so desired.

Maria shook her head in disbelief at the horror-movie predictability of anyone actually deciding to enter a forbidden room in the dead of night. And, not having an intense desire to push her luck, she ignored the impulse to go investigate and wandered gratefully back to bed instead.

But fear has a way of squeezing through the smallest of gaps. So, after firmly closing her new bedroom door, Maria considered a moment before sliding the room's large armoire, two bedside cabinets, and a particularly heavy armchair against it, before sleeping soundly through the night.

The first thing next morning, energy renewed, daylight blazing, Maria went downstairs, pushed her palm to the now unlocked door panel, and watched it slowly open.

CHAPTER 4
NINA

As the plane doors open a wave of tropical heat hits me. My muscles—tight from London life, from hours in libraries and lecture halls, and more recently in funeral directors' and legal offices—fight the heat's gentle invitation to loosen.

It's autumn back in London, and those last lukewarm days of British summer have done nothing to prepare me for this environmental shift.

As we disembark out onto the tarmac only a soft sea breeze breaks the scorch of midday sun. After less than a minute in its full unfiltered gaze, I am glad to reach the cool escape of the terminal building.

Funny how something can feel so good and so bad all at once. A death, a holiday. The prospect of getting to the bottom of things, and the things we might find there.

A taxi takes me and my one small yellow piece of luggage through the lush, palm-strewn countryside that separates the airport from Road Town, the capital of Tortola, and the entire British Virgin Islands.

From the open taxi window I drink in this other world, so far from the clammy cold of London with its gray buildings and gray-brown weather. Beyond the window, the bright landscape flashes past: thick jungle vegetation that gives way to sparse, sunbaked fields lying abandoned in the still heat. Coral-pink, aquamarine-blue, and emerald-green houses. People walking in the hot roadside dust, smiling, happy, their bodies looser, more lived-in than my own. Perhaps life is different here. Perhaps *my* life could be different here. But then everyone who's ever been abroad thinks that, don't they?

I can't help but wonder if that is why my father came out here—a paradise thousands of miles from his staid life in West London. Perhaps he wanted a different life too?

I shake off the morbid thought as the taxi breaks out into the sunlight from beneath a forest canopy, the burst of light momentarily blinding me.

As my eyes adjust, I see we are on a ridge, the vast sweep of Road Harbor visible in the distance, the creamy beach-lined horseshoe of it meeting the sparkling jewel of the Caribbean Sea.

The driver rolls down his window too, and the warm scents of salt and my own hastily applied sunscreen create a sensory gut-punch of childhood holidays. *Except we never came here, did we, Dad?*

Almost as if he can hear my thoughts, the driver turns with an easy smile. "That was Road Town. Good for shopping, restaurants, sightseeing," he singsongs happily. "But you are staying in a nice hotel so maybe you won't want to look around. Your hotel is very good, very nice. Too expensive for me," he confesses, then laughs uproariously at his own joke, which I imagine in a sense is me. Because as far as he is concerned, I'm paying the price of a medium-sized monthly mortgage to stay there every night.

For some reason I find it important to correct him. "Oh no. I'm not staying there. I'm just meeting someone."

HALFWAY THROUGH LUNCH WITH A younger-than-expected James Booth, one of the only certainties I have about the house turns out to be wrong.

"Oh no, the house isn't here on Tortola, no." He places his fork carefully down into his Michelin-starred lobster salad and hastily wipes his already immaculately clean mouth.

He looks genuinely horrified at the misunderstanding. "I can only apologize. It appears I didn't make that clear in our previous correspondence—the location *is* stated in the beneficiary letter but I see that it might not have been immediately clear to you as a non-national. The Islands can be confusing to visitors. I should have talked you through it. You see, most *business* gets done here on Tortola. And while Tortola is a lovely island it is really more of a port or a business hub for the BVI than a final destination. *The house*, your father's house, wouldn't have been on the island here. Just our offices."

I look around the beachfront terrace of this beautiful five-star hotel he has brought me to and wonder how the hell I'm supposed to get to whichever island I *am* supposed to be on.

"*Okay*," I hear myself say, my tone vague, two flights in and jet-lagged to hell.

Looking past James to the pool, where bathers drowsily stretch out on loungers and dip into the crystal-clear waters, I find myself wondering if I should just blow the entire inheritance and book in here for the next few nights. Hell, indefinitely.

"Let me explain," he continues, sensing he has lost me.

"The plan was, and remains, to accompany you across to the house on Virgin Gorda after lunch. If that still works?"

My focus snaps back to James. "Oh, I see. Sorry, so transport there *has* been arranged and—"

"Of course. All covered in the expenditure budget compiled in line with expediting your father's wishes." He takes me in, notes my confusion, and simplifies. "In other words: we have extracted and retained the necessary funds from estate assets to cover all necessary expenses in beneficiary handover."

"Ah, I see," I say with a nod. And then look down at my own mango-infused lobster salad, which I now see that I have indirectly paid for. Then I take a healthy gulp of my half-sipped champagne and refill it from the bottle. If I'm paying for it, then I'll have it.

"So when do we sail?" I ask him with a fresh injection of positivity.

James, his mouth full of mixed leaves, gives a shake of the head. I wait for him to chew.

"Helicopter," he says after a big swallow. "Flight's at two."

CHAPTER 5
NINA

The sound of rotor blades is deafening until I slip on the headset James hands me. Silence hugs me, soft and close. A crackle, then I hear his voice.

"Our takeoff slot is in two minutes. But these guys tend to be pretty on it. We should be there in around ten, fifteen minutes."

With that, I feel the helicopter lift beneath us. Beyond the Plexiglas door beside me the tarmac of the helipad recedes quickly, the surrounding grasses and palms flattening in our downdraft. Tortola sweeps out underneath us, its colorful buildings, vibrantly painted buses, and cars winding, now in miniature, through the lush landscape far beneath us. Then our speed increases and we glide over the golden sand halo of the coastline, immaculate powder beaches blending seamlessly into emerald sea as we fly out over the water.

I look back at the island we have just left, with its airport, its connection back to London and my real life, and instead of concern I feel an unexpected lightening. I cannot help but wonder if he, my father, felt this exact feeling. If he felt a lifting at leaving our world and me behind.

The thought doesn't stay long as a gentle nudge from James's elbow redirects my gaze.

He points out his window to the island coming into view in the hazy distance. Virgin Gorda is smaller than Tortola, its luminous sea halo brighter, more unspoiled than the one we have just left behind.

I try to imagine the approaching island as my father must have seen it the first time he caught sight of it, but try as I might, I can't wrap my head around why he would even come here. The studious, kind, easily pleased man that he was. But as Maeve so accurately said, he never did anything without a reason. And I remind myself that I am here to unearth that reason.

On the way to the heliport James had been circumspect about the details surrounding the house. "It appears from the documentation that the property, or at least the land it was built on, was bought a little over twenty years ago. A property management company successfully applied for non-belonger status in your father's name on purchase, and it was granted. The building was then specifically designed and custom-built over a period of three years. I couldn't find any information regarding the specifics of the design and planning though of course the companies involved are all in the public record and if you have the time, and the desire, I'm sure you can track down whatever you need."

My father had the house built from scratch. He has left me one more surprise, one more puzzle to solve.

"Are there floor plans? Blueprints?" I ask James.

"I haven't been able to source original copies. But there may well be within the property. We have recent survey drawings and a valuation markup but not the pre-build architectural drawings. I will, of course, keep digging if that is something you would be interested in pursuing?"

My curiosity to find out if father's name is on any of those architectural drawings is almost too much to bear. As a civil engineer it wouldn't have been too far out of his remit to design a home of his own.

His greatest achievement, certainly the most lauded in the slew of obituaries after his death, was his work on the development of Dogger Bank, the colossal newly constructed offshore wind farm, the largest in existence, that now loomed like so many frozen giants 290 kilometers off the east coast of Yorkshire, England. My father was central to the design of the subsea cable infrastructure and deep-sea monopile foundations for the monolithic 277-turbine-strong farm.

And now the idea that he might have designed a house. A mystery house.

I think of his Edwardian townhouse back in London, locked up and safe pending exchange to a wealthy young couple with three children. I always associated *that* house with my father. But that's about to change. I am going to see more of him, get closer perhaps to his inner workings.

Maeve was right about something else: he didn't let you in. He loved me, he listened to me, he celebrated life with me, but he didn't let me in. Maybe that is as it should be with a parent? Boundaries. Healthy boundaries. We should not know everything. And yet the idea that I might find out everything, that it might be possible, seems as thrilling as it is terrifying.

THE LANDING IS SMOOTH. I slip my headphones off aping James as he helps loosen my harness and then his own before opening the door and, rotor blades still thumping, steps out onto the tarmac. He turns, offering me a hand as my hair wildly caught in the downdraft blinds me. I take his hand firmly and follow, exhilarated by the noise and threat of it all.

In the car that waits for us I attempt to straighten myself out.

"Is it far?" I ask as we pull away, the helicopter already lifting across the tarmac and disappearing into the air back to Tortola.

James pulls a face. "No. Everything is close on Gorda."

I consider whether or not now is the time to broach my next concern.

"James, you said earlier my father applied for and was granted non-belonger status in order to acquire the land and build. Does that mean he wasn't seeking full citizenship?"

James frowns at the question, or at least the question implicit within my question. He takes a moment before answering, the lush sun-drenched landscape flashing by as he considers it.

"If you have fears, as many do, around the gray areas of domicile and non-domicile tax obligations, then rest assured your father raises no concerns. There are no additional hidden funds, other than those disclosed in the wishes, so from a legal standpoint—and from a layman's standpoint—everything is as it should be."

I feel something inside me relax. That fear, at least, that my father was involved in something not quite legal, has been taken off the table.

It's James's turn to question me now. I see him teeing up.

"From my brief look into your father's affairs and lifework I see he was an impressive man? A civil engineer? Is that correct?"

"Amongst other things, yes. He was a bit of a prodigy. Maths was his strong suit. Adapted some theories young, and yes, he built turbines, infrastructure. And other things."

"And wrote the crossword?" James says now with a sly smile that I believe is intended to express the sentiment: *Come now, don't be modest.*

"Well, he set them, yes. For a period. In *The Times*. Yes." I try to lower my heart rate but I feel my rage building. Talking about Dad like this, to strangers, explaining him to them, is bizarre and awful and I shouldn't have to do it. "He had a lot of passion projects. So—"

"Yes, I read an article," James interrupts, his interest now truly piqued, and I have to squeeze my eyes shut to stop from grabbing his pompous BVI yacht club tie and throttling him. When I open my eyes he hasn't noticed or cared. He continues unfazed. "Yes, *The New York Times* called him 'the last of the true Renaissance men': puzzles, codes, word games. And the wind farms, structures, mathematics. I didn't even really understand certain aspects of what he did in the article but overall, very—"

"Yes, yes. Overall, *very* impressive. He was. Yes. Yes. He was," I say, by rote, echoing James back to himself with a tone I hope expresses benevolent thanks for his opinion on a man he never met but was absolutely everything to me.

I look up to see the car has stopped in front of a gatehouse, the entrance to a walled property.

The gatehouse is shuttered up with no one present to let us in. James seems to snap out of his Renaissance-man-based reverie and I watch professional James, the James I actually prefer, reappears. He turns in the seat beside me.

"This is it. No security team employed at present but I've got a gate fob here." He pulls it from his jacket pocket with an expectant smile. "Welcome to Anderssen's Opening."

For the second time this week I feel my jaw slacken and my mouth drop open. "Excuse me? What did you just say?" I ask, looking at James in disbelief. I sit up in my seat—every fiber in my being alive again for the first time since my father's death.

"Gate fob? Anderssen's Opening?" he hazards.

"You're telling me this house is called *Anderssen's* Opening?"

He frowns. "Yes, why?"

"Sorry, I must be misunderstanding this." I take a breath before attempting to make sense of it. "That name, is it connected in some way to the area here, the bay, or—?"

"No, no. We're between bays here. Pond Bay is that way," he says, gesturing left. "Mahoe that way," he adds, signaling right. "*Anderssen* has no significance to the island. It's just a name. Perhaps it had significance to your father?"

I feel a tight knot form inside my stomach. It most definitely did. And it does to me. It is a message, a challenge. My dead father *is* communicating with me. To leave me a house and name it this—

James is staring at me.

I feel a hot flush in my cheeks as I formulate a response. How to explain—

"Anderssen's Opening is a chess move. A challenge. A very strong, very rare opening move. Adolf Anderssen beat Paul Morphy with it in the 1800s. Anderssen's Opening was sneaky. Is sneaky. You move your least important pawn one square forward and you wait to see what the opponent does next. It's a non-move, a taunt almost. You put the ball in their court—and then you watch and wait to see what they do next."

"Okay," James says, his bottom lip curling. "And does that mean something?"

"Of course, it means something. Everything *means* something, James. I'm just not sure exactly what this means yet. What he means. But he wants me to find out."

CHAPTER 6
MARIA

The door, now open, reveals what lies beyond it: the room is very large, white, with smooth walls that are ambiently lit as if by daylight, though being beneath ground, there are no windows.

It is completely empty.

The lights change slightly in tone as Maria peers into the space, as if sensing her.

Maria steps back from the threshold quickly, instinctively, and the lighting returns to normal. She takes in the cavernous room from the safety of the hallway. A small metal plate just inside the hydraulic doorway reads: THE ATRIUM. But the room doesn't look like one, at least not to Maria. She searches her mind for atriums and finds only remembered images from coffee-table books: old European courtyards, Italian vestibules, open-air cobbled sun-traps. But the space in front of her now is internal, a sealed room. Then Maria's mind finds something else, the other meaning of the word: a word she recalls vividly from her days at Cornell. The atrium of a human heart. An anatomical cavity, or passage. The chamber of the human heart that receives blood from the veins and forces it on into ventricles and then on and on around the body. She shivers, the memory of cutting open a human cadaver suddenly flashing through her mind. Strange, it didn't bother her at the time. And though she shelved medical school after the second year, it wasn't for squeamish reasons. She wasn't a delicate person; God knows she wouldn't have lasted long in her life if she were. She worked her way up to Cornell the hard way, from nothing and nowhere.

There is nothing in the room before her at all.

Except, she suddenly makes out, something on the far wall.

On the farthest wall from the door, at chest height, a green button begins to glow. It pulses as if willing her to walk across the vast, empty space and push it. Maria watches it intently for a full minute, her expression tight with suspicion.

"Hm, okay," she says finally, appraisingly.

Then Maria shakes her head, definitively steps away from the room, and lets the door automatically close in front of her—the room, button and all, safely out of sight again.

Probably best not to get involved in any of that, Maria reasons.

And then her thoughts go again to her absent client and his two children, and whether they will ever arrive, whether they even exist. The room's strangeness breeding stranger thoughts: *What is it for, and why had it been locked?*

Back upstairs, Maria considers her options. She could call the woman with the too-tight chignon again and request an end to this job.

Or she could ignore the room downstairs completely until the electrician she was promised arrives, resets the fault, and restores the locked room to its former secured setting.

Or, of course, she could march straight into the white room

and smash her hand onto that pulsing green button. What could it possibly do?

She stifles a giggle. Imagine if she was that fucking stupid.

Instead Maria makes her way across the living room to phone the woman. Best to cancel the job; it's getting a little too weird. Canceling now could secure her at least a percentage of her fee as a goodwill gesture.

But then again, that would rely heavily on the client's sense of fairness. She stops just short of lifting the telephone receiver. Fairness isn't a common trait at this level—at any client level. Fairness, if it ever exists, is only optics. And there are almost never optics in dealing with hired help.

Her hand pulls back slightly from the receiver at the thought of losing her fee, of losing what should rightfully be hers.

And just as Maria decides she will stay a little longer, the sound of the front doorbell cuts through the empty house.

Maria turns to the chime, momentarily baffled, her thoughts caught short. Then, remembering the electrician, she heads toward the hall.

Through the front entrance's floor-to-ceiling glass, she sees a man in his fifties with a kind face wearing a chain electrical company uniform. He gives her a hopeful smile, morning sunlight blinding him so he has to squint to see her through the glass. Clearly uncertain that he is in the right place, he gives her a hesitant wave.

Maria studies him a moment before deciding to smile back, return his wave.

He raises a security lanyard looped around his neck, the same as the one the gatehouse guards gave Maria the day she arrived.

Maria remembers that the property is surrounded by security. If this man was a threat, he wouldn't have gotten this far.

His voice is muffled, reedy, through the glass. "Hi, it's Joon-gi. They sent me up from the gatehouse. I've got to check the electrics." The statement is half question.

The man misconstrues Maria's curious gaze and adds, "I'll be quick. Thirty minutes max?"

Maria remains silent for a moment then raises a finger and says, clearly, so he can hear her through the glass, "Just one minute."

She disappears back into the living room to call the woman with the too-tight chignon.

Three minutes later, Maria lets the man in.

Twenty minutes later, he is packing away his tools and folding up his dust blanket. "Just a loose connection," he tells her when she pops her head around the doorway of the master bedroom. "Happens sometimes with new builds. Things need to settle."

For some reason Maria finds herself looking up at the ceiling as if it might be something other than a ceiling, knowledge of the strange room beneath them weighing on her mind.

A thought occurs to her. She watches the electrician as he fills out a service docket with a small red pencil. She is considering what she is about to say very carefully.

When the man looks up, he finds Maria staring at him. Misconstruing her look again, he reassures her, "Oh, you don't need to sign anything. I'll just leave the docket with you."

Maria's question solidifies in her mind. She raises herself up to her full height and gives him a winning smile. Then, seemingly as an afterthought, she adds, "Actually, I don't suppose you could take a look at something else, for me, could you? Downstairs?"

THE ELECTRICS IN THE MASTER bedroom may have been successfully reset but down on the lower floor the locked door's panel still glows green.

Maria explains that the door should be locked. The two tilt their heads in unison as they consider the problem.

"So, it was locked. And it just unlocked itself?" he asks.

Maria nods.

"And you want it locked again?" he says, aware something strange is going on here but also that he is not yet able to grasp its extent.

"Yes, if you can that would be good," she answers simply.

The man raises his eyes to meet hers. "Why do you need it locked? What's in there?"

Maria gives a noncommittal shrug. "Nothing."

"There's nothing in there? Then why do you need—"

Patience wearing thin, Maria leans past the diminutive man, and presses her palm to the lock panel.

The hydraulic door slides smoothly open to reveal the empty room.

The two stare in.

"Empty, see?" she comments.

"What's that?" the little man asks.

"A green button," Maria replies.

"What does it do?"

"I don't know," she answers. Then with absolutely no intention of entering the room herself she asks, "Do you think we should press it?"

The man turns to Maria, studying her face: her beautiful, feminine features, her thin frame, her soft immaculate uniform— and he finds whatever reassurance he was looking for there. He looks down at the room's threshold and after a moment's hesitation steps across it into the wide-open space of the white room.

Once inside, he looks up, taking in the size of it. He spreads his arms like Christ the Redeemer and spins surprisingly un-selfconsciously then lets out a chuckle. "It's big. Big room. Must have cost a fortune to dig out of the cliff rock. Is it a gallery?" He points to the pulsing green button. "Rich-guy art?"

Maria lets out a grunt of appreciation at the logic. It hadn't occurred to her that this could just be a piece of ludicrous over-priced contemporary art. And now that he is in the room, even he takes on a relevance, a specificity that perhaps he did not necessarily possess before. Living art. Everything he does is somehow brought into focus by the clarity of the room, so that when he suddenly pulls up short it is almost as if he has shouted back across the space to her. She stares at his unmoving back—he is transfixed by something on the wall surrounding the green button. He walks over and leans in to take a closer look.

"What's wrong?" Maria asks.

"It's weird," he calls back. "There's no access panel for the button." He turns back to her, his face suddenly a little ashen.

"Oh, okay. What does that mean?"

He gives a strange shake of the head. "Well, we're under-ground here. This whole basement level is carved out of the rock. They dug down. The walls should back directly onto more bedrock, so it follows that all the building's electrics should be accessible from inside the house. I mean, you can't get outside the building down here. But this button doesn't have an internal access panel. There has to be a way to get to the wiring—" He breaks off, touching the smooth white walls in broad, wide strokes either side of the button.

He steps back from the button, suddenly a little fearful.

"If there's no access to the wiring *in this room* then that means there *is* access on the other side," he says, carefully, pointing beyond the wall.

"So what you're saying is there's more house? Beyond this room?"

"Yeah." The man swallows and nods. "Must be."

Maria thinks she follows the man's line of thought and why it might surprise or even concern him. The proportions of this room alone are enough to pose the questions: who would build a room like this and why?

He turns his head slowly back to the green button as if it had spoken. "Have you tried it?" he asks Maria, gesturing to its green glow.

"No way," Maria answers. "I haven't even been inside the room. To tell you the truth, I thought the door might lock behind you, and trap you, as soon as you walked in." She smiles, hoping he might place her honesty in higher esteem than her blatant disregard for his safety. "But that didn't happen," she reminds him. "And to be honest, I think I've just been freaking myself out about it."

The man weighs her words, then his posture softens. "Yeah, it's just a room," he says, as much to himself as to her. And with a sudden reassurance and confidence that the world is ultimately a known quantity, he lifts his hand and pushes the green button.

CHAPTER 7
NINA

The house finally comes into view as we reach the midpoint of the steep stone steps. Anderssen's Opening.

"This was all just headland before the house was erected. The house's private beach was only accessible from the sea but they carved a staircase into the rock, just like this one, so it can be reached from the house," James huffs back to me as we climb, one arm stretching down in the direction of the sea far below us.

"They cut into the rock?" I ask and watch the back of James's head nod.

He catches his breath and continues. "Yes, the whole property structure is grafted into the rock. As far as I can see from the planning permits, a geological survey was done by a British company. There's a cave system under us, so the lower level of the property might not have required much excavation given the existing spaces. But I can send you the original sub-surface geomatic findings if you're interested." He pauses, momentarily, turning back to me with an amused smile. "If you're concerned it might all fall into the sea in the night, be assured that your father oversaw construction."

The least of my concerns is anything my father built falling into the sea.

"He was here, though? During construction?" I ask a little too fast off the back of James's last comment, forcing him to snatch another hastily labored breath before answering.

"Perhaps not for the entirety of the project, but yes, he would have needed to sign off the individual stages of construction in person."

I let that sink in. James reapplies himself to the steep staircase, and we continue our ascent.

The gardens pool out around us as we ascend, tightly grouped split levels of manicured tropical plant life, bright florid flowering monsters vying for space with spiky hardier vegetation accompanying us on our climb. James huffs on ahead as I note the blooms, looking for signs from him, signs *of* him.

"Two hundred and thirty steps up to the property from the gatehouse," James says, chuckling, then splutters a cough as his breath catches. "I imagine deliveries were problematic," he continues, breathless. "If I recall correctly, there are even more down to the beach, but the view is truly breathtaking there—so the time passes quicker." In the heat I am finding this hard and I am ten years James's junior, and a regular runner. "Not far now," he sighs, head dipped with exertion, and that is when I catch sight of it above us.

The clean glass and steel of it bobs into view overhead, each step up revealing centimeters, meters of it to me. It is not a sprawling millionaire's mansion but a tightly contained series of glass boxes: modern, minimal, and perfectly formed. It is by no means big but I know its size is deceptive, seemingly a bungalow from our approaching angle. I have to remind my-self of what James has told me, that the building goes down also, into the rock, with rooms looking directly out of the sheer cliff face below us.

We reach the top and James gives an expansive grunt. "Here she is. Three thousand square feet of prime real estate built into the rock of the British Virgin Islands. And she's all yours."

All mine.

The edges of the glass-and-steel building glint and glim-mer in the sunlight. Blue sky and passing clouds reflect from its immaculate surface.

Everything about this house is diametrically opposed to my father's townhouse back in London—its dim rooms, restrained pomp, original moldings. And yet I see as plain as day that the house in front of me *is* entirely my father. The clarity of the lines, the purpose, the simplicity and synergy with the natural world around it. An emotion I had not anticipated shifts deep inside me: loss, profound loss. I feel my eyes fill and I quickly tear them from the building.

At the summit, James has collapsed into a sympathetically placed bench at the crest of the stone staircase and is invested in checking his phone while he recovers his breath—and dig-nity. I move past him, tacitly acknowledging that, perhaps, we both need a moment.

I head along the terrace that wraps around the entire prop-erty, my need overtaking me, then I stop dead in my tracks as the front, or rather the back, of the property reveals itself.

The terrace drops to three separate levels. On one, the gleaming blue-green of an immaculate infinity pool, around it thickly cushioned loungers. As if pulled by the tide, my eyes flow across the sweep of the architecture, everything posi-tioned perfectly to direct the eye to the view: the vast expanse of the calm, crystal-clear Caribbean Sea that stretches out beneath, beyond, and around us.

My gaze finds the beach steps James mentioned and I follow their line down the cliff face, through the palms, to a small cove. Down there, my beach: through the foliage, I see the outline of loungers, a hammock, and pink-white sand.

Maybe he built this house *for* me. I let my thoughts roll and revel for a moment before shaking myself back to reality. He did not build this house for me; it was finished long ago and I was never made aware of it. My eyes prickle again, because I am tired, and I miss him, and I want to lie down.

I hear James rise behind me and I pull myself together. There will be time to cry and sleep later.

James draws level with me and takes in the view too. "I've seen a lot of properties on the islands but this is up there. Beautiful. Not the highest price tag, obviously, and certainly not the most ostentatious. But efficient luxury, as they say. Perfectly made. Everything you need. No more, no less."

He points down to the next terrace level, and I see the large glass windows built into the rock face, and through them, into the indoor pool glowing like a jewel in the dimness of the lower level. "If it rains," he says with a smile.

He indicates for us to head back to the entrance with a grand gesture. "Shall we?"

INSIDE THE HOUSE THE TEMPERATURE drops, pleasingly. "Fully integrated air-conditioning throughout. Integrated speakers, entertainment systems, lighting. A smart system with voice activation for pretty much everything. There's no phone signal inside the property due to the concrete, so the integration is a practical choice rather than a flourish.

"What's your favorite song?" he asks me, and I look at him

blankly for a moment before I can make sense of the question. And for some reason Dad's favorite song, the last song the university quartet played at the end of his memorial service— a joke of sorts—springs to mind.

"'Always Look on the Bright Side of Life,'" I say, with perhaps a humorous lack of humor.

James gives a little chuckle. "Ah, excellent choice," he mutters then raises his voice in a declamatory fashion to say, "Bathsheba, play 'Always Look on the Bright Side of Life.'"

I feel my eyebrows shoot up. Bathsheba was our cat when I was growing up. And biblically, of course, the lover of King David, who, having seen her bathe, lusted after her, killed her husband, and married her. Then God struck down their firstborn as a kind of bizarre punishment. The sins of the father and all that. I just liked the name.

The music kicks in, flooding the house with jaunty tragicomic joy, and it takes a lot of facial energy not to let a smile break across my face.

Instead I give James a nod of appreciation.

"Yes. Fitting."

JAMES GIVES ME THE TOUR. The biometric door system is explained and my own hand scanned into the central control panel. So far, so bizarre. But again, very like Dad, and a modern house deserves a modern security system. I see the logic in it, even if something about it sends a shiver down my spine.

The house is everything I might have expected from the outside.

Vast sweeps of marble counter. Cool tiles underfoot. Perfect, immaculate, but somehow anonymous, a blank canvas.

A state-of-the-art, chef-grade kitchen—an odd inclusion given my father could at best boil an egg, perhaps at a push bake some asparagus. I struggle to imagine him here, apron on, amid all of this.

"It's immaculate," I comment. "Who has been maintaining it?"

James smiles as if he himself has chipped in with some hoovering. "Your father hired through various companies. But we had the house deep-cleaned ourselves, and stocked, prior to your arrival. Again, as specified in the will, with funds set aside."

"The will specified the type of food that should be here for me?"

James nods. I immediately head to the fridge and open it.

A shudder in my chest as I see what is inside. Familiar brands stare back at me. Our usuals. This could be our fridge back home. Driscoll's strawberries, Alpine yogurt, Red Leicester, Ploughman's Chutney, all our favorites are there.

For a second, my father is alive again, he is here, in this house. I half expect his warm hand to land reassuringly on my shoulder and welcome me home. But it does not. Because this is not my home.

I am lucky my back is turned to James as I quickly wipe away my tears and close the fridge door.

James is looking away when I turn back. Of course he is, ever the professional, he's done all this before.

The kitchen gives way to a large open-plan sitting room, a sunken area with custom seating built in. Contemporary art hangs from the bright-white, gallery-style walls.

I study the artworks that he must have chosen, that must have spoken to him in some profound way, and try to guess what he saw in them. But their abstract starkness rebuffs any attempt at connection.

I try to work out if all of this—the minimalism, the money, the cool clean lines and empty brutalism—was in truth the kind of thing my father *actually* liked instead of our warm, book-littered home. I think of his wind farms, cold and silent and monolithic off the coast of Britain. Was that him, really?

The paintings stare back down at me, impassive, their tone understated, blurred shapes, endlessly open to interpretation. But then isn't that a sign in itself? What he is showing me here is something different.

I vow, there and then, that I will find him in all this: I will grind out the meaning of this inheritance even if it kills me. After all, it's not like I have anything better to do: I am not expected anywhere else.

"It's all cataloged in your beneficiary pack," James pipes up, then points to the giant giclée prints hung high on the wall above us. "Those pieces are Pamela Rosenkranz, and the triptych we saw back in the lobby was Bacon." I pull my eyes away from the gleaming photographic prints of stark empty rooms above me—a liquid submerged pink room, a brilliant white room—to look back at James.

"He has a Bacon?" I blurt, certain I have misheard.

"Well, you have a Bacon. Though it is an *early* Bacon," he adds. "He was still a furniture designer back then, of course. His work was still all very light and jolly. But it's a Bacon nonetheless."

I open my mouth to ask the question that every fiber of my being now wants to know—*how the hell could my father possibly have afforded all this*—but the words do not make it out of me. Instead my lips open and close soundlessly, a little guppy fish caught in a strong current, because I guess I know.

My father must have been paid a lot more for his work than I ever could have imagined. I am sure there will be a trail of deposits in whatever bank accounts are listed in the pack James has provided. I look down at it in my hands, and I want to tear it open and pore over it on the floor in front of him, but thankfully I still have the strength of mind not to do so. I can wait another hour or so.

There I was all these years thinking my father did what he did for the love of it, for the pioneering legacy building of it—but no. They must have paid him an absolute fortune.

And the truth is, he kept that from me.

Of course we never wanted for anything, but he kept all this—this immense wealth, this potentially ethically question-able hoard—from me. He must have been a genius for hire. A genius who, it seems, had little issue with lying to his daughter.

There is a trail here to follow, and my father is finally lead-ing me to an answer.

"Should you decide to part with any of the art collection, now or in the future, we'd be happy to assist at Mitfield & Booth," James says with an admirable level of disinterest.

I give a nod of acknowledgment as my gaze moves on to the enormous wall-to-wall glass doors across the front of the room. Outside is the immense curve of the island's coast, the tops of the palm trees beneath us, the cove with its perfect crescent of sand, and out into the shallows, the graduating greens of the island waters dropping out into the deep hue of the Caribbean Sea—the sun twinkling across it, glittering everything.

James moves behind me. Momentarily unnerved by his proximity, I spin, my shoes squeaking on the marble. He looks surprised by my nerves but recovers quickly, giving an airy gesture toward the staircase. "If you're ready I can show you downstairs?"

CHAPTER 8
MARIA

The electrician looks back at her with a smile that says: *See? Just as I predicted—nothing happened.*

Something inside Maria shifts, and she realizes with odd clarity that she wishes something had happened—to him. She wishes something bad had happened when that lovely, helpful, kind man, with all his misplaced male confidence, had pressed the button just to prove to her, and himself, that the world was as *he* expected and not as *she* feared.

That wish, that the world had opened up and swallowed him whole for his baseless assumptions, no doubt springing from anger built up over a lifetime of having to anticipate every eventuality in her own life as a woman: just in case.

Of course *he* can just press the button. But Maria knows bitterness is a pointless emotion. So instead she gives him an enthusiastic cheerleader clap for his bravery and ushers him safely back out of the room.

"I guess the button must just be for show then," she says, a hand gently leading him out into the dim hall. "That's so great to know, thank you so much for taking a look in there." The signals she's giving are clear, she hopes. She's telling him he has done what he was asked and now it's time for him to go.

Social order gently reintroduces itself to the equation.

The man looks momentarily deflated that their tiny adventure, where he was the hero and she applauded on the sidelines, is over but as they reach the stairs his ego rallies and makes sense of it all somehow.

At the front door, goodbyes are oddly exchanged and then he is gone.

MARIA SITS BY THE POOL, her limbs loose and warmed to the bone as she sips an iced coffee, hard won, from the professional-standard coffee machine she's finally managed to work out how to use.

The client and the children are not coming. She feels it now as if it is fact.

She lets the cool drink slide down her throat and closes her eyes. She tries to forget the green button, the man, the white room. She listens to the wind in the palms and she almost, almost lets it all go . . . until the sound of the house phone brings her eyes flashing open.

IT'S THE WOMAN WITH THE too-tight chignon checking on the work completed.

"Yes, he fixed the lighting issue. Yes." Maria almost stops there but decides to continue, her newfound anger still there, like a will-o'-the-wisp, rolling deep in the hidden parts of her. "He couldn't fix the problem with the locked room, though," she adds with an odd relish.

The woman at the other end falters a moment at this new information. "Excuse me?"

"The room you told me not to go in. It's open, unlocked. The man you sent tried to fix it but it's broken. Well, not broken exactly, the room just isn't locked anymore," Maria explains.

The woman on the other end makes an odd clicking noise, half tut, half hesitation.

"*You* haven't entered the room, though?" she clarifies.

"No, I have not entered the room," Maria tells her, with a strange jolt of satisfaction.

The woman is silent for a moment before answering, "Good, that's good."

"Great," Maria counters, "so I'll just stay away from the now *unlocked* room, right? That's what you're telling me to do? Right?" Maria isn't entirely sure what exactly she's asking but it seems to require specificity.

"Yes, that room is off limits, correct."

Maria gives the woman another moment to stew before filling the awkward silence. "Okay, understood," she says, before adding, "And I take it they're not coming. The children? The client?"

Oddly, the woman doesn't disagree. "We are still attempting to contact—"

"Right. Well, I'll be here. Until the final contracted day. Unless you'd like to cancel the rest of the booking?"

"No, no. Let's stick to the plan," the woman counters.

MARIA CONSTRUCTS A NEW PLAN: stay until the end, don't go near the white room, and collect the full amount of contracted money in ten days. No client is coming. It will be easy money.

———

THE NEXT EIGHT HOURS ARE some of the simplest, most carefree moments of Maria's life.

She lies on the warm sand of the beach, her skin gently bronzing as she reads. She swims in the warm emerald shallows and feels the sand ooze satisfyingly underfoot.

Then she lunches by the pool, sleeps on a sun-warmed lounger, swims in the cool chlorinated water when the temperature gets too much, hotfooting it across the baked-earthenware tiles back to the comfort of her towel. That evening she showers, drinks a glass of wine, and eats dinner while music drifts from the overhead speakers. She feels as close to free as she ever has. No one to tend to, no one to impress, just life to be lived.

Before bed, she goes through the house, closing up as she goes. She places the docket the electrician left her earlier that day on the hall table under a small ebony sculpture.

Downstairs, the door to the white room slides open as she passes it carrying damp towels from the indoor pool area to the laundry. Something new inside it catches her eye.

On the floor about a foot into the room lies a small object. She recognizes it immediately. She doubles back, squats down in the hallway, towels in hand, and squints into the room. A pencil: short, red, chewed at the end. It was the electrician's; he must have dropped it.

Maria considers the pencil for a long while. Then seemingly on a whim, she reaches out the short distance from the hall and tries to grab it, careful all the while to remain firmly *in* the hallway. But the little red pencil is just beyond her reach.

Of course it is.

"Oh, for fuck's sake," she huffs, and goes to get something long.

Spatula in hand, she tries again, wafting and leaning until she bites the bullet and crawls with both hands into the room, her knees still *in* the hall.

Overhead the lighting, sensing her presence, suddenly changes.

Surprised, Maria looks up quickly, loses her balance, and falls, whacking her elbow hard onto the floor. Pain shoots through her funny bone and instinctively her knees pull into the room. She freezes. Then lightning quick, realizing what she's done, she leaps back up, and jumps back out into the safety of the hallway. But nothing happens. She stares back at the room, almost disappointed. Nothing happened.

"Huh," she says.

The red pencil is still on the floor in there. So she just walks into the room and picks it up. Still nothing happens.

She looks around the space, her confidence growing. She spreads her arms now, like the man did earlier, like Christ the Redeemer, and she spins. Still nothing happens.

She walks over to the pulsing green button and stares at it. Then, as the man did before her, she smooths her hands over the white walls surrounding the button. He was right: no join, no access panel. But regardless, nothing happens.

So she too presses the green button.

A bassy low-frequency alarm is emitted, the lighting in the room immediately changing again, this time from white to pink.

This definitely did not happen when the man pressed the button.

Panic flares inside Maria. She spins but—as fast as she moves, and she moves fast—she does not make it back across the space before the door to the hallway seals shut in front of her.

CHAPTER 9
NINA

The next half level down, James shows me the bedrooms, three in total. A large, clean, impeccably designed and fitted master bedroom. The other two rooms smaller but no less perfect. The rooms are seemingly without personal effects, but I decide that I will scour the place—cupboards, wardrobes, shelves—for anything and everything once James is gone. I am shown the bathrooms, the wet room, then down another flight of stairs.

To the indoor pool, a mirrored spongy-floored gym, a cedar-scented sauna, a sterile white utility room, and then James brings us to a halt in front of another much more substantial-looking white metal door. Unlike all the others in the house, this door's lock panel glows blue instead of green.

"Blue means it's locked?" I surmise.

James gives a brisk nod. "Yes, we've had several firms out to look at the problem but, as yet, no luck. It appears to be jammed. No way to remove the door without substantial damage to the surrounding walls and structure. We weren't keen to move forward with that work without your prior consent."

He waits for me to say something and when I do not, he continues. "We have been in contact with the company that created the security system and they've agreed to reconfigure it free of charge, if that's something you'd be interested in arranging."

"Um, yes, I guess so," I tell him, taken aback at the oddness of the situation. "Sorry, just to clarify. What exactly is in this room?"

James frowns, pauses, grimaces, and then sighs. "Well, *that's* the question, really, isn't it," he says finally.

"Excuse me," I say as silence descends between us.

James clears his throat. "Well, I imagine: a home office, perhaps?"

I give him a moment longer but nothing comes.

"You *imagine*?"

"Yes," James replies simply.

"Okay, and what do the floor plans say is in there? There must be architectural plans?"

James straightens, still not quite on stable footing. "Ah, well, as I said earlier there are no structural plans. Well, rather, we haven't been able to locate specific structural plans. Of course, the recent survey only took into account the accessible areas of the property, but as you see, access to this particular room has been an ongoing issue. Once the door has been reprogrammed, though, I'm sure we can amend the plans. If that would be something you would be interested in doing?"

I try to wrap my head around what he is telling me.

"So this house, my dead father's house, has a locked room that doesn't appear on any architectural plans of the building and no one has been able to access it since his death. And that is not a cause of concern to anyone, potentially?" I stop abruptly,

the urge to explode into hysterics almost unmanageable—
with all my father and this house's high functionality and mo-
dernity, it is clear that, at the end of the day, nothing can open
a locked door except perhaps a large hammer.

I take a breath and regroup before continuing. "Does my
father's will mention anything about the room—a code or
something? Anything? You mentioned Melissa might pass on
a letter of wishes?"

James gives a tight smile and pats his pockets performa-
tively before the soft crush of paper reveals itself. He pulls a
thick duck-egg-blue envelope from his inside pocket and hands
it to me. "Yes, here we are. Though as I said it isn't of a personal nature. Purely a division of assets and so forth. His last
will solely for the executors, you understand."

He watches me thumb the grained paper. I feel exposed,
triggered by the sight of my father's handwriting in my softest
of soft spots, I clear my throat decisively and pop the envelope
directly into my bag.

"Yes, right. Probably best to take a look later."

James takes a step back from the door. Suddenly I can't
think of anything else I want more than to get rid of him—and
to his credit James seems to feel the whisper of it himself.

"If we wander back up, I can talk you through security
company options for the property," I hear him say, but I am
already mentally unpacking the house, scouring its rooms for
traces of my father. Besides, security hardly seems an issue if
it's impossible to even get into some of the rooms in the house.
"Almost all the properties along the coast of this size and
value," he continues, "have some form of security staff. Perimeter, gatehouse, grounds. We've been running a minimal ghost
service to keep the insurance valid but you might want to consider something more robust."

"Of course," I say as we reach the hall, orange-tinged sunlight streaming onto us through the vast windows as nightfall approaches. "Can we pick this up again when you bring the final documents over next week?" I hope he will pick up on my flagging focus and just leave me in peace.

"Not a problem," he says, his expression understanding but a little cloying. "The bulk of the paperwork I have left in the living room. You have the letter and the gate fob; you're entered into the biometric system. Everything in the house should be explained in the materials provided: oven, electrics, all that fun stuff. But you have my number."

I give him a weary smile, by way of thanks. "Thank you, James. You've been fantastic. I think I just need a day or two to acclimatize to it all, to have a think. I mean it's all obviously so incredibly beautiful, but practically, well, my life is back in England. I can't imagine staying here longer than this trip. I just want to get a feel for it before . . . He built it after all."

"Yes, understood. Well, take your time. We are here, whatever you need. If you decide you want to place it on the market, or whatever you decide, just call."

SILENCE DESCENDS AS JAMES'S REASSURING presence disappears down the steep stone staircase to the car park and gatehouse far below. I close the glass front door and squeeze my tired eyes shut, thankful there will be no more talking for a while.

Through the vast sitting room window, the sun is dipping toward the horizon, the sky now alive with peaches and pinks, breathtaking and calming. I watch the colors deepen until the sun slips into the sea, the house's exterior self-illuminating when darkness finally falls. The house glows in the new night air.

I fetch my suitcase from the hallway and wheel it across the marble, pausing to fully take in the Bacon triptych.

Astonished I did not place it sooner, I see it is a three-paneled screen: *The Three Furies.* The three goddesses of vengeance: Unceasing Anger, Vengeance, and Jealousy. But the triptych is beautiful, still, becalmed, with the pretty panels rendered in muted 1930s abstract geometric forms.

Odd subject matter for Bacon, and clearly well before his screaming-blurry-man period. This art is soothing more than anything.

Then my eye falls to a small ebony sculpture, a woman about to be engulfed by some unseen force, on the table beneath it. The figure's posture is tensed and ready for a wave that will never come. The air-conditioning catches on something hidden beneath it. An edge of white paper, flapping every so often as the fan's flow hits it.

I walk over, tilt the sculpture, and pull the paper out from beneath. I unfold its thin page. It appears to be some kind of invoice for electrical work undertaken. A small pencil-filled docket.

CHAPTER 10
NINA

After I haul my suitcase onto the bed in the largest of three generous bedrooms, I take in the room again now that James is gone.

As the largest of the three bedrooms this must have been my father's room—his bed, his sheets, his pillow.

I walk over to it and gently place a hand onto the soft give of it. I know the sheets will be long changed, fresh for my arrival, but I bend and inhale, hoping for his soapy citrus-and-cedar scent. A smell that has a direct line to my parasympathetic nervous system. But of course it is not there, just the scent of crisp, clean bed linen.

He is not here, not in that sense. But I know he will be somewhere.

I spot the large built-in closet lining one wall and head over. Inside is full: immaculately dry-cleaned shirts, trousers, cashmere jumpers folded. I run a hand over a tomato-red sweater, its texture telling me its quality, and I guess at its brand. The clothes in this closet are all expensive and new. I know they likely aren't actually new, but in comparison with my father's usual wardrobe of ancient Jermyn Street attire, this collection of garments looks rarely worn.

I look through each garment and imagine how he might have looked thirty years ago, how he might have looked before I was born. When he and my mother were together, back when she was still alive. For the first time in a while, I feel a different kind of heartache, perhaps a less selfish one—a heartache for him: for the life he could have had with my mother if she had lived. He raised me alone, a brilliant man forced to raise a child solo. Forced to hold his world and mine together after losing the woman he loved. He never married again after her death, never took off his ring, never so much as went on a date. Though I would have to take others' words for that as I was only a few months old when she died from post-birth complications.

He raised me, he had time for little else, and yet look what he achieved. In spite of me, perhaps, or if I credit myself, *for me*? I cannot even begin to think what he might have accomplished without me. It's funny, a thousand thousand days of selfless care and devotion to me, and my education, and my life, and the few times he was disappointed with me seem to lurch out at me from the past since he went.

I try to push a memory away but I can't.

I was eleven, it was my birthday. It was after bedtime and I was sneaking back downstairs to get a chocolate bar I knew was unfinished in my bag of gifts. I passed his office and heard voices. A man and a woman. My father and someone else.

It's funny to think that I didn't know the sound of her voice until then. He never talked about her, not really. He told me she would have loved me, that she would have been proud, that she liked flowers and Earl Grey and marzipan. But who she was, in her heart, was his. She was his and she was gone.

I walked in thinking he had a visitor. But he did not, his

voice was not coming from him but from the old tape player on his desk, the whir and clack of it now obvious. His voice from before I was born and hers too, just talking. A soft laugh. The sound of tea being drunk.

They must have recorded themselves for fun. She sounded a little self-conscious as he asked her what she made of the book they had just read.

My father looked up at me standing in the doorway and clicked off the tape, his eyes on me filled with a disappointment I still can't quite fathom to this day. And all I could think was, *He wishes she had just walked in, not me.*

I know I didn't kill her. She died from complications after birth. Medical failure. Oversight. A million tiny mistakes that meant her heart stopped working. But the truth seemed so clear in his look. The truth was that I was there and she was gone. That brilliant, beautiful woman, a woman bright enough to match the genius of my own father, had been exchanged for me. A moderately gifted, moderately attractive eleven-year-old albatross. He barked a "Get out." And a core memory was formed.

I did not mention the tapes again. Or her. She was his. And he would mention her when he did and when he did, she was still his.

Maybe I should have asked more? Maybe he wanted me to? A new type of regret blossoms in me.

But my thoughts have gone down a cul-de-sac and I know it. I push them away and gently close his closet. And it occurs to me that this place might just be a holiday home: that my father might just have needed more of the world to himself. And after a lifetime of service to me, wasn't he entitled to that? If he kept his wealth to himself, wasn't that also his right?

No one owes all of themselves to anyone else. We are all individuals, and what we give of ourselves, we must choose to give freely.

I feel a wash of guilt at having assumed my father did anything nefarious to secure this house, at having grown jealous that he had kept something more for himself and not told me about it. He was a human first and foremost—he was my father too, but he had a life outside of that, a life he did not owe me.

This house must have been part of that life.

I SPOT THE SMALL NIGHTSTAND next to the bed and am drawn to it instinctively. The little drawer in the nightstand, beckoning me. I lower myself to sit on the thick carpet in front of it and tentatively pull it open, its contents rattling as I do.

Piece by piece, I lay the drawer's contents out on the carpet in an arc around me. A set of keys, silver metal with a red float fob. I hold them up, turn them. It is unclear what their use is in a house with an integrated electrical locking system. I place them down and let my thumb find the grained black leather cover of a pocketbook. A small Moleskine notebook. Peeking inside, I see it is full, his handwriting bunched and scrawling through its pages as I flip.

I look across the room at my handbag, resting innocently on the low armchair by the door, and think of the *letter of wishes* that lies still unread inside it. Though the contents are purely functional, I know I will get more of his handwriting there too. I consider the other articles in front of me. A dog-eared Alexandre Dumas classic—not one of my father's favorites, I note, but a topical one given our island location. Then my eyes move to a small sterling-silver pig figurine, no bigger than a fifty-pence piece.

Beside it, a red pencil, stubby and chewed at one end.

I lift it and study the teeth marks in the wood. They don't look like his, but how much can you tell from a chewed pencil? It could be anyone's bite. And the house has been full of people since his death, after all: surveyors, appraisers, and solicitors. It might have just ended up here. Or else I could infer that someone else was here with him. I hold the idea in my mind for a moment before dropping it. It would be quite a profound change in character if I found out my father had shared a room, a bed, with someone else after thirty-odd years alone. Perhaps that is what he has brought me here to see: his truth, whatever that may be?

I reopen the small black notebook and flip through. It is a workbook of sorts: anagram wheels, sudoku panels, plays for chess games long past. Random quotes interspersed with his familiar line sketches. I linger now on one quote, scrappily penned under some undefined calculations: *For a man to know himself, he must be tested.*

So far, so Dad. Seneca. His favorite philosopher, a Roman stoic, famously exiled for adultery and forced to live out his days on the island of Corsica. Pleasingly topical, was this my father's Corsica?—although what crime he committed to end up in exile I do not know. It certainly wasn't adultery.

The quote's sentiment tracks, though. My father was always one for a challenge, for setting them, for accepting them.

He would leave puzzles out, my childhood and early adulthood peppered with increasingly complex problems. Whenever life was hardest for me—a new school, problems at work—the games would materialize, and the challenges would get harder.

Maths problems, riddles, translations, all pointing to some meaning, some answer. The distraction always bigger than the last, more taxing than the previous but also more rewarding.

I look around the room again. Is this one of them? After all, this is the hardest year of my life. Wouldn't it be just like him to set me my hardest challenge yet. A game bigger than we have ever played before. A game that seems to begin with Anderssen's Opening, with the ball in my court.

If this is a game, I will need more clues.

I head into the kitchen. He hated cooking, or rather it seemed to baffle him. So I'm more than a little curious as to what on earth I will find in this house's incredibly well-appointed food preparation area. The fridge I know is full of my favorites so instead I open the first cupboard I come to and take in the neatly arranged tins: chopped tomatoes, five different varieties of beans, artichokes, bisques, all stored pristinely. In the next cupboard, rows of baking ingredients: flours— brown, white, strong bread flour, self-rising, gluten-free— muffin sleeves, cupcake cases. I stare at them agog. Neither of us baked. Images of my father dusted in flour, rolling pin in hand, suddenly flash through my mind, more than a little baffling. Perhaps he developed a secret late-life love of *The Great British Bake Off*? I close the door on that and open another, this one full of spices and herbs: their seals broken, clearly well used. Another cupboard of dried goods, a fully stocked fridge, and several cupboards of chicly minimal crockery and I have completed the kitchen. There are enough basic ingredients here to make almost any dish. And while I am aware that James's company has obviously just had the kitchen restocked, it is clear that some of these items have been here for a while.

My father did cook, then. Or he had a cook. Or someone else was here who cooked.

I jolt out of my search abruptly as that thought lands: my father wasn't living here alone. There could have been a woman out here with him, or a man: a lover I never even knew about— a secret kept—as heartbreaking to me as it is unsettling.

I make a mental note to ask James if there is any record of another inhabitant.

I STAY UP LATE INTO the night scouring every inch of the house, every cupboard, shelf, drawer, and ledge.

I find little of substance, though every now and then I do stumble across a knickknack, or well-thumbed book, that I recognize from the house back in England. Objects that must have slowly made their way back over here with him. A small travel clock from his desk. His well-used Montblanc fountain pen, a gift from the university faculty after he won his first award. A rare first edition of *The Waste Land*, my mother's unfamiliar hand scrawled into the insert.

For the greatest man I know by the greatest I do not. All my heart, your Hyacinth Girl

I stare at her words.
Your Hyacinth Girl.
As Maeve said, he was a private man. I knew he loved my mother, I felt it to my core, more from the way he handled her memory and what objects of hers our house retained, than from his direct address of the subject.

I reread her words: words from beyond the grave to the man she loved, and now to me. All that love and now both of them gone. The fleeting nature of love and life is almost tangible to me for a moment—and then it is gone too.

I turn the book over, in hand, and look at the cover art. I am familiar with the text. T. S. Eliot's "The Waste Land." Strange material for a lover's gift, strange and sad, and heavy and portentous: as if she somehow knew her fate long before it befell her.

I try to remember what I know of the poem inside this book and what her reference here to a Hyacinth Girl could signify. Then the words tumble back to me: *"You gave me hyacinths first a year ago; They called me the hyacinth girl"* . . . *Looking into the heart of light, the silence.* A shot of hope, of transcendence, in an otherwise melancholic poem.

Was my father on the cusp of genius and madness—was she his shot of hope in the darkness? If so, he hid it well. But parents hide a lot of the world from their children, especially if they love them. He was happy and kind and content, I think.

I think.

But then here I am in a house of his making that I knew nothing about until now.

I slot the thin volume back into the bookshelf and continue my search.

Having run out of movable objects I turn to the walls themselves. I carefully check behind his priceless paintings for provenance—where and when each was bought—though I know James's firm will have notes on each in the beneficiary pack.

I am tired and sad and looking for my dead parents behind abstract paintings.

THEN MY MIND INEVITABLY TURNS to the room downstairs. I head down, the glowing blue light of the locked room's door panel pulsing at the end of the corridor. The one room I have not scoured, the one room I cannot enter.

Anderssen's Opening: an opening move, a locked door. A move that seems simplistic, innocent, that could almost be made in error. But it has a clear and targeted purpose: to make the other player make the first move.

Every answer I could ever want might be hiding just a few inches from me. An answer as to why he had this house, what it was for, who lived here with him, and why he never told me it existed. I walk over to it and touch the thick white-painted metal. The hydraulic door is warm, warm like a living thing.

I try the lock again. It does not open.

————————

THE BLUE LIGHT PULSES ON, slow and mesmerizing—it couldn't look more like an invitation, an opening move, if it tried. And suddenly I am certain that the reason my father has brought me out here is just behind that door.

In my mind, the house takes on the form of a puzzle box with this room at the start of it.

Somehow I need to get in there.

CHAPTER 11
NINA

There are sounds in the night. Things move in the darkness outside the house, or perhaps inside—I can't be certain if it's both, or neither. I try not to think of what lies beneath me beyond the locked door in the basement.

I tell myself that the noises are nothing, just the palms rustling in the breeze, birds screeching, creatures moving about. Or the clanking of the building's metal as it cools after a day in the hot sun—nothing more.

These are the sounds the world makes, I remind myself; I just couldn't hear them over the constant rumble of city life.

London was full of other noise: crime, sirens, violence, and humanity, but now, here, there is almost nothing and I find myself scared for the first time in a long time.

Silence sets the imagination on fire. And my imagination is primed with fears, death high up there, death front and center of everything right now.

And when you are alone there's a lot to be afraid of: intruders, accidents, or perhaps, worst of all, the slow unspooling of your own lonely mind.

I WAKE TO SUNLIGHT STREAMING through the edges of the blinds. I check my phone and let out a low grunt.

I overslept. Though it is hard to quantify oversleeping when there is no immediate reason to get out of bed.

I step out regardless and it is only when I am on my feet that the usual morning wave of memory hits me.

I am treated to my very own highlight reel of pain: guilt, shame, my father's last days, the last thing I said to him: "Thank you for loving me every day of my life, Dad." And the last thing he said to me: "It was the simplest, best thing I ever did." And the empty house back home, my advancing age, my lack of family, my stalled career, and ultimately the knowledge that in spite of what he said I must have been a disappointment to a brilliant man.

With that morning shot of *joy* I head to the kitchen to sink a coffee as fast as humanly possible.

The emptiness yawns inside me. It takes me an inordinate amount of time to understand the coffee machine, and then to operate it, but eventually I triumph. I sip gratefully and push all other thoughts away.

I pull open the terrace's wide sliding doors and pad out onto the already warm tiles of the pool terrace, then place my cup on a table and sit. I inhale deeply, the sweetly fragranced air slowing my racing thoughts. Eyes closed, I try to imagine that this house, this life out here is mine. But then I suppose it is, in a sense. Eyes fluttering open my gaze falls to the terrace wall. It takes me a moment to focus properly on what I see there.

A note is flapping in the warm breeze on the wall, a rock

holding it in place. I down a massive gulp of coffee and head over to get a better look.

As I get closer my pace slows, the words coming into focus. It is definitely not a note from James.

I stop abruptly as I read it, a warning, or a threat, roughly penned in Sharpie.

You need to leave. Now.

CHAPTER 12
MARIA

The door in front of Maria seals itself. It is locked. And for the first time Maria notices that there is no door panel on this side of the door. There is no way to reopen it. She is trapped. Beside the door there is only a simple metal plaque with the word ATRIUM engraved into it.

Maria places a palm carefully against the door, its coated metal warm to the touch, a living thing. She stares at the space on the wall where a lock panel should be.

This does not seem good. She will definitely not be paid now.

The room gives off a low-frequency whir now and its new pinkish tone deepens in hue. Something else is going to happen; she can feel it. The muscles in Maria's legs tense, ready to move again if she has to, but what she is not expecting is a voice. A calm computerized female voice fills the room.

"System activated. Please make your way to the vestibule door," it intones. Maria touches the locked door in front of her—she could not have made her way more to the door than this.

"I'm already here," Maria says out loud, hoping the voice is some type of voice-activated assistant, like the speakers on the floors above.

The voice does not respond. Maria retracts her hand from the warm metal.

An idea. She steps back and tentatively waves her hands around the doorway, as if it were a supermarket exit, as if there might be a motion sensor she isn't activating. Her waves broaden in span, then intensify, desperate.

But the door remains shut.

Maria looks around, certain suddenly that this is all some form of elaborate prank, a wave of relief coursing through her. This can't be happening; it must be a trick. Her new client and her new wards will appear from behind the locked door and announce they have been watching her the whole time and secretly judging if she is a good fit for their family—as in so many reality shows. She lets out a chuckle of disbelief.

But the door does not open. Nobody appears to disabuse her of the reality of her situation.

The room remains still. Maria reassesses. The electrical fault opened the door; it might have also locked it. There is a strong possibility that the door is just broken. That the voice / computer / room / whatever-the-hell *wants* to let her out, but it can't. She may be locked in for a while, at least until someone comes to check on her. And in her mind Maria carefully steps around the thought that there is a chance no one will become aware she is locked in, down here, for quite a while.

The client is not coming and the woman with the too-tight chignon won't be back to sign her off for another ten days. There is a chance the woman may call and then, not receiving an answer, investigate, but there is no knowing how long any of that might take. Maria is fully aware that she herself has been the primary driver of contact between them up until this point.

The only other person she has seen over the last few days has been the electrician. But he had a lanyard, he had to get through security to even reach the house, and there would be no reason for him to return. Unless he wanted to collect his stupid fucking red pencil. She looks down at the offending pencil in her hand as if somehow she might be able to MacGyver her way out of the room with it. A humorless chuckle croaks out of her, like a toad.

Maria is thirsty. She tries to remember how long a person can live without water.

From the depths of her half-forgotten med school knowledge, the answer comes and with it a wave of urgency.

Her palms fly to the door as she tugs, gripless, at its smooth edifice. Her panic-slicked skin makes that act even harder to achieve. She fumbles for the edges of the hydraulic door, the seals, with her nails, in an attempt to pry it open, a simple truth driving her on: human organs begin to shut down after three days without water.

Three days is all you get. As a general rule, no one survives over a hundred hours. No one survives beyond four days.

And Maria is fairly confident that she might, safely, go unmissed for well over that time. And though she is clearly aware there is no point, that the room she is in, that the house she is in, will be soundproofed, this is when she begins screaming.

"Attention," the computerized voice intones calmly, obliviously, interrupting Maria's hoarse screams, freezing her midclaw. "Please make your way to the vestibule door as soon as possible."

And in spite of her mounting panic and the sheer quantity of adrenaline now pumping through Maria's body, to her credit she forces herself to stop and think.

What am I being asked? She is being asked to walk to the door. But she *is* at the door. But then the question may be: is this the only door in the room?

There must be another door.

Maria spins around, her eyes flashing over the broad sweeping walls of the dim, pink-tinged room.

"Attention, this is your final warning. Proceed to the vestibule door immediately."

Everything in Maria's line of vision is degrees of white, the depth and perspective of the room hard to judge. Then her vision trips on something. On the far wall, a slight variation in depth, but no variation in light or color. But it is unmistakable now that she sees it. A new opening. The vestibule door. And through it, presumably, the vestibule. A low whirring tone begins, seeming to emanate from beneath her, and just like that, as Maria watches, the newly seen door slowly begins to close now too.

"No, you don't," she spits, springing into action and plowing full-tilt at the closing door, crossing the vast space of the room in a matter of seconds, to slip through the tiny closing gap, just in time, thwacking her other elbow hard into the wall just beyond the entry.

It is only when the vestibule door is firmly shut behind her that Maria, catching her rasping breath and clutching her incandescently painful arm, has the headspace to question whether going through was a wise next move.

Instinct has to count for something. After all, it's been keeping people alive for millennia.

And, she reminds herself, her instincts have always sent her in the right direction.

She assesses the situation.

Either she has accidentally stumbled on something she shouldn't have, something she was specifically asked not to stumble on—or none of this is an accident. This room, this situation has been meant for *her* from the very beginning.

Maria begins to realize that she never met the client, she never even met his children, only receiving jpegs of two smiling tots. She received emails from her agency, and flight information, and transfer details, but she never spoke to anyone in person. The only person she spoke to was the woman with the too-tight chignon.

She wonders if the woman is watching her now somehow.

Maria's gaze whips around, half expecting the woman to be behind her. But the vestibule stretches out ahead, empty, a long, bare passageway with another door at the far end. She scans the corridor. There must be cameras in here, she decides, though it is impossible to tell where they might be located.

The room didn't trigger when the electrician pressed the green button earlier in the day—it hadn't played fair. It had been waiting for her.

About a hundred meters down the corridor from Maria, another door opens. She shivers, though it isn't particularly cold, but the slight drop registers in an internal setting. The room beyond isn't fully visible, but the light within is bright.

Maria starts walking toward the doorway ahead of her.

Someone knew exactly what was going on here. They had a plan and they were watching.

The next room slowly reveals itself as Maria approaches it. With a flush of relief, like no feeling she has felt in her lifetime, she recognizes the sound of running water coming from somewhere within.

Whatever happens, Maria thinks, *at least I won't die of thirst.*

Through the doorway the room is now fully visible. It's much smaller than the first, though also pure white and immaculate. On one wall a tap is flowing, its water pouring down onto a grate and disappearing out of sight. Every few seconds the tap stops and restarts in automated pulses. Above the tap a flatscreen panel is built into the wall showing what looks like instructions.

Once bitten, twice shy, Maria waves her arm through the doorway without going any farther, her motion activating the computerized voice.

"Welcome, Yossarian, Maria. Proceed to the control panel to begin."

A shudder of dread passes through Maria.

That is her *real* name, a name she has not used with this client. It is not the name on her contract; whoever is doing this knows her birth name. They know who she is, her history, where she comes from, her damage and no doubt the series of leaps she took to get away from her old life and to arrive here.

She feels the twinge of her past awakening inside her. Her trauma—as always, buried just as far down as she can stuff it—twitching back to life. Her very own Frankenstein's monster, a shadow self, made up of off-cuts, bits of memory and faded scars and half-remembered images. The journey she made as a child—the hunger, the thirst, the deep yawn of both inside her, deeper than the cold, or the heat, or the fear, and the dread of the adults around her disappearing, dropping away, the memory of only the three of them surviving. The three of them, alone, made it through with the forest dirt and the shiver of what it took to do so.

Maria inhales sharply. The realization hitting hard—she was not invited here to care for children, that is now a stone-cold fact, she was brought here to do this. This has something to do with the past. Her past.

She looks back the way she has come, down the blocked white corridor, but there is no way out. She reassures herself: sometimes the only way out is through. She knows this fact as implicitly as she knows how to stand and walk and run as fast as she possibly can. She learned it young. Sometimes the only way out is through.

The flow of water is the only sound in the silent rooms and Maria is already thirsty.

She has survived before and she will again.

And with that thought she steps into the next room, the door closing slowly behind her.

CHAPTER 13
NINA

I squint to reread the note as it gently flaps in the breeze across the terrace.

You need to leave. Now.

I don't know why, but it makes me angry. I rush to it and grab it, accidentally dislodging the rock holding it in place and sending the stone tumbling over the side of the wall and down the cliff where I hear it smack into the stone steps leading down to the beach. I look over the edge, down toward the sea, the rock shattered on the steps beneath.

Whoever left the note must have come up to the property that way, from the beach; there is no way they could have gotten past the locked gatehouse and perimeter walls.

I study the note in my hands. Someone obviously wants me to leave, but for my benefit or theirs? Is it a threat or a warning?

I wonder if they knew my father, if perhaps he never told me about this place because it was in some way dangerous. I bat the idea away: he would not have left me a house he knew to be dangerous, at least not without some kind of warning. But then isn't that exactly what I'm holding, a warning?

Someone knows something about this house that I don't. Or my father could quite simply have enemies. The idea seems ridiculous—that my kind, soft-spoken father could have ever made an enemy—but I suppose sometimes enemies find you.

I think of who else, aside from James, might know anything about my father's life out here. Someone on the island must have known him, and someone must be able to tell me something, anything.

I look at the note again and shiver. *Leave. Now.*

And then the thought occurs that, given my secluded location, how does anyone, other than James, even know I am here?

I lean over the railings and look in both directions, but there is no way to see out of the property to any potential neighbors. And no way to see in. There is no way anyone could know I was here unless they saw me arrive yesterday or if they work for James's firm.

I call James from the seating area beside the pool where the cell reception is strongest and he is blessedly quick to answer.

He is surprised to hear from me so soon and even more surprised when I cut to the nub of things and ask him if anyone else has access to the property except for me. If anyone has been out to the house from his firm. I do not immediately mention the note.

"No, you have both sets of keys and you are the only person entered into the building's biometric system. Aside from me yesterday, and the supervised servicing team last week, no one else has been to the property. But if you'd like to add anyone to the system, I can set that up with the company?"

I decline. I ask James about the neighbors: does he know them, what they are like?

"I'm not sure offhand, I'll be honest with you, Nina. But again, I can look into it. Privacy is at a premium on the island obviously, so sometimes it can be tricky to nail names to faces, as it were. But I can certainly make inquiries. Is there an issue at the property?"

I look down at the note in my hand and consider not mentioning it but then remember I am out here completely alone and I don't care if I sound paranoid.

"Yes, someone's left me a bizarre message on the terrace."

"Oh. Really?! What kind of—"

"It just says, *Leave now.*"

I hear James clear his throat. "Er. Right. Okay." This is obviously not in his wheelhouse. "Very strange. Would you like me to contact a security company? Perhaps hire a staff to monitor the access points."

Suddenly I feel a little mad. I find one note written in Sharpie and I need a twenty-four-hour security crew.

"Have you checked the CCTV footage?" James continues.

"Oh no, not yet. I haven't set that up yet. And I'm not sure security is necessary. I just thought I should tell somebody."

"Yes," James concurs, "that's a sensible instinct, I should think. Would you like me to contact the local police perhaps on your behalf?" Again I feel like a loon, the A4 sheet feeling flimsy and unthreatening as it flaps in my hand.

"No, no, I think it will be okay. Perhaps I just need to leave the terrace lights on at night—set up the CCTV system."

"Yes, well, not to play things down but I do imagine that perhaps it might just be the work of local kids. It is the school break after all and there isn't as much to keep young minds busy on the island as you might imagine. I'd say, sit with it for another day and see if it's something that reoccurs. It may just be a kind of prank. Also, the CCTV system is very easy to operate if you do want to activate it. Everything is explained in the pack."

After I hang up, I have a strange feeling: I am simultaneously embarrassed and unnerved.

I head inside and search out the CCTV setup information. There is no way I am sleeping another night here without the security blanket of those cameras.

THE SYSTEM IS UP AND running within the hour. I flick between shots across the property but of course in the warm light of day there is no one there. Until I flick onto the kitchen camera and leap into the air at the sight of a woman in her thirties leaning on the kitchen counter staring into a laptop. It is of course me. And at this point I make the bold decision that perhaps it is time I left the house and got out amongst people. And by people, I mean my neighbors.

Someone must know something about the note, prank or not, and I'm fairly confident that I will be able to sniff out a local issue if there is one. Either way someone might be able to tell me something about my father and this house.

Dressed in hastily steamed linen, I decide I have done all I can do in terms of dressing to impress my new neighbors as I sling a straw bag over my shoulder. After all I am who I am: and at this moment I am not the person with the identity problem, my father is. And both he and this house have a lot of explaining to do.

As I leave, I raise my voice self-consciously to Bathsheba—it still feels odd talking out loud in an empty house, to something I know isn't a real person. "Bathsheba, turn off all electrics."

My command is ignored. The room remains lit and the

kitchen radio continues to pump out the reassuring tones of the BBC World Service. I try again.

Bathsheba does not respond. Huh, weird.

I head to the main system console and manually use the touchscreen, sliding off the mains. There is a chance I pressed something I shouldn't have while setting up the CCTV system earlier. I will have to get James to send someone out to look at the system.

Luddite that I am, I have probably disabled something.

I stuff my phone, some water, and the note in my bag—on the off chance, I suppose, that someone might recognize the handwriting. Then I give the house a cursory look to make sure everything is fully secured and locked before I head out the front door.

At the bottom of the steep stone steps, I look back up at the house, but down by the gatehouse it is blocked from view by the ascent. Down here you would never know what was happening up there—if there was a problem there would be no way to tell.

I shake off the odd thought and tear my eyes from it before heading to the gatehouse. Beyond the fob-activated security gates is a rough-hewn untarmacked Caribbean country lane, tufts of sunbaked hardy grasses springing at intervals along the caked central mound.

As the gates close behind me, I look up and down the road. To the left it curves down to the public cove, our own private beach inaccessible from there—though since receiving the note on the terrace this morning I am not so certain it is truly *inaccessible*. The road to the right leads back inland and to the nearest neighboring properties. I look up its slight incline and with a deep intake of breath head inland, making a pact with myself to knock on the first neighbor's building I come across no matter how daunting it may look.

IT TAKES ME THIRTY-FIVE MINUTES at a brisk pace to reach the next property from mine. Flushed with exertion, I attempt to tidy myself before pressing my nearest neighbor's gatehouse buzzer.

As it sounds, I step back and take in what I can see of the property over the electric gates. It is larger than Anderssen's Opening, a three-story, Caribbean-pink-sandstone colonial-style villa. Its proportions are intimidating, though I remind myself that Dad's house, or rather, my house, has its own beach, so . . .

The buzzer sound stops and the entrance camera flares to life.

"Yes," a female voice answers abruptly, the tone blunt.

I lean in toward the camera so the speaker can hear me better even though I am aware there is no need, something stupid, and British, inside me desperate to be amenable. "Yes, hello. My name is Nina. I've just moved into the place next door." I wait, then add, "To you."

"Okay?" the voice asks, clearly not getting any inherent social cues from our apparent connection. She needs more to go on . . .

"Oh, right. Um, my father—well, it's a long story—I was wondering if I could pop in. Say hello. Ask you a few questions?"

"Ask me questions? About?" the voice asks, clearly appraising me.

"Well, about my father."

"I don't know your father. Who is your father?"

I let out a short sigh and regroup. "He lived next door to you. He left me the house. The next house along from here. I just moved in. I'd like to speak to you, as a neighbor. If that's all right? About the house. The area?" I give the voice a second then dig into my bag and pull out the note, holding it up to the camera. I follow up with, "Also, I got a weird note this morning."

A moment's silence, then, "Huh. Interesting."

"Could you open the gate?" I prompt hopefully.

A tart huff on the other end of the line then the mechanical sound of the gate's motor being engaged. It rolls back on its rails to reveal a cobbled courtyard, fecund with bright tropical blooms. Beneath a heaving imported ancient wisteria bough, the front door opens slowly as I approach, a young man in uniform giving me a gentle nod.

"She says you can stay for a cup of tea, as neighbors, but she is very busy and then you will have to go."

CHAPTER 14
NINA

"Okay," I manage, unsure if I should be grateful or insulted by any, or all, of that.

Regardless, I follow the young man through the opulently chintzy house—the polar opposite of Anderssen's Opening—out onto an enormous French-Riviera-style terrace overlooking a long Greco-Roman-style pool and beyond it a lake with a small blue rowboat bobbing on its surface.

At a wrought-iron table, a well-preserved woman in her late fifties, with perfectly coiffed hair and a wide-brimmed sun hat, turns to take me in.

"Sit," she tells me brusquely, waving a hand vaguely at the chair beside her. I'm not sure if it's her accent, or her age, but I do as I am told.

She extends a hand toward me expectantly, but when I offer mine, she looks at me like I have completely lost my senses. "No. Note. Let me see note." The hand flaps at me, again, brusquely, so I quickly divest myself of the crumpled paper.

The woman squints at the words, her bottom lip jutting.

She grunts then hands it back to me, her eyes skimming me up and down.

"You are English?" It's a rhetorical question but I nod regardless.

She looks past me and clicks her bony fingers high in the air for the man in the uniform. "Iced tea," she croaks at him.

Then she leans across to my seat and touches my arm, giving it a gentle squeeze, almost as if to gauge my body-fat ratio. "Cake?" she asks me, lowering her sunglasses to reveal two amused eyes.

"Lovely, yes, please."

"Cake," she shouts past me. "Bring trolley."

The man disappears and the woman stares out at the view. She doesn't look at me as she talks.

"Note is a warning. Not a threat. Warning."

I stare at her in profile, and after a beat of silence she turns to look at me again.

"A threat would be 'or else.' There is no 'or else' here." She jabs a finger at the creased paper on the table before us, then changes tack. "You know, company is nice. I forget it is nice to meet new people. What's your name, new little neighbor?"

"Um. Nina. Yes, it's nice. Sorry, what was your—?"

"Oksana." She pauses for a moment before adding, *"Zaytsava."* I can tell from the way she breezes over her surname that I am supposed to recognize it, but I do not. I do know it's Russian, though, having had an art history housemate at Cambridge with *very* present Russian relatives. I can only assume, by Oksana's inflection, that her family, or a specific member of it, is famous—or, perhaps, infamous.

"Well, nice to meet you, Oksana," I say, then jump slightly as the man in the uniform appears beside me with a drinks tray and places a frosted glass of iced tea down in front of me before gliding around to furnish Oksana with the same.

Oksana takes a sip and gives the man a grunt of appreciation, which he acknowledges, like a connoisseur, before heading back inside.

"He is very good. You need good people out here. There is nobody on the island—everybody has a job already. You have to find people back home and bring them out with you. Nightmare. You have people?" she asks, side-eyeing me.

"No, no people. I just, as I said, I just took possession of the house."

"Ah, divorce?"

"No, my father died. He left me the house. I didn't know we even had a house out here. It's all been a bit odd really. I mean, wonderful, I guess, but incredibly odd." I look at the woman I am nervously jabbering at and I wonder if our ideas of normality and oddness would even tally.

But she nods.

"Ha, yes. Death opens a lot of strange boxes," she muses. "You can't hide anything once you're gone. God knows what my children will find out when I go." She lets out a little chuckle.

I look at her afresh, this otherworldly woman, with a realistic lens, and I know for certain there is no way a woman like Oksana knew my father.

"Oksana, did you ever meet my father? Do you know any of your neighbors?"

She erupts with another chuckle. "Of course not. I come here to get away from people. I don't give a fuck. What am I going to do—have a barbecue? Small talk? No. But *you* are fun. Little red face. You can be my new friend." She pats my leg like you would a medium-sized dog as the uniformed man approaches with a shuddering cake trolley.

Little red face?

I instinctively raise a hand to my cheeks and they are burning hot. I forgot sunscreen, of course I did.

Oksana peruses the cake trolley then singles out a slice of Black Forest gâteau that glistens in the sun as the man places it on bone china.

"I'll have the same," I tell him when his gaze falls on me. "I don't suppose you know anything about the house, do you?" I ask her as he places the cake on my plate.

"Your house? I see them building it, trucks in the road. Years ago, now. And there was a woman—" She stops to fork a chunk of dark sponge into her mouth.

"A woman?" I ask, trying to mask my deep sudden interest.

She nods, chews, swallows, then sips her tea. "Yes, young woman about your age. Nice. Pretty. She stayed there. I don't recall when exactly, but she stayed. I never saw a man, though. But I saw them build it. They took a lot of rock, on trucks, they dug down, deep. It is a big house?" she asks finally.

I consider, then look back at the proportions of her much larger property behind us. "No, no, it's three bedrooms. But there is a private beach, so—"

Oksana tuts. "Perhaps rock was from another house," she muses. "You have a basement?"

I pause long enough for her to look back at me and lower her sunglasses.

"Yes, yes, there is a basement," I tell her.

"And what you got down there?" She chuckles. "Basketball court?"

"Funny you should ask: I have absolutely no idea."

CHAPTER 15

NINA

Thirty minutes later I am getting in the taxi she has booked for me in spite of my protestations.

With the address of the harbor construction company Oksana knows to have worked on the excavation in hand, and with her advice to also see the marina while I am there and lunch at Milos, I slip into the hot leather seat of an island cab.

At the marina gates I disembark my ride and let the sea breeze cool my hot cheeks as I walk the walls, my eyes scanning for the building number written on the slip in my hand.

I think of the note, folded in my bag, and its exhortation to: *Leave. Now.* And I think of Oksana's take on my predicament— no "or else"—and her odd disclosure about the sheer amount of rock removed from the site of the house when it was constructed. I think of that locked basement door and what might lie behind it—and now of how much house there really is down there.

I shiver as I pass under the awning of a building, the sun blocked suddenly by its shade.

This is the door I have been looking for: M. LOMAN AND SONS, LOGISTICS SOLUTIONS.

It is underwhelming, a dusty brown tinted-glass door, the brass name plaque beside it scratched and rusting. Next door a bustling boat shop and marina chandlery. There is no buzzer or bell and beyond the door only a staircase up, its thinning carpet balding on the rungs. I push through the entry door and, unclear as to what else to do, decide to head straight up the narrow staircase to the first floor. The landing reveals only one open door, beyond it a small grubby office where a tall, broad-shouldered man, in his thirties, in worn construction clothing, looks up at me with surprise.

"Hello? Can I help you?" he asks. He's American, and his tone clearly implies that he assumes I have wandered into the wrong building.

"I hope so," I tell him. "I was hoping to speak to someone about work that was done on a house near Pond Bay several years back. Anderssen's Opening?"

The man squints and straightens, then lets out a "Humph?"—the name clearly not resonating. "Where is that again, just remind me? You're the owner?" he asks after a moment.

"It's out near Pond Bay, the house on the clifftop. I've just taken ownership of it, yes," I tell him, with no small sense of awkwardness.

He nods, then thinks a moment. "Lemme get my dad. He's the boss."

I feel my body relax slightly as he disappears into the office and through a connecting doorway. I wait in the humid little hallway, the sounds of the marina filtering through to me from outside. The man returns with a slightly short but older, similarly uniformed man, who smiles generously before stretching out a hand.

"Mick Loman. I hear we worked on your building?"

I shake his hand, and again relax a little more. He seems nice, sensible, someone who might be able to get to the bottom of all this and put my concerns to rest. If he worked on the build he should know my father, he should know all about the house.

"Nina Hepworth. Yes, I was just asking about Anderssen's Opening—sorry, the house on the clifftop. If you remembered working on it? Or had any information about its construction?"

Mick looks back at his son briefly before turning to give me a confused smile. "Yes, Nina Hepworth. Yes, we've spoken. I sent you the floor plans, didn't I?" He pulls a confused face now, as if I have gone completely doolally but he's being very restrained about the whole thing. I am genuinely lost for words. I look between them completely back-footed, and for a second I even consider that he may be *right* and we have spoken and I *am* mad.

He continues, "You said you'd received them. Of course, they weren't the full plans, obviously. I mean, I did explain on the phone that we were only given area plans. But the ones I sent you were all we had to work from at the time—"

I raise a hand to stop him. "I'm sorry. I think there's been some kind of misunderstanding here. I've never spoken to you before. You or your son. I didn't even know about this company until this morning."

The pair exchange a glance, a shred of concern.

"Okay. Well," Mick starts decisively, ushering me into the office. "Let's take a quick look at the emails and perhaps that will jog your memory."

I follow the father toward his desktop inside the messy office, a growing sense of unreality imbuing what is happening, but I am careful to keep my one eye on the son as he hangs back, just in case I am walking into something. The warning on the note this morning blazes brightly in my mind.

Mick brings up an email thread on his computer but suddenly seems to remember something and blocks my view of the screen. He calls over to his son: "Can you get the contracts, Joe. NDAs. Bottom drawer."

Joe drops from view and rises with a small paper folder. He brings it over to Mick.

"Sorry to have to do this but do you have any ID on you, Nina?" he asks.

"You want me to sign a form?" I ask, confused.

"No, I just need to see some ID," he tells me plainly.

Bemused, and more than a little concerned, I cautiously root out my passport from my handbag and open it to the picture page without handing it over. Mick squints at the photo and then my face before rereading my name once more. He lets out a huff, clearly as baffled by the situation as I am.

"Okay. So, Nina. Obviously, we just needed to check it was you before discussing the NDAs. But here they are as you requested. Signed." He opens the folder to show me two slightly dog-eared, signed nondisclosure agreements. I bend to inspect the counter signature: it is my name but it is not my handwriting. I pull up quickly to find them both staring at me.

"You think I made you sign these? You think we spoke on the phone, emailed?" I ask Mick.

He nods, then turns his desktop screen toward me so I can see the email chain I have apparently been involved in. It has been running for months. I look at the email address, apparently my email address, and I do not recognize it. But I make a mental note of it.

"You first got in contact just over three months ago now. It's been on and off since then."

I take in the horror of what he is telling me and quickly jump to my own defense.

"Well, *that's* not me. I don't know who you spoke to. I only found out about the house a week ago."

The father and son share a look again.

"What was this person in contact with you about?" I ask. They hesitate for a second, unsure whether to tell me, confused as to whether the NDA they both signed prevents them from telling me, as I am not the person they contracted it with—or if the NDA itself is null and void for precisely that reason. They land on the side of the latter.

"She wanted the plans. And then she wanted the plans to be unavailable to third parties, hence the NDA. But it seems we might have made an error of judgment in terms of this person's credentials. Though why anyone would request the information she did, if she wasn't you, is beyond me. It's not like she could have done anything with it. And then to prevent us from passing on the information—I can't see why anyone would bother," Mick confides with a shrug.

"Can I see the building plans?" I ask.

Joe wordlessly turns to look in a large filing cabinet.

"Of course," he says, before continuing, "I mean, it was an impressive job, no doubt. A big dig, sure, but big digs aren't unusual out here. They're our bread and butter. So I don't know why someone would be particularly interested if the property wasn't theirs."

"Did the NDA she made you sign prevent you from passing information on to anyone? I mean, did anyone ask for the information and have to be turned down?"

Joe looks up. "Yeah, a solicitor firm a few weeks, maybe a month ago. But aside from that no one else has ever asked."

I realize that the solicitor firm must have been James's firm trying to sort out probate. But he told me he came up with nothing.

Joe lays out a partial architectural blueprint in front of me. I lean in to take a closer look, still wary of the two muscular men sharing this confined space with me.

The plan shows a partial outline of the basement. The locked room's dimensions are suddenly visible. I catch my breath.

"Oh my God. It's big." I jab a finger at the locked room's outline. "It's so much bigger than I thought."

Joe frowns. "You haven't visited the house yet?"

"No, I have. It's just locked. I can't get in there. That room. It's why I came here, to ask you."

"So you can't access the connecting rooms then," Mick asks. I flounder for a moment before his gaze draws mine back to the plans. Before the plans cut off, three additional rooms are visible branching off from the main locked room.

"Oh my God," I whisper. "And this is only a section of the plans. There could be more down there, can that be right?" I ask.

Mick's gaze holds mine.

"Yeah, we took a lot of bedrock out of that site. *A lot.*"

CHAPTER 16
JOON-GI

Yang Joon-gi has thought about the woman in the house a lot. *Maria.*

It has been three days ago now since he took the boat from Tortola to inspect the woman's property on Gorda. His sleep has been off since. Strange dreams. He wakes now, in his tiny apartment, sweating. This new dream was too real. He was trapped in the walls of the house—and they began to close in.

The dream had started with the woman, the house.

It bothers him.

It isn't just that she is very beautiful. Most women who work in the big houses are beautiful. Nor is it that he wasn't paid, because he received a notification of payment on his phone before he even left the island. No, it is instead the sense that she was there, alone, and not in the normal sense that one might be alone, like he is, but in the sense that she was clearly waiting for something. Waiting for something to happen.

And that room, the room she had been told not to enter; he cannot stop thinking of that strange white room.

His dreams circle it, its smooth walls, its lack of perspective, its echo and the question of what it might be for.

On the few private islands that he has worked on, they had far more extreme shit: climate-controlled art storage lockups, panic rooms, cryo-chambers—it seems to him the richer people get, the stranger their lives become. Fears become visible when the super-rich try to combat them. These people seem to fear being stolen from, and aging, more than anything else. The threat of death through the actions of others or through time itself unbearable.

But *that* is none of his business. Moving to Miami by the age of fifty *is* his business, and he can be as polite and unassuming as they all need him to be as long as their money keeps stacking up in his savings account. He is on his way out, off the islands, as soon as his money is made.

Usually when he has trouble sleeping, Joon-gi thinks of his future, what his savings will afford him in Miami. A state-of-the-art two-bed high-rise apartment in a new building overlooking the ocean, nice and high, a balcony, a small kitchenette—he likes to cook. His mother taught him a few recipes before he left Seoul to study in America. He has riffed on them and created a whole repertoire of options since.

He will have plants in his Miami apartment, and time to water them. He will sit out on the balcony furniture and read with the sun on his skin and the breeze in his hair and he will never need to speak to any of his customers ever again.

But since visiting the house on Gorda, his dreams of the future cannot lull him back to sleep; instead his thoughts always fly back across the Caribbean Sea to that white basement.

His thoughts slip, like ghosts through that house. There was more house beyond those basement walls. Wiring does not lie, and the power to that room does not come from the building's main access panels.

That was the strangest thing about the whole experience: that she didn't know there was more to it. That she was not supposed to access that room in any way. Why would that be, and who could have told her that? More important, why does the house have staff with no employer present? She didn't seem to be opening up the house for an imminent arrival.

Inevitably, his thoughts drift to the security at the gatehouse. It had not seemed out of the ordinary. But the thought vaguely occurs to Joon-gi that they might somehow be keeping her *in* rather than keeping everyone else *out*.

No, he reassures himself, of course she isn't there against her will: she opened the front door for him; he watched her head out, barefoot, onto the terrace to have her lunch while he worked on the electrical fault in the guest bedroom.

It all seems normal, for that world, until he thinks of the green button in the room.

But he reminds himself that the button didn't do anything.

He goes back over the incident in his mind. Now that he really thinks about it, he realizes the woman didn't enter the room with him. In spite of everything, she remained on the threshold as if she did believe, in some sense, that something else might happen if she entered.

He thinks of how, on the boat back from the island, he tried to make a duplicate docket and realized he had lost his pencil. He must have dropped it being an idiot in that room. He cringes at his lack of self-consciousness. He wonders if the pencil might still be in that room—he can go back for it. He can see the room again.

If he goes back, he can check on her. He can tell the gate security that he arranged with the woman to return the next week to recheck the wiring in the bedroom. He can even invoice them again for the visit.

And then perhaps, if he can put these questions to rest, he

will sleep again. He can stop thinking of the woman and the room. He can focus on his plans. His big plans.

So the next morning, when the call comes through from the agency to attend another property on Gorda, Joon-gi says yes.

And as he packs a lunch in his kitchenette, he promises himself he will finish this new job early and walk back to the house on the cliff. He will tell his lie about checking the rewiring, and once inside, he will ask the woman if she is okay.

He will ask to see the white room again.

He slips his food into his rucksack and then heads to the storage cupboard to collect his tool bag; he rifles through various boxes looking for something specific before finally pulling back with a triumphant laugh. And feeling like he is already winning the day by 8 A.M., he places his wall scanner neatly into his rucksack with his lunch. If he gets into the room again, he will find out for sure how far the house goes. Bag packed, he heads for the dock.

CHAPTER 17
NINA

When I finally emerge from the excavation company's building, daylight hits me once more, and I am momentarily blinded by the midday sun.

Blinking and dazed, I head to the marina railings and grab a firm hold—the solidity of it reassuring. I let the cool sea breeze hit me, the low hum of harbor life, the gentle slapping of waves on the hulls of the ships quieting my fevered thoughts.

I try to put what I have just found out into focus.

The discovery of the existence of more house beneath Anderssen's Opening is deeply unsettling in itself, but the thing my thoughts snag on more is who on earth has been pretending to be me for months. I cannot help but wonder if this woman, whoever she is, has contacted other people under the guise of Nina Hepworth.

I didn't even know about the house, so she had free rein for months to do as she pleased without even raising suspicions. And my father was still alive for some of that time; how did he not know? I can't help wonder what else there might be that I still do not know about that she may have gotten to before me.

And the question of who she is or what she might hope to gain from any of this is truly baffling.

Suddenly, something Oksana said that morning flashes back to mind. She had never met my father but she mentioned seeing someone else at the house: a woman, a woman about the same age as me. Could that have been this other mysterious Nina?

But I do not get to follow the thought as a hand lands on my shoulder and with a yelp of surprise I spin abruptly around to face the figure behind me.

Joe Loman, Mick's son, looks down at me, a surprisingly handsome, apologetic smile spreading across his face. Caught unprepared for the realization that Joe is actually an incredibly attractive man, on top of the fact that he just scared the bejesus out of me, it takes me a second to tear my eyes away from his deep-brown ones.

"Sorry, probably should have just cleared my throat or something," he says with a laugh. He extends something in his hands toward me and I see it is my sunglasses. I must have left them in their office.

"Oh, thanks," I blurt, totally unaware I was missing them until now. I take them from him and to my eternal embarrassment, I somehow manage to fumble them and they drop to the ground. One tinted lens pops clean out of the frame and springs toward the marina railings before skittering over the edge and into the water. We both lean over the railings and watch it bob for a moment on the water's surface before inevitably sinking out of sight.

"*Fuck,*" I splutter, with more weight of meaning than a pair of airport sunglasses could ever really warrant.

Joe bends to pick up the broken frame, one winking lens still intact, one empty.

"Not a great day, I'm guessing?" he asks gently, proffering me the broken carcass. "Judging by the bits I've been involved in, at least." I accept the wire frame and lean past him to pop it straight in a recycling bin.

"No, not a great day, week, month, or year really. You know? Not that one should ever complain. We have our health, so—" I break off, suddenly exhausted.

"That we do," Joe concedes. "But I don't think anyone could be blamed for aiming a little higher." He looks back toward his father's building, unsure if he should leave me in my current mood. I try to rally with a smile but my hands are trembling.

"Hey, listen. It's lunchtime. I have an awful sandwich back in there that I have absolutely no desire to eat—so can I buy you lunch somewhere? Or a coffee, or something? Milos is really nice."

"Oh God. You feel sorry for me, don't you? Listen, that really was not my intention. Please, have your sandwich, I'm fine. I'm a grown woman. I can lunch alone."

"I know you can lunch alone. I've seen people do it, it's an impressive sight. But I would *like* to have lunch with you because I like you," he says with disarming straightforwardness.

"Well, you don't know me," I bat back quickly.

"You just found out there's another house under your house. You're dealing with it in a pretty incredible way. So unless you're unnervingly good at subterfuge I think I've got a pretty good measure of your character. And you're beautiful and funny." He winces at his own words, before asking, "Too much?"

I laugh for the first time in a while. "Yes, too much. And I'm not funny, I'm just grumpy and British."

He grins. "Okay, noted. So, lunch?"

"Okay, lunch."

JOE LEADS US ACROSS THE marina to Milos, a chic seafood bistro with white tablecloths and silver cutlery. He shrugs off his well-worn high-vis overshirt to reveal a surprisingly spotless white T-shirt beneath, and as we head into the restaurant it is clear he is a local figure. I bask in the warm glow he seems to elicit from the staff and a few friends he bumps into.

On his recommendation we order a selection of seafood tapas and sip some cool drinks as I watch the world flow by below. The marina is beautiful, as Oksana described, and blessedly full of people, life, and distraction. I let it wash over me from the safety of the terrace.

Below us families sightsee, couples wander hand in hand along the lower terraces, and lone travelers solo lunch.

A pleasant, sleepy calmness pervades everything.

"How long have you lived out here?" I ask Joe, after catching him looking at me in silence.

"Since high school. Long story, but my mom got sick. We moved out of Chicago. They'd honeymooned here and loved it—he thought it would make her better. And then we just stayed here."

"And did it make her better? Out here?" I ask, hope evident in my voice.

Joe is silent for a moment, before he grins. "Yeah, she went into remission. Full recovery. Signed off. It worked. But then she divorced Dad a couple of years later and moved back to Chicago. We stayed here, though. All my friends are here, you know, and Dad's company, our company. Nothing back in the US now."

"Wow. She divorced him after. That's not how that story usually goes, right? Wow, I'm sorry. I can understand you wanting to stay, though."

He smiles. "Yeah, it's beautiful, obviously, and life is pretty simple but—I'll be honest, you don't see a lot of new faces."

I let out a bark of laughter. "Well, I guess that explains lunch then."

He grins. "Yeah, maybe it does." He looks at me again curiously. "And you, why are you here?"

"At lunch or on Gorda," I ask.

"Both I guess?"

I sober as I consider. "My father died. He left me a house. It's all very bizarre and confusing and it just seems to be getting weirder, to be honest. I didn't know there even was a house out here until last week."

"He left it to you, no explanation?"

"Exactly, and as you can see it is a very weird house. And now apparently it comes with a giant subterranean locked room, unknown others, and apparently a random woman who has been pretending to be me for months. Oh yeah and this."

I pull the note from my bag and smooth it on the white tablecloth.

You need to leave. Now.

He reads it then looks up at me, eyebrow raised. "I hate to agree with your bizarre and terrifying death note, but they might have a point. No?"

"That I should leave?"

"Yeah, one hundred percent." He chuckles. "I would be gone so fast. Sell, sell, sell. That's prime real estate."

I take a sip of my drink and try to couch my—clearly unorthodox—reasoning for not immediately flying home in terms that another human might understand.

"This is a lot for a first date, or whatever the hell this is, but I feel we've been through some stuff already. Fast-tracked or whatever. So the truth is: this is all I have left, of him, of my dad. And I don't understand it. And I feel like he wants me to understand it. I have this great job back home—overshare— but I don't have much else, and I can't go back there empty-handed."

Joe takes a moment to digest what I've said before nodding. "I get it. I think we never left here because this was the last place we were all happy together before she left. You know. Even though I outgrew this place years ago. Yeah, I get what you're saying." He smiles a sad smile. "Thing is this house. This house your dad left you, but never told you about, the one you're certain he wants you to understand. You might not find what you're looking for. You know that, right?"

"Well, good or bad. I'd rather know."

His expression breaks into a warm smile again. "So I guess you'll be sticking around for a bit then?"

"I guess so."

CHAPTER 18

NINA

After lunch he gives me his number and I tell him I'll text him. Suggesting he might get a kick out of taking a look at the locked basement door.

On the cab ride back to the house I remember the problem that morning with Bathsheba and I call James.

He doesn't answer so I leave a vague voice message, unwilling to get into the strangeness of the whole bizarre "other Nina" situation within earshot of the cabdriver.

I am reminded again of the woman Oksana mentioned seeing at the house and I can't help but wonder if it might be the same woman. Oksana remembered her as being about my age, pretty, and she had been staying in the house. She must have been staying when my father was still alive. A friend perhaps, or the daughter of a friend. I trawl my mind for any friend of my father's I haven't spoken to since he died but come up short. His funeral and memorial were well attended and I can't think of anyone, even a passing acquaintance, who wasn't present.

At the memorial, I'd even met students who'd only taken one class with him, so well loved was he.

I look up quickly, an idea flashing into my mind: what if this woman had been exactly that, a student of my father's? I let the thought simmer, and I do not like the questions that bubble to the surface. Why would a female student of my father's be here in my father's secret second home?

The idea that he was having an affair, perhaps a long-term one, and that this woman whoever she was had tried to lay claim to the house is unsettling. And yet oddly grounding. There is an understandable, pedestrian humanity to it. If this unknown woman was solely a jilted lover, then perhaps the note, the odd behavior make a kind of sense—it would be easier to scare me off than sue me for land rights. But what can she hope to gain other than squatting in the building until I get around to selling?

The taxi takes a windy corner and I slide into the warm door panel with a thump; we are nearly back now, the roads thinning. As I rearrange myself and recover my line of thought it suddenly hits me, dread seeping into every pore of my body: what if she is squatting in the house already? I think of the locked basement room, the plans I saw earlier and this unknown woman's desire to keep knowledge of those rooms secret, the noises in the night. And I cannot hold back the thought anymore: she might be down there right now.

Back at the house, when I make my way cautiously up to the top of the stone steps, body pounding with exertion and tiredness, it takes me a second to notice that something isn't quite right.

Plastered across the front door is another note. It is taped to the glass, and as I approach, I read the words on it.

Do not go down there

It is as if whoever wrote it had just read my mind.

I tug down the note and turn to scan the terrace, suddenly certain someone is still here, the hairs on my arms rising as my eyes fly over everything in sight. But there is no one there. I slip my hand onto the door panel and the door mechanism clunks open as I quickly push into the house and shut the door hastily behind me.

And yet inside I feel no safer, the thought of another person lurking beneath me, around me, anxiety inducing in the extreme.

Then I remember the CCTV footage. I set the alarm before I left and I know for a fact that I am the only person with access to the security system. Whoever left the note will have been captured on video.

"Bathsheba," I articulate, raising my voice to activate her, but she does not respond. I forgot that she stopped working. Instead I quickly head to the main console in the kitchen and manually activate the lights and air-conditioning myself before opening the CCTV system. The footage is there, recorded, intact.

I scroll back to when I left the house and watch myself, ghostlike as I head out of sight down the stone staircase. I scrub through the footage quickly, hoping to catch sight of anything, then to my huge surprise I do. I freeze the footage.

A man.

A man coming up the beach staircase. A man, not a woman, and coming from outside, not inside, the house. I zoom in. He is older than I would have expected, perhaps in his fifties, about five foot nine, wearing some kind of work attire. I press PLAY again and watch as he heads around to the doors and tries to enter. He cannot. I relax ever so slightly and watch as he cups his hands and peers into the darkened house. He must see nothing of note so he then heads around to the front door. I tense again as I watch him write the note and affix it. He steps back from it, a thought occurring, and then disappears around the property. I pick him up on another camera as he walks toward an outbuilding I had not noticed before. Perhaps a pool pump room or something. I fast-forward as he does something to the door and eventually it opens. I watch him step inside and then the CCTV cuts out. There is no more footage. I look at the last time stamp; the power was cut to the system almost three hours ago and has not returned.

I look up from the console, confused. It doesn't make sense. All the lights and electrics in the rest of the house appear to still be working, which means the CCTV must be on a separate system. I run to the window to see if I can see the small outbuilding the man must have entered. It is just visible through the foliage, but the door is shut once more. I think about going out there to investigate but I don't like the idea of that at all.

Back at the console I cannot restart the cameras. Fear mounting, I call James again, but the concrete prohibits the signal. I need to go out onto the terrace to call him. Instantly panic rises at the mere idea of going out there. But what choice do I have?

OUT ON THE TERRACE I call James but he does not answer. I leave a brief message: "James, it's Nina. Sorry to bother you again but I'm not sure what to do. There's been another note. I have the man on CCTV. He somehow disabled the CCTV but it recorded him before then. There's no damage to the property that I can see but I'm just a little shaken and not really sure what I should do—anyway. Call me if you can or email the house and I'll call you back. Just a little concerned."

I hang up and quickly text the only other person I know on the island.

Joe, thank you for lunch and listening to the whole mad situation. There's been another note and I'm absolutely bricking it. You have the address. I promise this isn't a cry for help—though in fairness it literally is a cry for help. I have coffee, wine, two spare rooms—so don't worry about all that. Please come keep me company in a non-sexually-threatening way. Nina (The real one, I think). x

I hit SEND, run back into the house, and lock the door.

I stand in the kitchen, lost for a moment, before the cold breeze from the air-conditioning unit makes me realize that I am drenched in sweat, its dampness cooling against my skin.

I need a shower, especially if anyone is coming over.

I quickly scan the CCTV footage again, concentrating this time solely on the locked basement door, scrubbing through for any movement whatsoever.

There is nothing. No one is living down there.

It is only when I head to the wet room, lock the door, and slip under the hot rainfall shower, steam tumbling around me, that I see *another* note, this time stuck to the giant floor-to-ceiling mirror opposite me. A note inside.

I leap back from it, almost losing my footing in the shower. The man was inside the house too. He might still be here.

I quickly turn off the shower and grab a thick white towel from the heated rail, wrapping it tightly around myself. Because I realize, with sickening clarity, that I didn't check the rooms when I got back.

I eye the locked bathroom door, the only manually locking door in the house. I am, at least, safe in here for now. But my phone is in the kitchen, on the counter.

I step toward the note, my wet feet slipping on tiles as I tug it sharply from the fogged mirror. The steam-weakened tape comes away easily.

I flip the note over but the back is blank. I reread its scratchy words:

Look in the mirror

CHAPTER 19
JOON-GI

There is no one at the gatehouse when Joon-gi arrives.

The guard building is locked, shuttered; a small blue light flashing intermittently on its door and two on the main gateposts, are the only signs that the property is not abandoned. The security system is active. He watches the security cameras, their beady crow eyes following in automatic judders as he approaches the property intercom.

He buzzes the intercom, waits, buzzes again, and then makes a show of hefting his tool bag in pantomime at the roving cameras.

Whether anyone is watching is impossible to tell, but no one answers the intercom. No one opens the gates.

He continues his show, for the cameras, of impatience and eventually of giving up. He walks away, seemingly accepting of the situation.

But he is not accepting it, because it's incredibly strange. For the property to go from high security to no security in just four days is notable. He distinctly recalls the woman saying she would be remaining here for the next ten days.

There is a chance that she has left early. That she has become bored of whatever it is she's waiting for in there and flown home to wherever she came from.

Joon-gi tries not to think of the alternative: that something bad has happened to her since he left. That the building is now empty because it has in some way swallowed her alive like the house in his dream.

His curiosity piqued, and aware that he can always plead ignorance or professional concern if caught, he considers another way to access the property.

If the cameras are viewed remotely then it will take the company time to respond with no one directly on-site. If he is interrupted, caught short by some hidden security personnel, then he can always tell them his lie: he is here to check the wiring again, as arranged on his last visit.

He feels confident that he neither looks enough of a threat nor presents much by way of motive that he would not be believed as a concerned electrician wary of a lawsuit from a lack of follow-up. Besides, Joon-gi has spent a lifetime cultivating the exact degree of inoffensiveness to these types of rich Western homeowners that he is absolutely assured they will assume he is a nervous jobsworth, rather than a genuine property invader, without too much trouble.

He walks away from the property and makes his way instead to the cove. The entire length of the coast of Gorda is public access. If you can reach it, climb over it, or crawl through it, then you can enjoy it—though the real estate developers and architects tried everything they could to make the beaches in front of the homes of the ultra-rich completely inaccessible. But Joon-gi has lived and worked in the BVI for twenty years now. There are ways around everything. Just as the super-rich find ways around everything in their worlds, so too do the people who live and work among them. Reaching the property's beach would require a scramble over rocks and perhaps a wade through the shallows, but it is doable. Anything is doable if you have the time and inclination, Joon-gi has found.

If he were to stop now, if the momentum of the day weren't bowling him on harder and harder, if he stopped to ask himself why he is doing any of this, he might not immediately be able to answer. But Joon-gi will have time over the next year and longer to consider what he's doing and why and he will eventually land on the answer that in a sense, he recognizes something of himself in the woman in the house. Both of them alone in their different ways.

He will come to understand that he believes what lies under that house, what might have happened to that woman, might be the event he has waited his whole life for. His moment to shine, to be the hero, to be the brave one. Because when he analyzes it, he felt of use during his short time with her, and not just in the sense that he was being paid to help her. For the first time in a long time he felt needed as a person. He felt part of something more. And of course now he cannot stop thinking of that room.

On the public beach of the neighboring cove, Joon-gi decants a few useful tools into his waterproof rucksack, hefts it onto his back, rolls his cargo trousers high, and wades out past the rocks that block the property's private beach from the public.

As his bare feet grip into spiked rocks and battle slippery seaweed-covered stones he plans what he will do, what he will say if he is caught, if he is wrong about all of this. If he reaches the terrace via the beach steps and there she is, the woman, lounging in her swimsuit, her expression aghast at seeing him there unannounced, he constructs a lie he will repeat. And then he will just apologize and leave. He tells himself it will all be fine.

BUT THE WOMAN IS NOT sunbathing on the terrace when Joon-gi finally hauls himself, wet and grazed, up the stone beach staircase to the house.

The traverse was harder and more involved than he'd expected, and now, sore and dripping onto the hot terrace tiles, he feels oddly foolish as he struggles to remember why he thought any of this would be a good idea.

But self-preservation reminds him that there are more important things to consider; he is on private property after all. If he's going to do something, he had better be quick about it. He has little difficulty locating the cameras around the building as he heads toward the main entrance. They turn, following his journey, and stop when he stops. It becomes clear to Joon-gi that someone is most definitely watching him.

When he reaches the front door he presses the buzzer again and waits, the camera's beady eyes on him. And even though it is clear they know that he knows they're watching, still no one replies to him.

He cups his hands and looks through the glass into the lobby. The house is dim; there is no movement within. On the hall table he spots one of his dockets wedged under an ornament.

Nothing within seems to have changed since he left four days ago.

He wanders back around the property to the terrace doors. He gives them a pull but they are locked.

Peeking through the clear doors he spots a half-full glass of water on the marble counter beside the sink in the kitchen. And a jolt of hope leaps up through him. For a moment he is certain she is in there, just out of view, just about to emerge from another room.

He pounds on the door, the sounds reverberating loudly

through the empty living room. He waits, eyes flicking from doorway to doorway. Then he calls too.

"Hello. Hello! Is there anyone there?"

The jolt of hope sinks back down inside him. He thinks of the room on the floor below, the white room.

She could be down there. She could be locked down there.

He has concerns, he argues in his mind, concerns for a customer's safety. Shouldn't he act on those concerns? If, indeed, they are concerning? He frames this carefully in his mind, and he finds that the answer is yes. If he acts out of concern, he may well save the day. If he is wrong then who could begrudge an over-efficient employee?

And with that his mind is set. He will check on the room. He will need to enter the house to check on the room.

He heads around the building to where he knows the mains enter it as camera eyes follow him. Once there, he removes his rucksack, pulls some tools from it, and sets about removing the external electrical panel for the building.

Five minutes later all the blue lock panels in the building fade, locking solid.

But around the back of the building, one door does not. This is the one mandatory emergency-release fire door that does not deadlock in the case of a full power cut—instead the door buzzes open.

Joon-gi gathers his equipment back into his bag, slings it onto his shoulder, and heads off to find where that one door might be.

THE SUN IS BEGINNING TO SET through the palms as Joon-gi slips inside the dim house, and the change in temperature causes him to shiver, his wet trousers clinging to his legs.

He moves briskly through the house, the way familiar to

him, branded on his brain through four nights of obsessive thoughts and unsettling dreams.

He takes the stairs down two at a time. When he reaches the basement, he sees immediately that the door to the white room is shut, and his pace slows. He stops outside the room and places a palm to the coated metal door.

After a moment he pounds his palm on it. He presses an ear to it, squinting to hear through it. He pulls back.

"Hello," he calls. "Is there anyone in there? Are you okay?"

He presses his ear again.

He shouts again.

His blood pressure rising with each new attempt.

He pulls back suddenly, as if hearing something; he can't be sure. He stares at the door inert for a moment, his thoughts whirring. Then just as suddenly he is racing back up the stairs and back out of the building, his face set.

Outside in the burgeoning twilight he quickly scans the grounds, jogging to the edges of the grassed areas to find what he is looking for. Then between the bright verdant branches of a purple-flowering frangipani tree he spots the gray bulk of something.

He sprints to it. A power substation. A small gray bunker. This is what he suspected; this is what his mind has circled around in the dead of night these last few days.

The electrics in the white room, in the rooms he suspects continue beneath the house, do not route back to the building's mains. They need a separate source. And here in the heady-scented shade behind a wall of frangipani trees, he has found it.

He tries to turn the handle on the bunker's tiny door but it does not shift so he puts his weight against it and slams his shoulder hard, once, twice, three times. Then he pulls back, takes a half skip, and rams his entire body weight hard at the little wooden door. It splinters and the rest he makes short work of with repeated kicks until the dark concrete interior of the bunker is revealed.

He steps inside the bunker, waistband flashlight flicked on, and three minutes later, inside the house, the door panel light on the white room fades, its hydraulic door sliding open into its emergency position, the room beyond it now visible.

And Joon-gi feels a kind of triumph he has not felt since his youth.

He cannot possibly know that he will only remain conscious for another ten minutes.

CHAPTER 20
NINA

ook in the mirror.

I quickly raise my gaze.

But I can't look in the mirror. Its surface is too fogged to see a reflection in.

Hesitantly, afraid of what I will see when I clear it, I raise a hand to wipe away the fog but freeze mid-motion, suddenly certain something is right behind me. I whip around, but there is nothing there except the dripping shower.

Skittish, I turn back toward the mirror, inhale deeply, and drag a wet palm across its surface. My own terrified face is revealed as I wipe, then my shoulders, the wet room behind me, my towel-shrouded body, and finally the bathroom around me.

I am looking in the mirror, and all I see is myself.

Maybe that is the point?

The note could be a metaphor, I suppose, or a word game. It is still unclear if I am being warned or threatened at this stage. But what is clear is that the man I saw on the CCTV footage has strong feelings about me being here in my father's house. Does he know the woman who stayed here? Are they somehow connected?

Look in the mirror

Did my father do something to that man? Did *I* somehow do something without realizing?

I shiver and step back to view the mirror from a distance. I force myself to perch on the toilet lid and consider the mirror, my own drenched, thin frame unsettlingly staring back at me.

It is hard to look at yourself objectively, just as it is hard to look at anyone you are close to in the cold hard light of day. Love can blind us, the day-to-day of our lives can blind us.

Looking back at me I see now what I perhaps couldn't see before my father died; I see the truth, or as close to it as I have ever gotten. I see a scared woman in her thirties with no family, no friends, a dead-end job, and nobody to come home to. The freedom that used to feel magical to me now re-labeled loneliness. I hold my own gaze. If I couldn't even see my own life clearly, how the hell could I have seen my father's? If I haven't ever really known myself, how could I have presumed to know him?

He had a house, a fortune, a life I did not know about; it seems fair to assume he may have had a side I did not know about also. But I find that this line of thinking takes me nowhere fast.

I look at the note again. What am I not getting? What does it mean?

I look at the mirror itself now. It begins about five inches from the floor and ends about five inches from the ceiling. I scour everything I can see reflected in its surface for meaning and it slowly dawns on me that these notes might not mean me harm but might be offering me help.

I wanted to find more about my father out here, in this house, on this island. The mirror, the notes, the man leaving them, might hold the key.

I don't know why but I suddenly recall a scene from years ago. I had won a prize at school for a poem I had written. A poem about silence. I was so proud; I took it to show him. I remember pushing open his heavy study door and wandering into that hallowed space. He'd looked up and smiled and taken it from me imbuing it with the same importance he would a historical document. And I sat on his ottoman and watched him read, the lamplight reflecting in a glimmer off his reading glasses as my words were acknowledged. He took his time, and in the gap, I imagined all his possible reactions until he finally lifted his eyes back to me and said, "It's well written, Nina. Well done. A well-deserved prize. Congratulations." And with those words all my pride, all my accomplishment drained from me. It was his tone. It was pragmatic. Nobody wants to be approached pragmatically, it is not indicative of anything good.

"You don't like it, though, do you?" I had asked, careful to keep disappointment from my voice.

He removed his glasses and gave me a consolatory smile. "Do you want me to be honest?" he said with as much loving respect as one can say those words.

I nodded, no longer certain I could keep the emotion locked down.

"I do not. No. Simply put: it takes me to sad places and I do not like sad places." He shook his head, knowing he was not fully serving his own meaning, not fully parenting me as he would want to. He tried again, "What you are writing about, it might seem very grown-up to you, but adults, adults like the light. Do you see?"

What I saw, for the first time, was that he was a person, not just my dad. A person with opinions, with judgments about life and me and about what gives something value. And the notion blossomed in me that not everything I did would have a value. To him, to the world. He had thoughts, and feelings, and a world inside him that I could not control or even touch. I was not his and he was not mine, but we were bound. And if I wanted to be valued, if I wanted my efforts to be valued, they would need to adhere to his.

I feel it again. That he is here, that man I do not really know. But this time I might finally find him.

I stand now, enthused, as if in a game somehow. A game where clues are given and there is ultimately an answer to be found.

He is here.

I reread the note.

Look in the mirror. Look. In. The. Mirror.

In the mirror?

I drop down quickly onto all fours. The mirror is, indeed, not flat. I can see, looking beneath its underlit rim, that it juts out from the wall a good palm's width.

I inspect the mirror, towel wrapped tightly around me, on hands and knees, and then I see something unusual.

One of the screws holding the mirror's bulk to the wall does not match the others. It is fresh, the metal brighter, newer, and it is not quite screwed back into its housing fully. Someone has recently replaced it.

I leap up, pull my towel tighter, and head for the bathroom door with purpose.

The house beyond the bathroom is silent. I watch for a moment and then decide to go for it, sprinting back to the bedroom and my phone. I grab it and quickly dial James's number. It does not connect.

The house around me is silent. I think of what the note said. *Look in the mirror.* My answers will be there, suddenly, I am sure of it.

I head to the utility room, pull open the cupboard under the sink, and grab the toolbox. I heft its weight along the hall with me, my phone held tight in my other hand. When I get back to the bathroom, I lock the door behind me. Sink to my knees and rifle through the toolbox for a Phillips-head screwdriver.

Squinting under the giant mirror I begin to loosen the screws holding it in place.

When they are free, I climb up onto the sink counter and lean over the top of the mirror to unscrew the top fastenings. When all the screws are free, I drop down onto the floor, hands on either side of the mirror as I lift it from its moorings, and for the first time I am the only thing holding it up. The weight is extraordinary. I only manage a few seconds, my muscles and the joints in my hands screaming for release as my grip slips and the edge of the mirror crashes down hard onto the floor beneath, inches from my bare foot, cracking the tile as it connects. I somehow manage to keep ahold of it as the entire mirror begins to swing out of my clutches, but the knock sends a hairline crack racing up the mirror's edifice and I am terrified the entire thing will burst into a thousand shards in my hands. I steady myself. I test the structural integrity of it and when I am convinced it will not shatter into tiny, lethal splinters, I gently begin to slide it toward the nearest wall.

When I am sure it is safely leaning against the wet room wall and not going to fall on me, I release it and step back.

I turn to the wall where the mirror was mounted and my blood runs cold, horror washing through me as I understand what the note was trying to tell me. The notes *have* been warnings. Two warnings.

In front of me, at head height, mounted into the wall, behind the mirror, is a camera, its power light glowing red, recording, transmitting. In its opaque black lens, my face is reflected back at me.

"Holy shit," I breathe, stumbling backward, pulling my towel tighter around me, suddenly aware that everything I have done in this room has been watched. And like a forest fire my thoughts catch light one after the other . . . because if there has been a camera here in this mirror, then there are probably more. There are probably more cameras in this house, and those cameras will have seen even more.

Horror, shame, and gut-wrenching fear jolt through me.

What is this house? And what does it have to do with my father?

My phone clutched tight in my hand, knuckles white, I raise it and snap a shot of the camera in the wall recording me. That is when I see that the signal bars have completely disappeared from its screen. My stomach feels like it falls through the floor.

"No, no, no," I hear myself mutter as I try to dial James's number again, but of course it doesn't connect. I try again. I try the iPhone emergency button, but it does not work without a signal either.

"Please, please, please," I hear myself breathe, my voice oddly dissociated from me.

Then my gaze shoots back up to the camera recording everything and I understand with absolute certainty what it is I need to do. I need to get the fuck out of this house now.

CHAPTER 21

MARIA

Maria is barely conscious when the siren begins to sound. The deafening hazard warning tone, reverberating back through the house she has repeatedly very nearly died in over the last six days, rouses her.

She tries to shift her starved, trembling body and using the wall behind hauls herself up to face whatever fresh hell is coming her way.

Maria knows how incredibly lucky she has been to survive this long, how her past, her childhood has helped keep her alive down here. And in a vague way she knows that all of this must somehow be inextricably linked to that past.

Her parents changed their family name after they got to America. Venezuelan refugees descended from Armenian refugees.

But in order to get to America, a four-year-old Maria Yossarian and her parents had made their way on foot across the brutal mountains, mud, rivers, and unmapped lawless rain forest of the Darién Gap, to eventually seek asylum in America. Others had not survived. It had almost broken them too, but it was that or risk worse by staying in a city that had pulled itself apart.

The Darién Gap—a five-thousand-square-kilometer strip of rain forest connecting South and Central America, one of the most dangerous places on the planet—had almost killed them. But somehow they made it out alive where others had not. And they arrived, starved, exhausted, caked in mud, and barely able to speak, in Panama and later on in Texas, where they applied for asylum on the border with hope of a better life.

The trip hadn't killed her parents but their health had never been the same after it, and when they had gotten sick in their late fifties they had gone suddenly. And left her alone but for a quiet, traumatized uncle.

She alone survived. It seems almost ingrained in her now, that ability. She knew how to survive.

The siren blasts on through the rooms and panic, like an old friend, pumps life back into Maria's jittery muscles. An urgency she feared she might no longer possess roars to life inside her.

Something is happening. She shifts her weight in preparation for whatever is coming. The warning siren grows incrementally closer, less muffled. She swipes away the blood trickling dangerously close to her eyes, knowing she will need all her senses operational for what is going to hit her next.

It isn't that the house is getting harder; she knows she is getting weaker, slower, less sharp. She looks down at her hand, post-wipe, a brilliant red smear, her most recent, most severe injury clearly not yet healing. Sepsis is one of her biggest concerns, and has been for days. She saw her reflection a day ago: a large lacerated, green-black hematoma on her left temple.

Her injuries are substantial, she knows, but she is still able to function. And as far as Maria is concerned that's all that matters right now.

She managed to bandage her arm with the torn hem of her top and cauterize a cut on her thigh in the other room, but her lips are dry and cracked, her energy low—she has had water but hasn't eaten now since day two.

Across the stifling heat of the room, the door panel light flickers, then fades out completely. Maria blinks hard, unable to believe her eyes, unable to trust the reality of what she is seeing as the door slowly, undoubtedly, begins to roll back to reveal the previous room. Beyond it, the previous, and then the previous, all their doors opening, on and on.

She has only a moment to take in what's happening before all the lights go out and she is plunged into darkness.

Her breath and the blaring siren the only sounds in the pitch black, Maria tries to remain calm. She tells herself to focus, to breathe. She has gotten used to doing that. Her eyes will adjust to the darkness, she tells herself, if she just gives them a moment.

Eyes wide open Maria waits, blindly staring in the direction of the door, hoping for some sliver of light to become apparent. She blinks again and again until the darkness slowly begins to graduate, though part of her mind is conscious that this is all just wishful thinking. Or a trick. But as her eyes adjust, the vaguest outlines of the open doorways become evident.

And with her last available jolt of energy, Maria springs from her resting place and begins to move.

In the darkness she shifts around the walls of the room until her fingers find the door's opening and she stumbles through.

The next room is harder, larger, the floor still slick with

water. She slips and skids across it, her hands desperately trying to grip, palms clammy, on to the smooth walls.

But time not being on her side, she begins to rush and a
moment later sprawls across the wet floor, landing headfirst
into the half-open door to the next room. The pain is intense
as she holds in her yells, its initial waves and throbs flowing
over her and passing, then scrambling up, she continues.

Maria slips through another doorway and another and to
her absolute, unbearable joy, she begins to see a lift in the darkness several doorways ahead. Risking everything, the alarm
system blaring bass-y and slow around her, she takes a final
risk, pushing off the wall behind her and propelling herself
full-tilt toward the light.

WITH A PRIMAL SCREAM, MARIA barrels out of the rooms and
back out into the hallway, her clothes ragged, her eyes wild,
her face blood-smeared and bruised.

BACK IN THE MAIN HOUSE, she propels herself toward the
stairwell, half collapsing onto its steel banister. Her eyes,
crazed, snap back on to the half-open door she just flew through.

She hangs on the banister momentarily, her breathing coming in high, tight, inhuman rasps as she clings to the stairwell,
knuckles white with tension, watching to see if anyone else,
anything else, will emerge after her and pull her back.

A clang, from deep within the basement, snaps her out of
her reverie and propels her once more up the stairs into the
natural light.

Twilight sky is breaking through the vast windows of the
living room. The natural light almost blinds her after only ar-
tificial light and darkness for days.

Maria skids and skitters across the marble living room, desperate to get to the terrace doors, but she slips, her hand saving her but leaving a smear of pure red on the once immaculate white bouclé sofa as she passes.

Then, as she nears the doors, she pulls up sharply. Someone is there. She isn't going to make it.

Two men approach the house. She sees them, one from the terrace, the other from the garden, backed by a bright pop of frangipani trees.

Thinking fast, Maria turns on her heels to bowl back toward the main wet room—the only room in the house that she is certain has a manually locking door.

As Maria flies into the marble bathroom, the sound of another alarm joins the siren from downstairs as all the lights in the property flick back into action.

Maria slams the bathroom door, slides the lock, and drags anything and everything she can move in the room in front of the door before backing away from it until she bumps hard up against the wet room screen.

She spins and jumps, catching sight of her own bloody, haggard face in the floor-to-ceiling mirror beyond it. She holds her own gaze, breath coming hard and fast.

Maria knows she needs to get out of here, dead or alive. Going back downstairs is not an option.

She knows the men will take her back down if she lets them and she will die there. Better to fight up here and risk death than to go back down and continue the game.

After six days in the basement, Maria's mind is functioning on an entirely different level than the men's outside this room. She has an advantage, however small.

She has been fighting for her life for 118 hours.

She listens for the men beyond the door. Under the blare of alarms, she hears their footsteps. There are only two of them.

There are *only* two, but two is more than one; Maria knows this.

The only other sound in the bathroom is the gentle white noise of the air-conditioning system above her.

Maria looks up. The sound is coming from a supply-and-return vent in the ceiling. She takes note of the little screws holding it in place, remembering movies where plucky heroes escape baddies through ceiling panels. She studies the one above her, with its small rectangular shape. An idea forms and she swallows hard.

A gentle knock on the bathroom door, and her attention is ripped away from the ceiling.

"Ms. Yossarian?" the man's calm voice asks with a degree of politeness in his warm American accent that Maria finds truly terrifying. "Would you mind opening the door?"

Maria muffles her breath and stares at the bathroom door, frozen.

Another rap comes, and Maria jumps. Then without a second thought she grabs the small hand mirror from the edge of the sink unit and smashes it onto the floor. She quickly grabs a shard, climbs up onto the toilet cistern, reaches up, and begins to quickly loosen the screws on the vent grate above. The screws tinkle one after the other down onto the bathroom floor.

Another gentle rap on the door but Maria is undeterred.

"Ms. Yossarian. We will remove the door if you do not open it."

The sirens blare on as Maria wedges her fingers under the grate and pries it from the ceiling to place it gently onto the floor beside the toilet.

Then after a moment's hesitation, aware she needs both of her hands free to climb, she places the large sliver of broken mirror between her teeth, wincing as the edges of the glass cut into the sides of her mouth, parallel streams of blood now giving her face the appearance of a ventriloquist's dummy.

Maria inhales deeply. Then, with a hand on each side of the vent opening, she hauls herself up, with trembling effort, onto her elbows, and from there pulls herself fully up into the shaft that snakes away from the bathroom, the sound of the property's alarms covering her muted grunts.

CHAPTER 22
NINA

I run to the bedroom as fast as I can and grab the first set of clothes I can find, then without stopping I sprint straight toward the terrace doors. But when I press my palm to the panel the doors do not open.

"*Bathsheba*, open terrace doors," I garble, desperately trying to make my voice steady and clear.

Bathsheba does not respond.

"Unlock doors, Bathsheba," I try again, now desperately wrestling on the clothes and shoes. But nothing happens. I run to the console but the screen is blank, disabled.

My blood runs cold. *Who the hell turned it off?*

That is when I decide to run. I rattle the disabled handles. Someone has turned everything off and they are watching how I react.

This is Anderssen's Opening.

I stop what I am doing. If this is a game, if their advantage is that they can see me, I need to remove that advantage.

I head over to the nearest mirror and speak directly into it.

"Open the fucking doors," I tell whoever is watching. I give them a moment but nothing happens so I turn on my heels and head to the kitchen counter, grab a large pan, and head back to the mirror.

I stare through it with intent then slam the pan as hard as I can into the glass, shattering it, sending twinkling shards down onto the marble. The camera behind is revealed. I grab it, yank it out, hauling it into the room and onto the floor where I smash the absolute shit out of it before tearing out its cables and throwing it farther into the room.

Then I head to the bedroom.

"Open the doors," I tell the mirror there, the one I imagine watched me sleep and cry last night.

The doors do not open.

I rip the little drawer from the bedside table, scattering its contents on the carpet before slamming it into the mirror, which bursts apart to reveal another camera. I pull it free, wrench out its cables, and lob it as far into the hallway as possible. Then something catches my eye. There is something etched into the wall under where the camera was mounted. Words seemingly scratched into the concrete.

Whatever you do, do not go in the basement.

I had completely forgotten about the basement, the locked door, the secret rooms yawning out beneath me, but now they are all I can think of.

Either the notes are warning me or they are leading directly into danger. What I do next will decide how this plays out for me. I know it.

In chess white always plays first, always. In Anderssen's Opening white plays first but it is not a real move, it gives away its advantage in order to force black to, theoretically, make the game's first real move. It's called playing white as black, wasting your first move to see what theirs will be.

What will the other player do.

All things considered, the last thing in the world I want to do is go downstairs.

But then, as if on cue, downstairs I hear the access tone of the locked door activating in the corridor.

There is no way out, the locked door is now open, and the ball is firmly in my court.

CHAPTER 23
MARIA

The internal air-conditioning system is thin, tight, and hot: a never-ending metallic coffin, disappearing around bend after bend.

Maria has processed this horror at some level but after the last six days she has learned to put aside what is not immediately necessary: and what *is* immediately necessary to her immediate survival is finding the way out to open air and freedom. She has blocked out everything else, not through strength of character but through sheer focus on need—she is not going to die here.

She knows what she's looking for. She sees it so clearly in her mind's eye, at the end of all these vents an external air-conditioning grate high on the property's wall, beyond its slats the lush garden.

She visualizes it in her mind: she will kick out the external grate, the fresh Caribbean breeze will hit her, it will cool her sweat-soaked skin, and she will leap or tumble down from the opening high on the wall onto the springy grass and she will run. She will run as fast as she has ever run toward the beach. She will take the beach stairs two or three at a time, down and down and down. She will splash into the sea and she will swim, in great arcing strokes, around to the public cove and she will flag down the people there, the few after-work sunset swimmers, and they will see her and run to her. And wide-eyed they will pull her, bruised and throbbing, from the water, and she will cry hot tears that it is all finally over. They will wrap her in soft towels and the police will arrive and she will finally know that it is really, truly over.

But it is not over yet, because tight in the ducts Maria cannot find her way out to that grate that she sees so clearly in her mind.

She crawls on fast and determined, slipping on her own sweat as she squeezes around another bend in the crawl space. As she rounds the corner and looks up ahead, there is no hoped-for sliver of natural light in the dimness.

The only luck she has experienced so far seems to be that the sound of the alarm system is still covering her movements as she thumps and bumps through the crawl spaces of the property.

She has a head start on them at least, though she expects they might have entered the bathroom now and are beginning to search the room vents for signs of motion. She doesn't have long. But then she's never had long in this house, and she has adapted to that with worrying necessity.

As she careens on, she thinks of the feeling of wind on her face again, she thinks of running across the grass, splashing into the water, pushing through the waves, then the hands of her rescuers pulling her from the water, the relief she will feel—and that is when the deafening sound of the house alarm cuts out.

Maria stops moving instantly, ringing silence filling the gap that the piercing wail of the alarm has left. She is exposed. They will be able to hear her now, find her. And as if in answer to her fears the duct around her lets out a sad groan of its own, the metal straining with her slight weight.

Maria tries to muffle her snatched breath, but she is exhausted and her body needs every rasping inhale. A sound in the rooms beneath her, movement in there. She strains to listen. A muffled voice. The men must be talking. Footsteps moving away—and then the sound of one of the terrace doors being opened. One of the men must have made his way outside to search there. She remains stock-still. The metal of the duct creaks once more but this time farther back behind her. Her eyes flash back into the darkness, suddenly aware that someone is crawling in the darkness toward her. But there is nothing there, just the dim sheen of more metal tunnel. The duct groans again and everything in Maria clenches just in time as the entire structure gives way beneath her and she slams down eight feet onto the marble of the kitchen counter, still encased in a section of duct.

Her eyes flash up to the shocked figure now standing across from her, a large stretch of living room between her and the man who, back-footed by the unexpected crash, pauses for a micro-second to process the scene—but Maria does not need to pause.

With wild desperation she heaves herself from the broken section of duct, scrambles onto her knees on top of the counter, fumbling for the first object at hand from the chef's-grade knife block across from her. And as the man runs full-tilt at her, she makes a decision: whatever happens next is going to be okay.

He barrels into her, wrestling her off the countertop onto the floor, all the while she kicks, bites, and wildly swings with the blade, knocking everything from the counter to the floor as she goes.

On the floor he straddles her, tries to wrest the knife from her. She fights him, but then changes tack; she releases the weapon, using his suddenly released momentum to force the stranger's head back hard into the side of the marble island.

His eyes flash shut on impact, he's dazed but not incapacitated. He does not lose his grip on the weapon, but his brief loss of focus is enough.

In the micro-second the man takes to reorient himself, Maria reaches for what was knocked from the counter in the scuffle: the wooden knife block itself. And with all of her body weight she heaves the heavy block over her head and into the side of the man's skull.

His head whips sideways, hard, smacking back into the island once more. His body then slumps into the unit, momentarily immobilized.

Maria does not exhale, or relax, or smile a little smile of triumph; she scrabbles immediately up, grabs a large blade, and drives it repeatedly into the man's body with the unrelenting fervor of someone who has learned the hard way that things are not over until they are truly over.

It is only the clank of another loose duct section high above her dropping that snaps her out of her purpose.

Maria sobers instantly, she looks down at the man, the overview of the situation coming to her in one burst of thought: she needs to go, there are more men here somewhere and the cameras are watching everything she does. Others will come for her—because her getting out of here alive is clearly not part of their plan. She needs to go now.

She drops the knife, rises from the blood-soaked body, and runs, bare feet skidding in blood, as fast as she can toward the open terrace doors.

CHAPTER 24

NINA

Nina looks up at the air-conditioning ducts. If the doors are all locked, the only way out is up.

Or through the plate glass of the windows.

She looks back to the terrace doors, then seems to make up her mind, marching toward the firepit at the end of the living room. She grabs the heftiest of the andirons and runs full-tilt at the doors, swinging like a golfer.

The metal makes contact with the reinforced glass, letting out a loud, angry reverberation that resonates back through the andiron to Nina, forcing her to drop the quivering weapon. Tempered glass. She remembers from her father that the only way to break tempered glass is to hit it on its edges. She looks at where the glass disappears into the metal and seals of the door structure—she won't be able to reach the edges.

She looks up at the ducts again and wanders the length of the room, following their direction in and out of bedrooms until she feels certain the exit point is through the wall above the smallest guest room.

She climbs on top of the chest of drawers and stands up on it to inspect the grate. The screws have been sealed over with resin. She wouldn't be able to access the grate or duct system even if she wanted to.

Whoever is doing this thought of everything. Well, almost everything. They didn't bank on the Korean man leaving her messages.

Or maybe he's part of it?

To ask who the note leaver was would be to ask who the one locking her in here might be—and ultimately, what either had to do with her father.

She listens to the silence of the house. She is locked in—but to what end?

She scans the walls of the guest room for mirrors and quickly finds one seamlessly embedded in the wall. Now that she thinks about it, most rooms in the house have mirrored walls or mirrors of some sort.

There will be a camera behind each, she doesn't doubt it. The house is a kind of set, filming the inhabitants. She sits down on the chest of drawers and stares at the mirror opposite, her wet hair and slack expression catching her eye and forcing her to look at herself afresh. Why would someone want to watch her: a thirty-something, recently bereaved English professor with no family and no life?

Did her father film people in this house? Is that what this is? Was he a terrible, terrible person and this is how she's going to find out?

Nina slips herself down off the chest of drawers and walks over to the mirror, as if proximity to the lens through which this person might be watching might help her glean more.

The thing is, she thinks, *my father is dead and whoever is doing this clearly isn't.*

Her father built this house, she has no doubt about that. Its name and Bathsheba's name are proof enough that her father had a hand in whatever this is—but he is dead. He cannot be doing this to her directly. Someone else is, either at his direction or in order to show her firsthand what kind of man her father really was.

A fresh dread spreads through her, like ink in water. What kind of man was he, to have a locked house full of cameras?

She snaps out of her reverie and wanders back into the living room once more, taking in the scene with fresh eyes.

Her father named the house after an opening move. The room downstairs was the bait to action for her and however many other people. She swallows hard at the thought of other people trapped here, filmed—other women. Are there other women still here, down there?

She casts her eyes with dread across to the staircase. Downstairs the locked-door tone sounds again as if deliberately calling to her.

The answers will be just down the stairs, she knows that. Whether she wants them or not.

A secondary thought occurs to Nina, sending a bright jolt of hope shooting through her. She asked Joe to come, and though the terrace outside is empty she feels certain he will get here soon. She said enough in her message to cause concern, especially if Joe can't reach her and can't enter the property. He does not seem like the kind of man who would simply walk away and assume she is fine when everything points in the opposite direction.

He will make his way up here. He will find her. He will call someone and they will get her out.

The tone beeps again downstairs and she knows with certainty that *they* want her to go down there. That's how they want this to go. And every fiber of her body tells her not to. Better to wait here for Joe. Or James even?

She tries to recall the last message she left James, and whether it might cause him enough concern to make him fly out to Gorda to check on her over the weekend.

She realizes shamefully that she knows nothing about James really: does he have children, a wife, a husband, or a partner? She has no idea. But it seems unlikely he will charter a flight on the basis of a slightly concerning voicemail message. When he does realize that he can't get hold of her he might alert the island authorities to perhaps check on the house—but there is no guarantee that that will happen before Monday. As far as he is concerned, her calls are work calls, and work happens Monday through Friday. Monday will come, but not soon enough. A shadow thought passes over her: perhaps James is in some way responsible for this, if he is aware of what this house is, or has been.

But she pushes the thought away. Joe will come first.

And she will leave him a note.

She turns from the terrace doors and heads to the stationery drawer in the side console behind the sofa, rooting out a pen and paper and a small roll of Scotch tape. She quickly scrawls a message then heads back to the terrace doors to affix it to the glass, its letters facing out onto the terrace.

Nina stops suddenly in her tracks, a thought occurring that sends a shiver down her spine. Joe helped build this house too. What if he is in some way connected, if he knows what is down there?

She stops the thought. She forces herself to recall elements of their meeting earlier that day. Joe is not a bad person, she tells herself. And in spite of this the simultaneous thought surfaces, in Nina's mind, that she spent a lifetime with her father and thought the same of him. Yet here she is trapped in a house of his making.

She physically shakes off the thought and turns on her

heels to head back across the room toward the staircase, then down into the basement.

Once she has left the room, the camera behind the living room mirror whirs, zooming in on the note left hanging on the glass, the sun backlighting the reversed words so that anyone looking can clearly read:

Joe, call the police! Not a joke.
Something weird is happening here.
The house is a trap. Be careful. Stuck inside.
I am going down to the basement now.
I think it's all to do with that.
Get help.
Nina

In the basement Nina stands outside the locked room that is no longer locked. She presses her palm to the door panel, which now glows green instead of blue. The door slides open with hydraulic smoothness to reveal an enormous empty white-walled room, reminiscent of an art gallery but completely devoid of art.

Nina's eye catches on movement on the far side of the cavernous space. A light slowly pulses: a circular green button, about chest height, in the wall. She stares at it mesmerized by the simplicity of it. If that is Anderssen's Opening, then it is a good one: a button that demands to be pushed.

But Nina does not push the button. She steps back from the room.

She thinks back to what she can remember from reading about the original chess match between Adolf Anderssen and Paul Morphy in 1858.

If she remembers correctly, Morphy didn't beat Anderssen in the first game, but he did win the subsequent matches.

Nina wonders what might happen if she does not enter the room, if she does not play on and make her move.

In chess you have 120 minutes from the start of play to complete your first forty moves—but it is unclear to Nina how many moves in either of them are at this stage.

She just knows that the big green button is a game changer.

Upstairs, either Joe is coming or he is not, but Nina knows that to find out more she must enter the room and play the game.

Suddenly music kicks in, loudly, Bathsheba pumping a familiar tune at volume into every room of the house. Nina looks up at the ceiling as the opening chords play out. It is a song that was performed by a string quartet at her father's memorial service, a fitting song, a song that matched his sense of humor and in a way Nina's too.

Nina's eyes rove the hallway for the nearest mirror. She finds it staring back at her from the end of the corridor.

After a moment's thought she raises her middle finger to the camera that she knows rests just behind the glass, and she mouths *Fuck you* as "Always Look on the Bright Side of Life" blasts merrily through the empty rooms of the locked-down house.

CHAPTER 25
JOE

J oe looks at the blank screen of his phone as he drives along the ridge road winding from the harbor out toward Pond Bay. She has not tried to call him back.

He's pretty sure he's doing the right thing, driving out there. She seemed nice—well, more than nice, great, which even Joe is aware isn't the most eloquent description of the incredibly interesting, funny, intelligent, and yeah, sure, very rich British woman he met earlier that day.

Her message wasn't a booty call, or at least it didn't seem like any he's had in the past—and being an islander, he has experienced plenty of booty calls. Hell, most of his relationships have been, essentially, just protracted booty calls.

But then she invited him over, just hours after meeting him—that sounds impulsive. But then he is coming, so what does that say about him? Joe wonders if he gets himself into situations like this deliberately. If there is something innate in him that means this is all he is good for relationship-wise.

He tried to reply to the voice message but quickly remembered the whole no-signal situation in the new builds across the island—she wouldn't necessarily get the message that he is on his way. But he can always leave if it turns out she's changed her mind and all is well. He tries not to think how embarrassing it would be that he traveled all the way out just to check on her after one lunch, but hey, the good thing about island visitors is that they don't tend to hang around to remind you what a disposable person you apparently are.

He shakes off the thought. She isn't like that, she's nice. No, not nice, great, she's great.

THE GATEHOUSE IS SHUTTERED WHEN he arrives. He pulls his car tight into the curb and locks it up before heading over to investigate.

The intercom doesn't seem to be connecting to the main house when he presses the button. He tries Nina's phone number again—it is unavailable.

He checks the time of her last message; it was over two hours ago now, though he'd only listened to it as he was leaving the harbor about half an hour ago. Perhaps she changed her mind. He tries to peek over the gates but it isn't possible.

He steps back and reassesses. He notes the camera mounted high on the gatepost above, trained down on him, and reasons that her "call for help" constitutes mitigating circumstances— a phrase slipped in on the two occasions Joe has had minor brushes with local law enforcement as an island-bound teenager to explain his potentially gray-area behavior.

He squints at the gate, head cocked. It's probably, what, ten feet? That's industry standard anyway. He is six foot two, so if he climbs over and drops, he won't likely break anything. And again, if he is caught on camera, it's her house and she invited him and it seemed like an emergency. He pauses a second, remembering the last time he slightly misread a situation, but he argues internally that that situation *had* been a booty call, and this is most definitely not. *Non-sexually-threatening* company is what has been requested. Joe pauses again. Does that mean *sexual* company was requested, just not *threatening sexual* company?

"Fucking hell," he mutters to himself. Things are hard these days. And the annoying thing is, he isn't even that bothered about sex. Well, of course he's interested in it, but, like, in a normal way. Jesus! He just likes her. He just wants to see her again and chat to her because—because she's great.

He shakes off his concerns and instead runs full-tilt at the gate, finding a foothold on a hinge halfway up the left gatepost and heaving himself up to straddle the wooden gate top. He looks up at the hill visible beyond, and memories of his brief time working on the site flood back.

He shivers in spite of himself at the memory of the floor plans from earlier that day, the idea that the house at the top of the hill goes down into the rock is creepy in a way he hadn't conceived of at the time.

Joe swings his legs over the gate, lowers himself as far as arm's length, and drops the final distance to the ground.

No alarms sound, no attack dogs are released, and so he dusts himself down and makes his way toward the steep stone staircase leading up to the house.

Halfway up the ascent the house comes into view. He hasn't seen the finished article; he and his father's company were only required for the excavation stage of construction. They hauled and removed the tons of rubble necessary to hollow out the cliff in which the property nestles. Now that he can see it, he stops in his tracks. It gleams in the sun, an unexpected jewel carved out of the rock.

It's sophisticated and minimalist. A lot of the luxury properties on the island are not. It looks like her in a way, the house, Joe thinks, then he grimaces at the stupidity of the thought and continues to ascend. It's a building; it doesn't look anything like her.

He is definitely putting too much on all this, he reasons. He should just get on with it, help her with whatever, and go home.

When he reaches the top of the steps the full experience of the house hits him: the terraces, pools, beach, the breeze rolling in from the ocean view. He pauses again.

Yeah, he thinks, he should definitely not read too much into this. It's unlikely that a university professor who owns a house like this would be interested in anything other than a booty call from someone like him. Not that he isn't a thinking, feeling, emotionally intelligent guy with—

Joe stops. All thoughts put on hold as a woman in a long flowing black dress emerges through one of the terrace doors. She is beautiful, but she isn't Nina.

"Hello," she says, a polite level of surprise in her voice—but perhaps not quite enough surprise given the fact she has just found a complete stranger on her secured property. "Who are you?"

Joe opens his mouth to speak and then stops. Has he vaulted the wrong gate? He thinks back through the last twenty minutes and then frowns. *No, this is definitely the place.*

"Joe. Nina asked me to pop over."

It is the woman's turn to frown now. "You're here for Nina?"

Her surprise is so genuine that Joe is suddenly certain this is all a joke. Perhaps this woman is Nina's friend or a sister playing a trick on him? He looks past her into the open-plan living room beyond and there sure as anything is Nina's handbag resting on the counter.

Joe cracks an amused smile and nods his understanding. He thinks he gets it: Nina wanted company, and obviously she didn't just message him. Her friend arrived before he did and she's got it covered, and now, apparently, the friend has been told to get rid of him.

"Okay, fair enough. Just tell her hi, okay. No pressure: she's got my number. Tell her I'm around if she wants to grab a coffee or something next week."

The woman tilts her head appraisingly. "You like her? Nina?" she asks, her tone curious, objective.

Joe suddenly feels something is off. Something about Nina's friend doesn't quite fit; he can't quite picture them together. But he answers truthfully, interested to see where this conversation might take him.

"Er, yeah. Yeah, I do."

"But you don't really know her, do you?"

Joe frowns in spite of himself. That's what Nina said of herself only this afternoon. In a sense it is true, and yet he does feel like he innately *knows* Nina. He *knew* her from the moment he saw her.

"I think I've got a pretty good sense of her. People like to think they're fairly complex but I find my first feel for someone tends to hold true. You can see the good and bad pretty much straightaway—and sometimes one outweighs the other. So yeah, to answer your question: I know her; I like her," he concludes, watching carefully to see how the sentiment lands on the woman in front of him; the woman he absolutely does not trust, even though he clearly doesn't know her either.

He watches her easy charm tense, almost imperceptibly, as she flashes an amused smile, but its edges are a little tighter than perhaps she is aware.

She doesn't like the response, Joe sees that. She is hiding it well, but he is good with people and she doesn't like what he just said one bit.

And it suddenly dawns on Joe that perhaps this woman isn't Nina's friend. This woman is the reason Nina asked for his help. Whether she is Nina's bizarre note leaver or the woman who pretended to be her, it's impossible to tell, but she is most definitely not Nina's friend.

"Well, that's good. Interesting philosophy," the woman muses, her gaze drifting out to the view. "But I'm afraid Nina isn't here right now. You're welcome to come in and wait? She should be back soon."

Joe looks down at his phone. If Nina is out, she would have a signal, but he just tried her number and it wasn't working. Joe looks back at the woman, hoping to buy himself a little thinking time. Behind her through the terrace doors, an immaculately clean living room and kitchen and there on the counter Nina's handbag. Odd that she would leave it behind.

"Where did she go?" Joe asks.

The woman gestures for him to enter the house. "She's just gone for a walk, to clear her head; it's been a tough few weeks: a death in the family."

Joe looks out across the terrace toward the stairs. He hadn't thought of that, that she might just be on the beach. No one needs a handbag on the beach.

"Oh yes, of course. I forgot. Nina's father. Are you part of the family too?" he asks with an appropriate level of sensitivity.

"Me. No, gosh, no," the woman says delicately.

He wonders now if perhaps he *has* misread the situation. And with that thought he lets the woman usher him inside. He will go in and wait and perhaps Nina would still like to see him when she gets back.

And as he enters the house, he catches sight of something odd through a half-open doorway leading off from the living room. Dread fizzes through him. The mirror in the room beyond is smashed, the floor beneath it swept but the facts crystal clear that something bad has happened.

But before Joe can turn to confront the woman, who is now calmly in the process of gathering her loose hair up into a neat chignon, a sudden flash of pain shoots through the back of his skull, turning everything into darkness.

CHAPTER 26
MARIA

Maria runs. She runs as fast as she has ever run and it still feels too slow.

She pelts across the hot terrace flagstone, her eyes flashing in every direction, certain she will catch the glimpse of another runner as she goes. Somewhere, she knows, the other man is still searching for her. And every second she does not see him, her fear mounts. Because she knows he is out here and as soon as he sees her he will be on her. Every second she does not see him coming is a second of advantage he will have over her. And Maria has nothing if she loses her advantage. At half the weight, strength, and fitness of these men, she knows she only stands a chance if she sees them coming and has time to out-maneuver them.

She skids to a halt as she reaches the steep stone steps leading down to the beach.

There is a chance he's down there already, that she might meet him coming back up the narrow staircase and be trapped.

She glances back to the house and curses herself for not having kept hold of that knife. Instead, she left it as evidence.

Her mind briefly rakes over the coals of what she just did. She killed a man. Not just killed him but really, really killed him. She wonders fleetingly if that level of killing still falls under the banner of self-defense.

One stab would have saved her; twenty or so had perhaps been unnecessary solely for self-preservation. But the animal part of her is the only thing keeping her alive and Maria has absolutely no intention of trying to rein it in until she knows she is safe. Safe back in her home, back in New York, back in her bed, duvet pulled up snug and tight.

She isn't safe yet.

If he is on the stairs, if she runs into him, she will kill him. She promises herself that. Even if she has to die in the process, she will kill him. Or rather the primal part of her will, it promises her, and she feels safe because it hasn't let her down yet.

Maria launches herself down the stairs two, three, four at a time in massive leaps, her bones jarring with each. Sharp stones embedding and freeing themselves from her bleeding feet as she flies on.

At the midpoint bend in the staircase, Maria notices for the first time the camera positioned high on the rail post. They can see her still; she is still part of it, she is still in it. She considers again her plan, to swim to the public cove, grab the nearest stranger, and scream until they pull her from the water and call the authorities. That no longer seems safe. How can she know who the people in the public cove are, who they work for, who they know? And the local police: how can they not know what is going on behind closed doors in this house? Maria knows she is not the first and will not be the last.

No, it isn't safe to scream for help. It isn't safe to swim to the public cove. As she nears the base of the stairs she slows, her senses heightening, as if already picking up on the presence of another person. There is no one there that she can see, but then she can't see past the rocky outcrop that blocks the public cove from view and keeps the house's beach private. She pauses in the foliage and waits, but nothing changes. No figure appears. So she takes a deep breath in and a slow steady breath out to calm her nerves and bolts from her hiding spot toward the water.

Her plan is to swim out, to swim in the opposite direction from the cove, to swim toward the next private beach and the next until she finds an empty stretch of public sand. Then she will clamber out and run.

She is almost at the water's edge when she sees him and stutters to a halt. He has been crouched by the rocks. As he stands, she sees what is in his hand, and on a cellular level she knows what it means.

A long black rod hangs from his hand. She has only seen them on TV but she knows what it is: some kind of tasing device, but longer, a cattle prod of sorts. Maria watches as the end of it crackles. Even from this distance, she understands the implication.

She turns to look back at the stairs up to the house. She can go back, try another way. But then who is to say there aren't more men up there. Down here there is only one man and one weapon.

Basic physics tell her that the weapon's charge will not conduct through water—but if she enters the water and begins to swim and that man reaches her and tases her, she will simply slip beneath the waves. She will in essence be killing herself.

Of course, that would be perfect for them. Her cause of death would appear natural, a drowning—she is sure those happen every day across the islands. The momentary shock of that Taser will not show on an autopsy.

It suddenly seems crazy to her that she has thought even for a second that they didn't have a backup plan, this whole time, in case of her escape. Crazy that after everything they have shown her already about how they operate, and about their level of efficiency and rigor, she would still think they would let things run on to this degree without good reason. They are going to dispose of her in the simplest way possible: she will kill herself. A solo swimmer who got tired and slipped under, her bruises and bangs explainable by an accident on the surrounding rocks.

Maria feels sick at the cleanness of it all and a new anger begins to rise inside her, an anger at the idea that her pain could be so easily deleted, hidden, erased.

Well, I will not make it that easy. Oh no.

Maria will get her murderer's blood and hair and cells under her nails and take him with her if she can. She will make their plan an impossibility. And even if she has to die herself just to fuck them over, she will.

Instead of continuing into the waves Maria begins to walk directly toward the man on the rocks.

He seems momentarily surprised, his eyes flashing to the blood splashed across her dirty cream polo shirt, soaked into her cream shorts, drying into the skin of her hands and splattered across her set face.

Maria wonders if perhaps this is the moment the man on the rocks realizes that he might have to try a little harder than he'd thought; or if perhaps he thinks nothing at all.

Either way it doesn't matter—she is going to die and she is angry as hell and whatever happens she is going to take it all out on him.

Maria's walk turns into a run. She is running directly toward the man on the rocks at full speed. The man seems unsure about what is happening and though he raises the crackling stick and prepares himself for her attack he is somehow back-footed and that appears ever so slightly to unnerve him: after all *he* has the weapon, *he* is taller, stronger, *not* covered in his own and other people's blood. He surely has the upper hand.

Except he doesn't.

Because while Maria might not have seen a Taser in real life, she has witnessed the medical treatment of tasered patients in the hospital at Cornell. She knows that the short five-second bursts of electricity Tasers deploy intermittently are not enough to cause injury in and of themselves. As soon as the five-second burst lapses faculties are resumed. You are only in danger of dying during that loss of control. If people end up in the ER after being tased then it is due to a secondary injury. Falling, drowning, choking. Tasers stun the nervous system, and apparently hurt like hell, but they can't kill you. The only way you can actually kill someone with a Taser burst itself is to apply the pulse directly to the heart and keep going over and over again.

Maria knows that. All she needs to do is not die in the five-second increments that freeze her nervous system.

As she reaches the rocks, she dips to grab a fist full of hard wet sand and scrambles up to standing six feet from the man. He is big and she is small, but she reasons that this means he has farther to fall, and falling from higher up causes more damage.

Her bare feet cling to the rocks as the two face each other, their bodies instinctively crouched, their centers of gravity low. He is farther out, nearer the water, waves crashing sporadically into the rocks behind him, clearly forcing the issue. As the next massive wave crashes behind him, she flings the contents of her hand at his eyes, his hands flying up to protect himself. His vision must momentarily blur because, fearful of attack, he lunges forward toward her, stick crackling. Maria dodges to the side but even her reflexes adapted over the last six days cannot quite escape it in time, the edge of the stick making brief contact with her upper arm as she pulls away. The sharp stab and tug of white-hot pain grab at her skin like a claw and pulse through her as if trying to hold on to her indefinitely as she slips past it. And that was only a glancing blow.

The man pulls back hastily and regroups, wiping his face, the lunge having cost him his footing.

Maria sucks in a sharp involuntary inhale as the charge dissipates and she focuses. That was probably a one-second shock. She will need to withstand five seconds. It's doable, she can easily remain conscious, it will hurt like all hell but as long as she doesn't fall, she'll be fine. And that is when the plan forms.

Maria can pull the goalie.

She backs up, feet clinging to the jagged rocks as she puts distance between herself and the man. He duly advances, cautious, alive to her unpredictability, his weapon raised. A brief glance tells her she has reached the edge of the rocks and she leaps back down onto the wet sand, eyes still set on the man and his weapon.

She needs to get somewhere flat and far enough from the water that there can be no risk of drowning. Luckily, she has a whole wide flat empty stretch of beach to choose from. As the man becomes occupied in making his own labored descent from the rocks, Maria spins and sprints out to a section of dry beach and lies down and waits, limbs stretched out on the warm soft sand.

Every fiber in her body tells her not to do what she is doing. Every cell yells at her to stand, to run, to *move*. But she refuses to listen. She has a plan. She is pulling the goalie.

She knows the strategy from ice hockey. It is only ever employed in the final stages of a losing game. You remove all your defense and switch it to offense to gain an advantage. The goal is wide open, but you have an extra man on the ice.

And right here and now, the facts are the facts: you cannot

die from a Taser—unless it is repeatedly applied to your heart, all it can do to you is shock your nervous system into falling, choking, or drowning. Well, now she is lying down so she can't fall, or drown, or choke unless the man carries her somewhere. And if he carries her, he can't shock her at the same time—she can fight, claw, bite, struggle, and all the while he keeps hold of that weapon, he will have only one hand to fend her off.

Each Taser burst lasts only five seconds and then the stick recharges before sparking again. If she can stay calm, if she can count out five, knowing how much it hurts but how little damage it's doing, if she can save her energy for that break—then she can get his weapon.

It makes sense in her mind but not in her body. Every muscle in her shudders to move as he tentatively approaches her. Maria wonders if he knows what she is doing. Even as the fear courses through her she thinks that he looks wary, but perhaps that's just her wishful thinking.

But when he stops near her, he keeps as much distance as he can between them, only the tip of his stick reaching her abdomen. And as it lowers toward her flesh, she squeezes her eyes gently shut and tries to relax every muscle in her body. She will not fight it until she knows it will matter. She takes a deep breath but does not get to finish it before the pain shocks through her. White light fills the darkness behind her closed eyes.

One.

Her body curves and arches beneath her and she lets the stabbing lashes of it roll through every muscle.

Two.

Her palms clench and release unbidden. She feels her bladder empty, warm and slow under her.

Three.

The stick is pushed deeper into her skin, the current running deeper, to her bones almost, as her spine flicks and spasms like a frog in a science lab.

Four.

It's almost over. Thoughts impossible to keep ahold of and meaning intermittent. She clings to the arrival of the next number.

Five.

And her body slacks into the sand. Now is her chance. Thought and the world are bleary but she knows she has only a moment before it begins again. And she knows beyond a shadow of a doubt where on her body the stick rests. She grabs for it, eyes flashing open, and tugs with all her strength.

And instead of letting go the man clings on, toppling forward onto her rather than releasing the weapon. But that is enough. She tumbles him down, under her, releasing her hold on the stick and double-fisting hunks of sand directly into the man's eyes and rubbing down hard—blinding him.

He yells out, writhing and kicking, but she stays low on him hugged tight to his core like a limpet. He releases the weapon and flails at her to get her off and she obliges, scrambling from his violent body onto the sand and snatching up the weapon. She turns it to face him, activates the charge, and applies it directly to his heart.

He fights it. She kicks more sand in his face, then applies a knee to his throat. At the end of five seconds, she pulls back, the stick recharges, she applies it again to his heart. And again. And again. And again. Until his movements stop.

Then she slides down onto the sand beside him, crying in deep shuddering sobs.

After a moment she calms her breath, carefully clambers up to standing, and makes her way toward the water.

CHAPTER 27
NINA

As Nina enters the room, the lighting state changes to a pinkish hue.

She notes the small metal panel on the wall just inside the door that says ATRIUM as she passes it on her way to the pulsing green button.

Nina's academic mind slips easily around the word's etymology. If the house is a puzzle box, then every word is important.

Atrium from the Latin: first room of the house, from which other rooms lead off.

Nina stops in the middle of the room to take it in, the cavernous space, the smooth white walls now bathed in pinkish light. Entrance hall indeed.

It's funny, now that she is down here she has never been so certain that her father truly did build this house: the cleanliness of line, the simplicity, the functionality. But why would he build this, what was he doing down here?

She turns to the pulse of the green button. Perhaps that flickering pulsing light has all the answers, she thinks wryly, but there is only one way to find out.

She cannot see a camera in here but she knows there is one. The music in the house beyond stops abruptly as she steps up to the green button.

They want silence for this. This is the moment they've been waiting for. She does not know who they are yet, whether the Korean man is involved or not, or the woman who had been emailing Joe's company for months prior to her arrival, or even if Joe himself is somehow involved. And she is even less certain how much of this seemingly awful situation is down to her father, her brilliant, kind, loving, gentle father. Her father with the secret house. The secret house with the secret rooms upon rooms beneath it.

But help is on its way. Joe is on his way, and she would rather know than not know what all of this means. Because part of her still is certain her father was a good man, and that he wants her to see, to uncover something. That all of this will turn out to make sense, somehow, if she can just get to the bottom of it.

And with that thought Nina presses the green button. Far behind her back, the door into the atrium slides shut. She does not run to it; she was expecting as much. Instead Nina remains where she is and waits for the house to make its next move.

Noiselessly a door begins to open beside Nina. She flinches from the movement momentarily until her brain makes sense of what is happening. Beyond the opening door she catches a glimpse of a long thin hallway, the door at its end sealed.

"Attention," the voice of Bathsheba intones, causing Nina to jump at the sound. "Please make your way to the vestibule door."

Nina looks back at the new doorway and what she can only assume is the vestibule. She steps inside, the door closing behind her. She turns back to view the sealed door. There is no door panel on this side; she suspected as much. The rooms seem to be individually sealed, leading her on like a rat in a maze, cutting off enter and exit points and funneling her on. A door at the end of the corridor begins to open and with it comes the sound of flowing water. Nina follows the sound. On either side of the corridor, mirrored walls.

She is now officially playing whatever game this is.

She reaches the doorway and takes in the new room. It's brightly lit, brilliant white, and much smaller. Perhaps big enough only for a single bed and a chair, though the room has neither. A twinge of claustrophobia yawns inside Nina, though she has never had it until now.

The room doesn't feel crushingly small, and as she looks up she notes that the ceiling here is notably higher than in the previous rooms, perhaps reaching fifteen feet in height.

On the farthest wall there is a tap. It's flowing, its water pouring directly down onto a grate and disappearing from sight. Every few seconds the tap stops and restarts in automated pulses.

Above the tap, built into the wall, is a flatscreen panel. Words appear on the screen as she watches, but she is not close enough to make them out. She would need to go in, and she is fairly sure what will happen if she does.

But she has come this far for an explanation; surely she isn't going to chicken out now, she berates herself. And yet she has never been a huge risk taker. Perhaps it's better not to go in after all, to wait here in this vestibule for Joe to arrive with the police, with other people. Best to wait to be rescued. Then they can tear this place apart, search the rooms, find out who is behind this whole setup.

Yes. She steps back from the doorway. That's the sensible thing to do. As she pulls back, more words automatically appear on the screen across the room. Nina feels the pull of urgency, suddenly terrified that there might be someone else down here trying to contact her, someone else trapped.

The message behind the mirror upstairs warned her not to come down here—but what that meant really relied on who left the message.

Nina turns to look at the large mirror panels in the hallway.

"I'm not going any farther until someone tells me what's going on. If you want me to keep going, you'll have to explain what the hell this is," Nina tells her reflection.

She waits, then she waits some more, but no one answers.

Across the room she can see more writing appear. Perhaps they are trying to communicate with her that way.

She warily leans forward into the doorway and strains again to read the words on the screen, but she can't.

Then she gives up.

"Okay, I can wait. You know someone's coming. You know and I know. And this is only a game if I consent to play it, and I'm not consenting."

Nina walks back into the vestibule corridor and sits down on the floor, her back to the wall, and waits. She can wait as long as it takes for Joe to get here, and unless they do something she is not going any farther.

OVER THE NEXT HOUR THE temperature in the vestibule steadily creeps from an ambient twenty-one degrees Celsius to an intensely uncomfortable forty-one degrees Celsius. Nina sporadically removes layers of clothing until she wears only her shorts and a hastily put-on sports bra. The heat is becoming unbearable. She paces now, no longer able to comfortably sit on the hot floor, her sweat running in rivulets down her spine onto the ground, her movement providing the only flow of air available. And she is parched now, the rhythmic stop/start of the tap in the next room impossible to ignore.

She is being flushed through the system, Nina knows that, but it doesn't stop it happening. She needs water.

And just like that she enters the room.

The door closes behind her as she heads straight over to the flowing water and bends to slurp furiously at the cool intermittent bursts of it: bursts that Nina can't help but notice are irregular in their duration, though clearly preprogrammed to be so.

However, she does not have time to contemplate that fact further as her ears prick up to focus on Bathsheba's voice.

"Welcome, Nina. Proceed to the control panel to begin."

Nina pauses, rising from her thirsty gulps at the tap, cool water still dripping from her chin as Bathsheba slips once more into silence.

Her eyes travel to the screen. Text flutters onto it, scrolling as it appears.

The door is now firmly closed, the vestibule, atrium, and other floors of Anderssen's Opening long gone. She is *in* whatever this is now. She is in the heart of the game. And her opponent is showing her their next move.

She wanders to the control panel, wipes her mouth, and reads the text. A poem or a riddle, repeated and repeated and repeated as it scrolls. Nina blinks, a certain part of her coming alive. That Thursday-evening-with-her-father part of her, the vast swaths of useless knowledge she gathered and tended in order to keep up with his mind now uncurling inside her. She made it her lifework to live up to her father, to keep pace or at least not slow him down. If ever anyone was ready for this sort of thing, then it would be her, surely?

She blinks and rereads:

Here is the man with three staves, and here the wheel,
    And here is the one-eyed merchant, and this card,
Which is blank, is something he carries on his back,
        Which I am forbidden to see. I do not find
        The Hanged Man. **Fear death by water.**

Nina realizes with a flush of triumph that it is a section from the third stanza of "The Waste Land," but her thrill of recognition is short-lived as the sentiment of the final sentence hits her.

Fear death by water. The phrase overtakes everything in her mind. Nina's hand rises to her wet mouth as dread blossoms neatly inside her. She just drank the water. Potentially poisoned water?

She bends quickly to the flowing water and sniffs. Then she pulls back, frowns, and sniffs again. Her mind filing through her complete knowledge of poisons.

There is no scent of garlic: *phosphorus.* Heart failure, coma, low blood pressure, death.

No scent of sulfur: *hydrogen sulfide.* Delirium, convulsions, blindness, death.

No scent of ammonia: *ammonia.* Shortness of breath, coughing, blindness, degenerative organ failure, death.

No scent of almonds: *cyanide.* Headache, dizziness, shortness of breath, slowed heart rate, vomiting, death.

She can't smell any of them, but then would she bet her life on it?

And then of course there is the possibility of *thallium* or *arsenic*—both scentless.

Fear erupts inside her, the absolute certainty that she has ingested one of them solidifying in her mind.

Nina looks urgently back to the screen, desperate for an answer or, at the very least, more questions. She tries to recall if either poison has an antidote.

The screen now reads simply:

Death by water is: _ _ _ _ _ _ _ _

It requires an answer. An answer might supply her with a cure.

The answer is eight letters long. Her death by water is: _ _ _ _ _ _ _ _ .

Thallium fits. And *hydrogen*, but not *hydrogen sulfide*. Would *hydrogen* still count?

Shit. Nina blows out a hard breath, her hands shaking with the tension. Then a thought occurs.

"Bathsheba, how many guesses do I get?" she asks, her voice assertive with an underlying quiver.

"Checking system," Bathsheba answers efficiently. "Question one will allow for two incorrect answers. Your third answer will be final."

Three guesses. Nina quickly types in *thallium*—because if it is thallium, she only has a short amount of time left, and if it isn't then she has two more chances.

The room emits a bass-y failure tone, the lights lower in hue.

"Oh fuck. Fucking fuck," Nina erupts, turning to the console again. "Think, think," she orders herself. She cricks her neck and shakes out her hands with a light bounce on her feet.

There is a splash, splash noise from the floor as she moves. She looks down. The small room is filling with water. She steps back from the console, her eyes roving the room for an explanation—which she finds beneath the stop/start tap. The grate that was previously draining away the flowing water is now pumping water back into the room at a frankly alarming rate.

The room is designed to fill with water: *death by water.*

That is it, not poison. She hasn't been poisoned; the water is going to kill her in a very different way.

Instead of fear, joy bursts through Nina as she rapidly counts out the letters on her trembling fingers. Yes, that's it. That's the answer.

She wades back to the screen, water now at knee height and rising. She taps out her answer, her finger hovering momentarily over the submit button, before squeezing her eyes shut and tapping. On the screen her answer pulses.

Death by water is:

D

R

O

W

N

I

N

G

Correct!

The lights in the room return to normal but to Nina's horror the water does not stop. It continues to inch farther up her thighs with every second.

"Bathsheba, what the hell is going on. I got it right. I got the question right!"

Over the bubble and lap of incoming water Bathsheba's voice remains as always unnervingly calm. "You are correct. Question one complete. Two remaining questions."

"What the fuck!"

Silence from Bathsheba.

The screen instead flashes up with the next question.

```
This room is filling at 3 cubic units per minute.
This started three minutes ago.
How long until the room is completely submerged?
```

A timer appears at the top of the screen expressing the three minutes already mentioned, seconds adding on as she watches.

"Maths, okay," Nina blurts suddenly, talking herself through it with a strange disassociated calmness, her hands trembling the whole time. "So, three threes are nine. We're nine cubic units in. The room's volume is—" She spins to estimate, then splutters out a "fuck" as she realizes she has absolutely no idea.

The water is now almost at her crotch. She takes a breath and forces herself to refocus.

Then the glimmer of an idea. Nina suddenly remembers a completely random and soul-crushingly embarrassing single-woman life hack that she found on YouTube her first week as a new homeowner back at Cambridge University. She had never lived alone before and had found the act of trying to get the house in order herself while working all the hours under the sun utterly soul destroying. There was never enough time, or the right tools, and the house still looked like an anonymous shell. So at 2 A.M. she'd watched a tutorial on hanging pictures without tools. She'd used a log from the wood burner stack as a hammer, some picture hooks, and her own arm span to measure distance.

Without a second thought Nina stands and sploshes her way to the nearest wall, water now at waist height, and presses her nose to the wall, one arm stretched out to touch the other wall. Then marking the spot where her other shoulder hits the wall, she measures one meter. She repeats the process across the first wall and can complete the action twice more, telling her that the wall is almost exactly three meters across.

She pulls away from this wall and repeats the action on the three: all three meters. She looks up: the ceiling in here is high for a basement. It looks about the same as her father's townhouse ceiling, perhaps four meters.

So three by three by four meters? Thirty-six cubic meters.

Nina quickly looks back to the screen. The timer is hitting four minutes, the water now at Nina's chest.

"Okay, okay," Nina mutters, trying to stay composed. "So, four minutes of flooding in the room at the rate Bathsheba suggested of three cubic units per minute means the room must now be twelve cubic units full. And if there can only be thirty-six cubic units in total in the room and those twelve units are already in it then I only have twenty-four cubic units left to go before I drown." She visibly shakes off the thought and refocuses.

"And if the room fills with three cubic units per minute, that's twenty-four divided by three. I have . . . eight minutes left," she concludes triumphantly. In front of her the timer counter clicks onward. "Shit, no, no, I have seven minutes now." With the water at her collarbone, lapping just beneath the screen, Nina waits until the timer hits five minutes exactly and then types her answer.

Correct!

The screen flashes up, the water inching up its own glowing edifice.

The screen will shortly be submerged, Nina realizes, and she will have to duck under to read it.

The water does not stop in spite of her second correct answer. And with that her tiptoes lose the floor beneath her as she begins to tread water.

"Come on, Bathsheba, next fucking question. Come on!"

CHAPTER 28
MARIA

Maria's body relaxes back into the airplane seat. The cabin doors are sealed and they are taxiing around to the runway, due for takeoff in less than ten minutes. She has made it.

She has somehow made it out of there alive.

She thinks back over the last forty-eight hours, her face still bruised, her muscles still aching, cuts and abrasions hidden now under a thin cashmere sweater she had bought from an airport boutique.

She somehow managed the swim, a swim she would later, from the safety of the US embassy business center, calculate had been more than a kilometer. Somehow she managed it in her own breathless fashion. And when she saw an empty stretch of public beach, she waded back to shore and, steering clear of the main road, made her way along the wild coastal path following signs to the Gorda ferry port.

Thankfully the blood had been washed from her during the

swim, but Maria was aware there was no way she would be able to take a ferry as she was; she had no money and she was soaking wet, covered in bruises, and shuddering with cold now that the sun was finally setting. She carefully picked her way through the undergrowth that was concealing her progress to take a peek at the shoreline beyond. A couple of evening swimmers dotted the water, their towels and bags left on the sand. She did not break cover yet, though; the single swimmers she saw were so solitary that they would easily notice her slipping from the cover of the trees to deftly take their items. She did not need more people chasing her.

She was certain the people she was running from would be looking for her at police stations and harbors. But she doubted they would have thought to cover the busy tourist ferry terminal—after all, how could she possibly go there without drawing attention?

Maria continued along the coast until she found the perfect opportunity: a mother with three children running and playing in the waves, the woman's attention split among too many potential dangers to notice Maria.

Maria had been there as a nanny many times. Caregivers were easy targets—she knew herself; if more than one kid was having a frantic half hour, you'd be lucky if you noticed that your beach towel back there was on fire.

She waited until the oldest of the woman's children, a four-year-old, dashed screaming into the foaming waves clearly intent on making his way out to a raft that was definitely not a child's distance away. The mother grabbed one toddler and firmly ordered the other not to move, then stumbled into the waves after the adventurous swimmer.

Maria slipped from the undergrowth and walked calmly but purposefully in the direction of the woman's beach spot, careful to keep a calm relaxed pace and pass as a sunset walker from some neighboring resort.

As predicted the swimming emergency metamorphized into a game in the water. The mother to her credit subverted the danger and somehow got the child to willingly stay in the shallows. But her attention was firmly locked on her brood as she tried to playfully negotiate an end to the increasingly post-sunset swim.

As Maria passed the family's array of towels, she did not break step, bending only to hitch the woman's woven bag onto her own shoulder and grab a thick sweatshirt from over the arm of the pram. Then she was away, seamlessly continuing her walk along the beach, listening behind her as the sounds of family life faded, all the while expecting a hand to roughly grab her and spin her around. But no hand came and the world continued to spin. Once she had made it around the curve of the beach, she slipped back into the undergrowth to inspect her haul.

A wallet with cards and eighty dollars in cash. In her head, Maria promised the woman she would leave the wallet in a public spot, use only the cash, and return the rest to a lost property.

She removed her torn wet polo shirt and slipped on the woman's warm sweatshirt. Her shorts were still wet but partially covered now by the thick sweater. She dug around in the bag and came up with a cheap pair of flip-flops, a worn sun hat, and a children's snack bar. She tore into the wrapper and inhaled the cereal bar, its oats and dried fruit hitting in a way she had never thought possible, all the magic of life suddenly present in the nutty tang of it. She let out a moan of enjoyment. It had been days since she had last eaten.

Snack devoured, Maria crumpled the wrapper, returned it to the bag, slipped on her new shoes and the sun hat, and headed toward the road.

She managed to buy a ticket and slip onto the ferry hidden among the passengers of a large American cruise ship returning to their ship in Tortola after a day trip. Sun hat pushed down to avoid the cameras she was certain would be across the ferry port, she boarded the ferry back to the main island.

It was easy to buy a flight home using online banking at an internet café. Her next move was harder, however. Having left her passport back in that house, she needed emergency travel documents to return to the US, and even after she applied for a replacement passport the process required a two-day wait. So wait she did, for forty-eight terrifying hours, in a cheap airport hotel. She checked her emails for evidence of who these people were and what they wanted from her, but all correspondence from the company that had hired her had disappeared from her email account. There was no paper chain. If she had died in that house, if her body had washed up on the shores of Gorda, it seemed unlikely anyone would have been able to identify her. They had made sure no one knew where she was or who she had been working for.

And yet now she is free. She is safe, she reminds herself, aboard a five-and-a-half-hour flight back to New York. Safe.

She thinks of her apartment, the tiny place she shares in Brooklyn with her now pretty much estranged best friend Freya.

The idea that Freya won't even have missed her yet is an unsettling one in Maria's mind, but then everyone thinks Maria is nannying right now. Nannying at some rich person's holiday home in paradise. How could they possibly know what occurred over the past week?

As the plane roars its way down the runway and lifts, engines deafening around her, she thinks of how the people who held her captive arranged everything perfectly, only emailing her the final address the day after she arrived on Tortola, so that no one but her would know the exact location of the house.

But she remembers—and once she is back home and recovered and absolutely certain she's safe she will tell somebody what happened out there. By then the bodies will be gone, she doesn't doubt, and her crimes will be as hidden as theirs.

The plane levels out high above the islands and Maria lets out a long-held sigh, tension slowly releasing from deep inside her.

She will get back to that apartment, she will tell Freya, at least some of it, and over the next few days she will find a lawyer, and she will make sure those people can never hurt her again.

EXCEPT FREYA IS NOT AT the apartment when Maria arrives at the door eight hours later. And Maria does not have a new phone yet. Or a key.

Freya's absence is not unusual. Maria and Freya met at Cornell the day before their first class commenced; they were in the same med intake. And Freya is now in her third year, her hours even more extreme to Maria's now "outside" eye than they were when she herself was living through them. The pair rarely sees each other most days and when they do, Maria can often sense Freya's discomfort around talking about anything, especially the career that Maria abandoned with such seeming ease.

Perhaps even back then Freya felt that age-old twinge people get when something, namely Maria's altered career path, seems too good to be true.

And wasn't that instinct borne out spectacularly in the end, Maria muses, as she makes the schlep down to the super's apartment to request a spare key. Her own key and phone no doubt now in some unknown landfill in the British Virgin Islands.

Best not to wait for Freya to get back. God knows when she might return home.

The super obligingly lets her into her own apartment, clearly pleased to have the opportunity to interrogate Maria once more on the habits of the rich and famous. Maria customarily bats him off with a few choice anecdotes but has neither the will nor the energy to do so today. Sensing a new frostiness to Maria, he soon disappears back to his own apartment.

HER APARTMENT SMELLS LIKE HOME—well, not her childhood home, but her New York home: the scent of cooking spices, laundry detergent, and Freya's calming shower gel. Freya obviously came back to the apartment and went out again not long before Maria's return.

Maria tries not to let her thoughts pull back to memories of her childhood home, her parents, long gone now, or the uncle who took her in for those final years of high school.

She tries not to think of them most days, but now more than ever she is not in the mental space to reminisce about lost loved ones.

Her uncle and herself rarely speak. She loves him and he her, she knows, in his quiet way. But they are not close, each reminding the other of what was lost. No, Maria is alone, and will be until she chooses to have a family of her own, or chooses not to.

She wanders from room to room in the apartment looking at everything as if for the first time, so certain she was that she would never make her way back here again.

Her room, just as she left it: a few unpacked items that never made it into her case, spilled makeup powder on her dresser, the last book she finished before the contract came through. And on the edge of the bed some folded towels Freya must have laundered and returned to her room. A gesture so potent in its everyday kindness that it makes Maria let out a throaty sob. Eyes blurring, she takes in her space, her things, the pictures on her walls, her possessions, things she used to care so much about, each item now seeming alien to her somehow. She rises and wanders to her dresser, the bottles of face cream, scents, nail polishes, strings of beads in all colors and styles all as if someone else's.

The feeling opens a worrying question in Maria's mind, the question of whether she has now outgrown her old life, if what she has witnessed has made her real life seem ludicrously naïve by comparison. She heads over to her DSR camera hanging by its strap from her door handle and sits down heavily on her bed.

She flicks on the power and scrolls through her old photos. She's always thought of herself as having a bit of an eye, spending hours on weekends wandering the streets of Manhattan and catching moments, but looking back now magic no longer glitters through her hard-won photos, only people trying their hardest to live their lives. Maria tries to shake off the thought but it sinks deeper into her and expands. There is no escaping it.

The truth is, the world is not the place Maria thought it was before she left. The world is a place where you can die, where you can be killed and you can kill and everything will carry on as normal—without you—without them.

She winces at the thought of the two men who tried to kill her, the men she subsequently killed. But wincing does not stop the memories from coming. The memories of the rooms, one after another. And the people she did not see, but who watched everything she did. She tries not to think who they were and what it was for, she tries to push away the questions of how many people died in those rooms before her, of what it was all in aid of.

She wondered back there, between bouts of terror, back

under the house, if it was just a kind of gladiatorial game for someone's sadistic amusement or if it had some larger significance? An experiment perhaps—but to prove what hypothesis?

The sound of the fridge clicking on in the kitchen shakes her from the thoughts. She is still hungry. Two days in she still has calories to make up, and even the thought of the fridge and what it might contain in spite of Freya's restricted diabetic diet is enough to get her up and moving.

In the kitchen she eats her friend's food, and when she's full she gathers some clean clothes and a towel from her room and heads to the bathroom. She runs a deep hot bubble bath and lies in it, certain in the knowledge that she cannot live here anymore; she can't slip back into this old life after what happened to her. She cannot pretend everything is the same when she has pressed up hard against the invisible line between living and not.

But she has savings, she has a lot of savings, from three years of living among the kind of people who could do this to someone. She could move, perhaps move out west, near her uncle? Perhaps a quiet life could work for her now. But she somehow doubts it. She needs to fill the silence that brings on remembrance, not encourage it. Because when her thoughts are free they run like lightning straight back into that basement in Virgin Gorda, they fly through those rooms right back to the final one, and they find her curled fetal on the floor, ready to let the pain take her and for it all to end.

The thought is interrupted by a knock on the door.

Maria's eyes fly through the open bathroom door to the hallway. She shifts in her warm bubbles and hugs her knees close. The knock comes again.

"Hello," she calls, and tells herself it's not them. It can't be, they couldn't follow her, could they?

"Hey," the voice comes back with barely covered disinterest. "Sign for a package: Freya Samuels?"

A wave of relief swims through Maria with such force, a chuckle erupts from her. "Oh, okay. One second. I'll be right there."

Maria rises, wraps a towel around her wet body, and pads to the door. She checks through the peephole, sees the package, and opens the door.

He grabs her.

A hand instantly over her mouth, her wet feet slipping and skidding back into the apartment as he drags her and slams the door behind them.

She tries to scream, to bite, but nothing gets past his thick leather-gloved hands. She struggles, but he is stronger. He steers her back toward the bathroom, toward the tub that moments ago was so relaxing, the tub full to the brim with warm bubbly water, and she knows his plan.

And that's when her old friend kicks in once more. The friend who has always saved her.

She stops struggling and lets her body go limp. When the momentum he has been using against her is no longer necessary it suddenly pivots him forward. Maria is momentarily loosened from his grip as he grabs for the doorframe with one hand, the other still tight around her mouth. She dips to the floor and skids back away from him. She runs to the front door, grabs the baseball bat Freya's ex-boyfriend bought them for self-defense after a homeless guy was found dead in the building's stairwell a year ago, and swings it wildly at the back of the stranger's head.

ONCE MARIA HAS CLEANED UP the floor where he fell and moved him to her bedroom, she washes herself again, dresses, and heads out onto the street to find what she's looking for. She is not worried the man will wake. He's dead now. She took one of Freya's old diabetic syringes from her used sharps box and filled it with air. She made sure he would not bother her again.

When she gets to the homeless shelter on East 30th Street her plan solidifies. She pays the men generously for their spare items of clothes until she has a full outfit, which she bundles into a carrier bag, holding her nose, and takes back—to much consternation—on the subway system.

Back in the apartment she changes the man, careful to match the colors of his original outfit she knows would have been caught downstairs on the entry hall cameras.

She pulls the mobile phone from his pocket and uses his lifeless face to unlock the screen and change the password.

Then checking the halls are clear, and for the first time in her life pleased that her building has no CCTV in the hallways, she hauls the 160-plus-pound man along the hallway to the unused stairwell.

WHEN FREYA RETURNS TO HER apartment that night everything is as she left it. Which is why she finds it so incredibly odd that all of her chicken is gone. She is sure she had a full container when she left that morning—but her hours were long and everything is stepping up at the hospital now that they're nearing the end of the year. She checks Maria's room, but everything there is as it should be.

Of course Maria did not eat her chicken. Maria is halfway across the world in some amazing resort or other with some new employer and their ungrateful spawn—she's not sneaking around their shitty Brooklyn apartment stealing chicken chunks in Cajun spice.

———

IT WILL BE ANOTHER THREE days until the smell from the unused stairwell alerts a neighbor to the dead homeless man lurking down there, and a minor police investigation into said death ensues. A query is briefly raised by Freya when she overhears the super charting his own movements the day the man entered the building. The super mentions that he had let Maria into their flat a few hours prior and then done maintenance work for the rest of the afternoon. The police ask Freya if she can contact Maria, but when both Freya and the officer involved attempt to call, their calls go to voicemail. But not before the international call tone sounds. Maria, to all intents and purposes, is still in Gorda.

And in a sense that none of them could possibly ever understand, and is of course purely metaphorical, Maria always will be Still in Gorda.

In reality, Maria is on a flight to London. A string of messages on the dead man's phone led her right back to the woman with the too-tight chignon. An office in Mayfair, an address, a name.

Maria verified her own death on the man's phone, confirmed the job was done, but it would only be a matter of time before the man does not show up where he is expected and Maria's story will begin to unravel.

But for now, she has a momentary advantage, and the savings she's been accumulating for her future to fund it.

The people who hired her to go to that house want her dead now, and it seems unlikely Maria will be allowed to move on with her life until certain conversations have taken place.

CHAPTER 29
NINA

Nina is treading water now, the screen impossible to see without ducking beneath the rising water. She snatches another breath and dips her head under and there the final question fills the screen:

```
Read with your hands, using your head,

the rhythm of the water is what the thunder said.
```

Nina looks down past the screen to the faucet about five feet below her. Even submerged she can see the stop/start of its stream.

Morse code. The realization coming to her as if directly from her father's mind. They'd learned Morse code together as a joke to get them out of boring visits.

She recalls a Parents' Day at her school; she must have been twelve or thirteen. A teacher of hers had been explaining as they both sat there that while Nina's work was technically perfect it lacked originality or spirit. This from a woman in Christmas tree earrings in mid-November, Nina had thought.

Nina had watched her father listen and nod, but around his eyes that telltale crinkle as he looked down at her. They both knew exactly how much spirit she had. And almost in answer Nina had let her hand pat the desk in time.

It would have looked like a nervous gesture to that woman, just a thoughtful pat-pat. But he saw it for what it was; he understood. The word *go* in Morse code—and if that wasn't spirit then God knows what could have been. Two slow palms on a table, one nail tap, and three more slow palms. Dash-dash. Dot. Dash-dash-dash.

Nina shakes off the immediate link between what's happening to her now and what happened that day. It raises again the question of why he would be doing this to her, of his meaning, of his intent. She does not have time to analyze the whys and wherefores of any of this while the room around her fills with water.

The point is, the tap is spelling out a word. A four-letter word. God knows Nina can think of a few of those off the top of her head right now without the help of a submerged tap but her words sure as hell wouldn't be the right ones.

She will have to dive down and watch the tap, feel the pulses.

The timer on the screen below gives her five minutes of remaining air. And with that she tips her head back up to the surface, the ceiling looming close above her, takes a deep breath, and dives down to the bottom of the room.

She grabs the tap to stop herself floating back up and waits for it to stop pulsing.

When the water stills, she places a hand beneath the nozzle and waits.

The first short jet comes hard against her fingers.

Dot, dash, dot, dot. That signifies the letter *L*. A pause and then the tap jet restarts.

Dot, dash, dash, dot. That signifies a *P*.

Another break and then: *Dot, dot, dot, dot.* That signifies an *H*.

The water stops then restarts in one sharp burst. *Dot.* An *E*.

These are the four letters. But they don't make a word. Four nonsense letters? *LPHE*.

Nina tries to still the panic avalanching inside her, tries to still the fear that somehow, she has forgotten how to do this. She has forgotten how to read Morse code. Treading water as she breaks the surface, head bobbing closer and closer to the ceiling, she sounds out the letters. Forcing herself to think.

"*L, P, H, E,*" she splutters and just like that the letters seem to rearrange in her mind. *HELP.* There it is, jumbled but there.

Nina gasps a breath and plunges back under the surface, kicking down to the screen and typing the letters into the keyboard.

Read with your hands, using your head,

the rhythm of the water is what the thunder said.

HELP.

The screen seems to be frozen but her eyes dart to the timer with one and a half minutes still ticking down. It's just taking too long. Her chest aches to push back to the surface but she holds fast and waits for the screen to change.

It finally shifts; the now familiar bright-green font appears, declaring:

Correct!

The timer tells her she has just under sixty seconds until the room is full, all air gone.

But that does not fully prepare her for what she experiences on reaching what she presumed would be the surface. Only half an inch of air remains at the top of the room between the water and the hard surface of the ceiling. She cannot bring her nose and mouth out of the water without adjusting to lie back prostrate floating in the water, gasping in breaths.

The world's least relaxing flotation room, Nina muses, spluttering a gallows-humor laugh then promptly sobering as her nostrils fill with water. The room is not draining yet; its final bursts of water make the level continue to rise, the last remaining inch covering her mouth. She forces herself to remain calm.

She holds her breath beneath the surface, a hand braced to the ceiling, as the deafening sound of the drains opening beneath her roars, her chest desperate to heave in a breath. She cannot rise, because there is nowhere for her to go.

Then with a wave of profound relief she feels the water level pull away from under her, the hand braced above her on the ceiling suddenly free from water. She bobs up into the new gap and drags air into her lungs greedily as the water level rapidly lowers around her. She drops fast, a grateful buoy bobbing on the surface until her toes finally brush back onto the floor and she is able to stand again. Her limbs weak and trembling from the exertion of treading water for over half an hour.

A great sob issues from her and as the water drains from chest level, to waist level, to knee height, she appears to crumple down with it until, room drained, she lies with chest heaving, muscles quaking on the cool wet floor.

Nina isn't sure how long she lies there, slipping in and out of sleep, unwilling, and possibly unable, to stop it washing over her exhausted body. She lets it until the *shush* of the hydraulic door opening breaks the silent spell the room has cast over her.

She heaves herself up quickly. Looking back, she sees that the door she entered from is still sealed; the noise instead came from a new door on the opposite wall. Another corridor stretches out beyond it, this one in an ambient pale-green tone. She looks to the screen above the tap as if it might suddenly decide to explain everything to her. But it does not. Instead it simply reads:

    Congratulations, Nina!
    You have completed Death by Water. Please proceed
    to the vestibule.

As if reading her mind Bathsheba promptly reiterates the command, "Please proceed to the vestibule immediately."

But Nina does not.

She stares at the words on the screen. *Death by Water.*

Nina knows the phrase well; it's the name of one of the five parts of T. S. Eliot's poem, "The Waste Land." And the clue included another part of that poem: What the Thunder Said.

She thinks of her father's first-edition copy of *The Waste Land* upstairs on the library bookshelf, of its inscription inside. Now she isn't quite so certain that the words etched into the title page by her long-dead mother were quite as innocent and hopeful as she had supposed. How she missed the significance of that book being upstairs, she does not know. After all, who in God's name gives, or receives, a copy of *The Waste Land* as a lover's token?

Nina knows the content of the poem, start to end, she's even lectured on it recently, among other things. It is not a joyful poem, not a lover's poem; it's a poem about disillusionment, emptiness, and the garble of humanity.

It was up there as plain as day. Nina, for the first time in a long time, certainly since her father's death, pronounces herself an idiot.

That book was a clue; the whole house above her was a clue. This is a massive escape room, and she is the sole player. And if she doesn't sharpen up, she will lose the game.

If this room is called Death by Water and she's heard What the Thunder Said already, then it's no stretch for her to infer that there might be other rooms down here with similarly themed names. There might well be three more rooms, at least, for the three other parts of "The Waste Land." She runs them through in her head: Death by Water, What the Thunder Said, then Burial of the Dead, A Game of Chess, The Fire Sermon. Clearly the rooms are not in the correct order down here, but taking the one she has just completed as first, this seems the likely order.

What the rooms are for, however—what any of this is for—she as yet has no idea. But her father must have built this place for a reason, and she has to believe it wasn't to try to kill people. He wouldn't do that.

And yet the rooms are named after parts in his dead wife's favorite poem, a poem that clearly meant a great deal to both of them. So maybe he did want to hurt people? But why, Nina demands of herself, why when he was such a rational man would he bother to do that?

"Please proceed to the vestibule immediately," Bathsheba repeats.

"Or what?" Nina screams back at the voice. "You'll try to kill me in here again? Good luck, I know all the answers to this one now, don't I?"

After all, Nina considers what can they actually do to her. Make her hot again perhaps, make her wet again?

"I want to know who you are! And why you're doing this! Did you know my father? Did he build this? What is it?"

Nina looks around at the whiteness on all sides. But no answer comes.

Her questions hang awkward in the air.

She could of course answer them herself. Why would anybody do something like this?

Because they can, because awful, evil people have always existed and sometimes you can't tell they're awful and sometimes those people turn out to be someone's lovely loving clever cuddly dad.

As she watches the vestibule door begin to close she does not move, she simply watches as the green-lit corridor beyond it slips from sight, the door sealing over it. And with that the room Nina is in plunges into darkness.

After a moment of silence Bathsheba's voice fills the pitch blackness surrounding her.

"Sensory deprivation initiated. Three hours and fifty-nine minutes remaining."

The only sounds after that are Nina's terrified breaths.

CHAPTER 30
MARIA

Maria sips her coffee as she watches the office building across from her.

London is cold. And though she is wrapped up warm against the chill, she shivers in spite of herself.

She knows she isn't at her best, she's still recovering from her injuries, from her rapid weight loss and trauma. She should be in bed somewhere, she should be recovering, family and loved ones surrounding her. But she has no family, not really, and the last thing she wants is people surrounding her.

No doubt that's one of the reasons she was chosen for the job in the first place. She fit the profile of a missing person perfectly, a woman working abroad on short contracts, a woman who—having quit Cornell after just one year—is evidently unreliable. A woman with friends in different states, with busy lives of their own and an understanding of their friend's innate unpredictability. Maria knows she might have been missing for months, even years without someone assuming the worst. And when they did, would this tie-less short-term woman be remembered at all by the few people she came into contact with on the island where she was last seen? Most likely not. She had wandered into her own entrapment without even realizing what an easy mark she had been.

Her joints ache as she places the coffee cup back down on the table, but her hands no longer shake constantly. She is making progress, and that's good enough for her.

It has only been a week now since she ran blood-soaked from that house and let the warm Caribbean Sea wash away the external traces of what happened to her. But the internal traces are still there, the bruises, cuts, and burns beneath her clothes are still there, and in her mind Maria is still in that house. Perhaps she always will be, the house blending in her psyche with that barely remembered past, blending again with the loss of her parents, blending with the never-ending strug-gle to live in a world she knows is not built for women as cer-tain and driven as her.

You have to tread water just to stay afloat.

But she would rather be *there* in her mind, still in the Darién Gap, still in the house, than dead. This will not be the end of her, these people.

She looks back at the thin glass building opposite as people come and go. Maria saw the woman enter this morning, the woman who showed her around the house, the woman with the too-tight chignon. Her name is Lucinda Hooper, and she works in some capacity for a blue-chip wealth management firm. Maria has been watching the building for three days now, from the comfort of the quiet brasserie opposite. Hidden under the safety of awnings and blocked from view by a sculptural outdoor heating unit and understated topiary, she has watched. A book propped up in front of her, to a passing eye she is just a tourist with a new favorite café. She switches locations on the hour and takes up the same view at each.

The woman arrives and leaves at the same time each day, slipping promptly at 6 P.M. into a town car that takes her back to her home, a coral-pink gated house on Millionaire's Row in Notting Hill. A housekeeper appears to let herself in, daily, an hour after Lucinda's departure, and leaves again an hour before Lucinda returns home.

No other visitors have come to the house, as far as Maria has seen, and no one else appears to live there with her, except a small bouncy copper-haired cocker spaniel that she promptly walks for forty-five minutes as soon as she gets home every evening.

Maria's eyes flick back up to the office building as a group of men enter the revolving doors, a woman in the lobby extending a hand to greet them in turn. It isn't Lucinda.

Maria hoped to see her with somebody, to extend her knowledge of who else might be involved in what happened to her out on Gorda, but so far all she has to go on is Lucinda.

And tonight, she will be paying her a home visit.

MARIA SITS IN HER NONDESCRIPT silver-gray hire car and waits.

Lucinda arrived home two minutes ago and disappeared into her house to retrieve her dog. Maria watches the town car slide away, not to return to collect Lucinda until eight-thirty tomorrow morning.

Lucinda will reappear from the house in a few minutes with dog in tow, wellies and puffer coat on.

Maria is nervous, of course, but certain of what she has to do. She lets her eyes sweep down the street to reacquaint herself with the lamppost-mounted CCTV cameras dotting the affluent area. She estimates they will catch her approach to Lucinda's side of the street, but where she sits now is not covered by the public cameras, nor are any of the private house entrances.

Lucinda's house has its own private cameras mounted above the gate and door, which appear to activate when the gate sensor is tripped on entry and exit.

Maria has rehearsed the plan in her mind for the last three days. If she keeps her nerve it will work, if there are no surprises it will work. She can't plan for everything, but if she stays present it might all be fine; that other part of her will come alive and save them both.

Again, she has the advantage, the element of surprise. Odd that she has an advantage now, after a lifetime of having no notable advantages at all, of struggling for everything she's received, but then life is like that sometimes, she supposes. Or maybe she only has the advantage now because she *has* struggled so hard and adapted to it?

She shakes off the thought as a deliveryman suddenly pulls up in the bay two down from her own and leaps from his truck, package in hand, heading to another building.

Maria's hand pauses on the handle of the car. She can't do what she needs to do with this person here, a potential witness. Maria has not factored this in, an unscheduled delivery, an on-street witness. Lucinda is due to exit the building for her dog walk at any moment. She watches the man ring the house buzzer and wait, shifting the weight of the package in his hands as the tone blips on. They are clearly not in. Maria feels her anger rise.

Just try another house, leave it with someone else, she screams in her mind. But he can't hear her and is clearly in no rush. Across the street there is movement. Maria's gaze flies over to catch sight of Lucinda pulling back her large cedar security gate and holding it open for her excitable dog, who yelps and spins in lead-tangling circles as she does so.

"All right, Penny, almost there, sweetie. Come on then," Maria hears her coo as she too pushes through and closes the

gate behind them. Her guard down, a softer, more off-duty ver-
sion of the woman moments before. "Right. Let's go, cutie."

Maria looks back to the delivery driver. He's still there,
oblivious to Lucinda's existence and to the fact he has so
soundly destroyed Maria's plan. He, having pressed the gate
bell, has finally also come to the conclusion that the homeowner is not in and he is now chaotically trying to scribble out
a missed-delivery slip while balancing the package with one
knee braced against their wall. Work completed, he slots the
slip into their mailbox and jogs the package back to his van
before slipping in, swigging at a fizzy drink, and speeding off
again.

Maria bristles in his disorganized wake. Lucinda is gone.
She could follow her on the dog walk but there's no point, because what she needs is in that house. She'll have to wait until
Lucinda returns. It isn't a big change to the plan, really, it just
feels like one. A snag that has knocked her plan forty-five minutes down the road. But if anything, things might be easier
once the light has fallen further. Sure, more people will be
home to hear, but witnesses will be less likely to see anything
at all. She'll go ahead with the plan, she decides, in spite of the
change of order. She just has to wait a little longer.

THREE-QUARTERS OF AN HOUR LATER, almost to the minute, Lucinda rounds the corner at the far end of the street and Maria
takes her cue.

To the casual observer it will look completely unconnected,
Lucinda's appearance and Maria slipping from her car and
crossing over to Lucinda's side of the street; just two London-
ers going about their daily lives.

Maria's face will not show up on any CCTV footage when
the police finally get around to checking months after Freya

reports her missing and flags her flight to London. Maria's rental car number plate is deliberately out of sight of the cameras, as she intended, her baseball cap down low, her collar up.

For all intents and purposes Maria will never be seen again.

CHAPTER 31
NINA

The lights flicker on after four hours of darkness and Nina squeezes her eyes tight shut at the sting of it. She blinks the room back into focus and rises to stretch her aching limbs.

She managed to sleep for a large portion of the sensory deprivation period, perhaps three hours, but she had no *real* concept of time alone in the darkness.

She paced the black in her waking moments, mapping out the room like a woman newly blind, using the edges of things and her own strides as maps and markers. She had water at least; though silent, the tap in the room had collected a few handfuls in its curved catch cup above the drain. She had that, and time to think; much too much time to think.

Standing now she reaches her arms up and stretches out her aching back muscles, too taut from the trauma of hours before. She knows something is coming and she knows she needs food and if she had to put money on it, she'd bet that's how they'll get her in the next room. And by God, she has thought a lot about that next room over the last few hours.

With a hydraulic whir the door across the room slowly slides open.

Bathsheba's voice returns, after so much silence. "Sensory deprivation complete. Please proceed to the vestibule."

Nina looks beyond the door at the thin vestibule corridor and the other room waiting. She turns back to the door she entered the room from, firmly sealed behind her.

She reminds herself that Joe is coming, he might be here already, he will have alerted someone, help will be on its way. It's only a matter of time until someone batters down the doors, one after the other, and rescues her. The only reason James's firm didn't do so before she arrived was because they didn't want to damage the property. But if she is clearly in danger no one will think twice. And James will get her messages soon, if he hasn't already; it will be Monday soon.

People are coming, she tells herself, and she will make it out. And she promises herself that whoever, or whatever, this is and the reasons behind it will be dragged into the light.

If she were to be honest at this very moment, she'd admit that she doesn't care anymore if any of this was her father's doing, though she feels a twinge of shame at the thought. She isn't even interested in the women whom she assumes have been through this house before her. She doesn't have space in her mind for that right now because she knows what's coming next. Not exactly, but she knows it will be hard, physically and mentally, and she knows it will be a game designed to test her very limits. And if she keeps going long enough, she will reach those limits.

She has considered her options.

She needs food. She will need more water. If she stays here in this room for another round of sensory deprivation, she might be too weak even to continue eventually. Better to keep her body healthy and try to delay whatever comes next than to waste time here and hope she isn't tested again.

Bathsheba repeats the request. "Please proceed to the vestibule immediately."

Nina knows they're watching her. She felt it in the darkness, in the silence of the sensory deprivation, eyes on her, night-vision cameras—in her mind's eye she pictured the scene like some kind of behavioral experiment. Perhaps it is that, perhaps it isn't. What this place is she still doesn't know. But she knows it isn't good. And she knows that she can, and fears she most likely will, die down here.

She presumes her father created it, all evidence seems to point that way, but his reasons are still unclear.

And yet, in spite of everything, she still believes those reasons will unveil themselves before too long and she will suddenly make sense of it all, either by the nature of what she finds down here or with the arrival of help.

But she knows she can't spend another four hours in darkness.

The vestibule is her only option.

And with that she steps out of the room and into the green-tinged corridor. Another door closes behind her, sealing Nina even deeper into the house.

CHAPTER 32
MARIA

Maria has played out the scenario obsessively in her mind for the last two nights.

She's watched people in Lucinda's neighborhood and knows how to blend in. She's purchased a toddler's scooter on Amazon, muddied it up in a park, and when she pulls it from the car and jogs lightly across the Notting Hill street with it slung in hand she looks every inch just another harassed West London yummy-mummy pre- or post-pickup.

She knows the flash point could be eye contact, but most people rarely make eye contact for more than a second in big cities. But she's alive to the possibility that Lucinda might recognize her, though she feels certain, given the heightened nature of the situation she's engineering, that it theoretically will not be a problem.

As a student doctor she helped save people's lives in triage, and those same people had completely forgotten her face less than an hour later. She held their lives in her hands and they wouldn't have been able to spot her in a lineup. She knows that the human brain has only so much attention available at any moment; people don't notice a lot of things when their attention is split.

Even if Lucinda gets a really good look at Maria, so much about her appearance has changed in the last two weeks that it seems very unlikely recognition will kick in quickly enough to be an issue. Maria's hair beneath her cap is cropped tight now, her long soft curls gone. Her eyebrows are gone too, bleached, completely changing the appearance of her face, making it appear broader and less easy to pinpoint without the framing effect dark brows gave her. On top of that Maria took pains to ensure that the clothes she chose—a trench coat, sweatpants, and technical sneakers—were as far from her own feminine softness as conceivable.

After all, the woman with the too-tight chignon only actually met Maria in person once, and that meeting was only perhaps half an hour long.

Besides, Maria has been confirmed dead already. The man this woman sent to kill her in a tub of bathwater in her New York apartment achieved his goal as far as Lucinda knows. Maria is a problem solved in this woman's mind, and until she becomes a direct problem to her again it seems unlikely that Lucinda will make a connection, especially during this brief interaction.

As Maria approaches her Lucinda gives her only a cursory glance and the vaguest of smiles. Maria returns them, and as Lucinda slows to approach her own gate Maria feigns recognition.

"Oh hey. I was just knocking on your door there. Hi, I'm Anna, our house backs onto your garden—on the Fairholt Gardens side?"

Lucinda turns, eyebrows raised in surprise at being engaged in conversation.

Maria has noted that neighbors in this affluent area of London don't appear to speak, know, or even acknowledge one another. They have priced themselves right out of the necessity for conversation.

Maria watches Lucinda squint at her in the fading light, searching for reassuring markers that she is who she professes to be. Already she knows her American accent is working on Lucinda; most of the locals around here were relocated overseas by American finance companies. Maria fits the bill.

She hoicks her cumbersome children's scooter and continues with warmth.

"I'm so sorry to disturb you but my eldest has lobbed my husband's signed Chelsea football into your back garden." Maria raises her hands, scooter too. "I know . . . the joys of parenthood. But we do what we can, right."

Maria is including her in that—as a dog mother. Lucinda gives an indulgent smile, Penny hopping around her feet with excitement at her mother's rare human interaction.

"Can I be a total pain and grab it from you? The ball?" Maria continues, with a quick look to her own watch, as if she too has a million other things she would rather be doing this evening.

Lucinda looks to Penny, the only other witness, as if the dog might have the answer. Penny nudges her, happy and eager to be involved in the situation. Lucinda gives the woman a final cursory look up and down: she is just one of the many mothers Lucinda often sees hurrying about at the ends and beginnings of days. A woman she will never be, nor has ever really desired to be.

"Sure," Lucinda answers. "I could go, take a look, and bring it up or—" She leaves the idea hanging.

Maria does not jump on it. She leaves Lucinda to finish her own sentence. It will be better if it's Lucinda's idea, easier.

"Or you could come through and grab it? Probably quicker. You know what you're looking for."

Now it's Maria's turn to give the impression of weighing up Lucinda. She looks back over her shoulder as if judging the appropriateness of entering another person's house—then gives a light shrug.

"Er, okay. I'll just grab it and leave you to your evening."

And just like that, social awkwardness and pre-planning have opened Lucinda's front gate and then her front door.

The pair wander into the marble-floored hall of Lucinda's beautiful townhouse, Maria catching sight of a staggering staircase spiraling up to the floor above and a glass one leading down to an open-plan kitchen and garden. Penny skitters in behind them and Lucinda closes the door.

"Garden's through the kitchen," Lucinda tells her, passing to lead the way. "Just down the stairs here."

Maria follows. And at the top of the glass staircase, when Lucinda's back is turned and Penny is following on behind them both, Maria pushes the woman's body hard.

Lucinda only lets out a small yelp as she flies forward. It has in it a tight mixture of shock and anger, as if halfway through the act of falling she's realized what an idiotic mistake she's made—given who Lucinda is—inviting a complete stranger into her home.

Maria knows Lucinda could not have, in that second, realized who she is exactly, but Maria knows Lucinda understands she has made a fundamental error of judgment and in that split second she registers as much.

As Lucinda's body tumbles forward, she flails for the glass balustrades on either side of her, but her fingers only graze the immaculate glass, leaving the faintest of smears as she slams forward into the midpoint of the staircase and slumps unconscious against its clear surface.

Penny barks twice from the top of the stairs before carefully walking down to meet Maria and lick her hand.

Maria waits a few more seconds to check there is no further movement from Lucinda before gently picking up the dog and continuing down the stairs to delicately step over Lucinda's crumpled form, Penny in her arms.

At the bottom of the stairs Maria takes in the expensive open-plan living space that rolls out into a large well-tended garden. Then her eyes land on what she's looking for: beside a large cozy Everhot range cooker lies a comfy dog bed. Maria heads over and gently places the slightly concerned Penny into it. Then she moves the dog's water bowl close so that, after her walk, she will have what she needs close. Penny looks up at Maria with wide eyes, as if unable to work out if she is a threat or a savior.

Penny dealt with, Maria heads back to the huddled mass of Lucinda. She checks for a heartbeat, and there is of course a strong one. The fall was short; it was the impact to the side of her head that knocked her out. Maria does not intend to kill her. She needs Lucinda alive and able to talk.

She carefully unfurls her and, with arms under the fallen woman's shoulders, drags her as gently as she can down the remaining five steps into the kitchen. Maria then lays her out flat and performs a jaw-thrust maneuver on her to prevent her from choking on her own tongue—Maria doubts a spinal injury, but it's always better to be safe.

Maria estimates, from the severity of the blow, that she has a few minutes tops until the woman comes around, the loss of consciousness likely due not to serious trauma but to a mild concussion that will quickly pass.

Maria scans the room for her next requirement but can't see it. She heads quickly back up the glass staircase and into the main sitting room, a large double room, one half of which appears to be Lucinda's minimal home office. She sees the small tablet screen on a stand on a shelf behind the desk. On the tablet's screen four boxes display various rooms in the house. The CCTV hub. She scrolls through the rooms and external cameras, the gate outside still annoyingly hanging open. She checks the kitchen footage where she sees Lucinda and Penny, where she left them. She disables the system, the room cameras each in turn going black.

In the bottom corner of the screen a small red dot is flashing. Tapping on it, Maria sees that it's an alert of the external gate remaining open; Lucinda must have left it ajar expecting them to be in and out quickly. Maria cancels the alert then scrubs back through the footage from the past ten minutes and deletes all footage of herself. Job done, she wipes the tablet surface clean of her fingerprints and replaces it onto its stand.

BACK IN THE KITCHEN MARIA pulls cable ties from her coat pockets and proceeds to bind Lucinda's feet and hands.

The plan is simple: Lucinda will wake up and Maria will get her to say who's responsible for putting her in that house, who was watching, and why. There should be simple answers to these simple questions.

Maria will find out who did this to her and she will end whatever this has been. She isn't interested in revenge, though looking at the way these people live, renumeration after the fact wouldn't hurt her. But her primary aim is making herself safe again and, of course, not ending up in jail.

A groan rises from the body. Lucinda is beginning to come around. Safe in the knowledge she is no longer being filmed, Maria removes her cap and coat because in spite of her not overtly wanting revenge she does want to witness the moment when the other shoe drops for Lucinda. She wants Lucinda to know who she is and to be afraid, very afraid; as afraid as Maria was in the bowels of that house for six days.

Maria does not hear the men enter the house above her. She does not know that the alarm raised by the open gate has been picked up by the private security company. She does not hear them glide down the stairs behind her as she kneels beside Lucinda, whose eyes are beginning to flicker open. She knows nothing about it at all until Lucinda's gaze flits momentarily away from her own to something behind and slightly above her. And then Maria knows nothing at all.

LUCINDA PACES BACK AND FORTH in angry strides across her open-plan kitchen, hands unconsciously rubbing at the skin where the cable ties left divots in her flesh.

Penny is awake but sleepy in her bed, her eyes following her human back and forth.

"I just don't understand how it got this far? How she found me? Explain to me," she says, hands now pressing down on the air as she stops in front of a man a good deal broader and taller than her. "Explain to me how she got here, how she got through all the layers of security we are supposed to have and made it into my actual fucking house."

The man in front of her seems unfazed by the outburst. Behind him another man, a private doctor, pops medical items back into his bag, his face a mask of professional disinterest. "We'll go back through the sequence chain and plug the gaps. I think you're aware this is the first time a participant has made it off the island. Since the changeover, we have had four non-paying participants, and this has been the only incident. This is a special case. It will not happen again. They want you to continue."

Lucinda splutters out a laugh. "I bet they do. I bet they fucking do. But what assurance do I get? What incentive do I get—because apparently, I'm not even safe now in my own home. God knows what she could have done before you got here. I'm lucky I'm not in a wheelchair after that fall."

"She wanted you alive. She wanted information. She had medical training—trust me, she wasn't trying to kill you. And you know it's incredibly unlikely that anyone will ever get out again. You know that."

Lucinda slumps down hard into one of her kitchen chairs to consider his words.

He advances on her, and part of her retracts internally. She knows she's important to the job, but she is perhaps not that important if she proves too difficult. The rewards for her are huge but the losses as she knows could be substantial.

"Going forward," the broad man tells her, looming over her now, "wear this under everything." He hands her what looks like a medical alert bracelet.

She takes the bracelet in carefully, studying its screenless face.

"It's an ECG, it tracks your heart rate. If you're doing exercise press the side button. If not then we'll come," he tells her with a tight smile.

"But it won't happen again?" she asks.

"It won't, no." There is a finality to his words. The discussion is over.

"And they want me to source another one?" she asks after slipping the band onto her wrist.

"They've sent you three new options. We need a choice by the end of the month. The house needs to be prepared; they want to start implementing the relevant information into the rooms."

"Tell them I will do it, but this will be my last. We discussed an exit strategy after the third, and now I would like to action that."

Behind the man the doctor stands to leave. The two other men who were present earlier have already gone.

"I will pass that on. If it's something you have discussed then I'm sure there will be a resolution soon."

"Okay, thank you," Lucinda answers, her gaze falling now on Maria's abandoned hat and coat, draped across her kitchen table. "And what will you do with her body?" she asks vaguely, certain she won't get a satisfactory answer. And she does not.

"Let me do my job and I'll facilitate you doing your job," he tells her, not without warmth, before picking up the coat and hat and disappearing up Lucinda's staircase. The sound of the front door shutting above her an almost physical release.

She squeezes her eyes shut in the silence that follows and tries to reset. She has reset after much worse.

Penny lets out a muted yowl from her bed. She is hungry. Lucinda rises and goes through the motions of filling Penny's bowl and settling her. Her own thoughts are on what must be done next.

LATER THAT NIGHT, LUCINDA SWITCHES on her desktop computer, pulls in her seat, and makes her way through the layers of security on the encrypted platform before finally opening a folder with three labeled files: PERSON P, PERSON Q, PERSON R. The next intake.

Person R's label has an asterisk next to it.

CHAPTER 33
LUCINDA

Lucinda settles into her seat and takes a fortifying sip of coffee before opening the first file.

Person P: Kidney disease, transplant incompatible, degenerative. Palliative care.

Current estimated life expectancy: -3 months.

Person P has clearly exceeded the expectations of their doctors and lived three months more than predicted. Lucinda reads on, and it's clear from a quick glance at their medical information that the condition is now, finally, deteriorating rapidly.

She is used to this. She has seen a lot of these files.

All the non-consensual participants, like Maria and the ones before her, were chosen this way. Each person chosen for the house was the sole remaining next of kin of a terminally ill relative.

This was how they found them, their participants: they were people specifically selected as least likely to be missed within a certain demographic.

Lucinda is sent the data, and she researches the solitary next of kins to find the perfect fit. The potential participants would not be Persons P, Q, or R. They would be their remaining next of kin.

Lucinda knows what she's looking for, what the remit is, and she reports back her findings on her chosen candidates with suggestions on how to package them as participants and suggestions on room and game content.

What she is looking for is simple: candidates must have no remaining family after their bereavement. They have to be unconnected, they have to be able to slip between the cracks.

She is sent patient information and then she further researches the remaining relative, the potential candidate.

From this research Lucinda cherry-picks the cream of the crop. Women are more popular, and those between the ages of twenty-five and thirty-five are the preference. Once a male guest was tried, but the results had generally been considered unsatisfactory, with only one room having been completed. Testosterone it seems is a hindrance in this particular set of circumstances.

Lucinda scrolls down to Person P's next-of-kin information. And there she is: female, twenty-six, a management consultancy senior partner from Connecticut. The job doesn't seem an immediate draw for potential clients, but Lucinda latches onto the fact that this young woman has already reached senior partner at twenty-six. Such a level of ambition and application will definitely garner interest with clients.

Lucinda tries not to think of the woman who made it all the way to her kitchen earlier that day. Of how she survived so much. Of all that intelligence and application and the extraordinary mind-boggling waste of it all.

Instead she scrolls down to the photo attached to the twenty-six-year-old senior partner's file. She stops abruptly as the young woman's image fills the screen. She tries to take her in objectively, as she always does.

Her name is Claire. She is pretty, with the first flush of youth on her, and an enviable cascade of glossy red hair teamed with that shrewd unflappable look of confidence that Lucinda has come to search for in candidates' eyes.

Claire looks like she has a lot of fight in her—and that seems to be, from Lucinda's limited experience, exactly what the clients are after.

Lucinda opens her medical records. Fit, healthy, low BMI, strong heart and lungs. She will certainly be physically capable of at least two rooms—though it's always impossible to judge how far participants can be stretched mentally. But then she understands that this is the draw of the enterprise. The thrill of the unknown. How much fight there is in the dog, so to speak.

Yes, Claire looks like she has fight.

Lucinda marks a double star against Person P's file and moves on.

Person Q: Car accident. Non-responsive. Life support.

Current estimated life expectancy: No prospect of recovery, advised terminating life support.

Lucinda scrolls to the next of kin. An older woman, at least by their limited standards, at thirty-five. Her medical records read well. She too leads an active life as a marine biologist in New Zealand. Her name is Krista, single, travels regularly for work, no financial, or familial, ties except her now incapacitated father.

Krista's job has the edge over Claire's, her backstory carrying more cachet, more packaging options; her rooms could offer more visually and psychologically rewarding options. Though her age might put the clients off.

It has occurred to Lucinda before now how similar this world and the commodified world of app dating are. The built-in misogyny and stratification of it. In a sense, she sees herself as the matchmaker from hell.

Lucinda scrolls down to Krista's picture and quickly triple-stars her. Beating out Claire easily.

Krista has clear visually bankable qualities.

Person R*: Late-stage lymphatic cancer. Hospice recommended.

Current estimated life expectancy: + 2–3 weeks. Rapid deterioration.

Lucinda had already noted the asterisk. She skips ahead; Krista will take a lot to beat.

Thirty-four, single, Cambridge University English literature professor, Cambridge, United Kingdom. The daughter of John Stanley Hepworth, the British public intellectual, polymath and she is an author in her own right of several well-respected academic texts.

Lucinda feels her mouth fall open. She recognizes that name. She knows who he is, what the connection is to the house, to all of this . . .

She swallows hard. His daughter, in his house?

She scrolls back up the file, the asterisk staring back at her. It's not a mistake; it's a preference. An order from the top, and she knows who the top is.

She licks her lips. It's unexpected for sure, but Lucinda feels the same frisson of having found something incredibly rare as when she had first learned of Maria's backstory in the Darién Gap.

This woman, Nina Hepworth, is at the older end of the scale, but her pedigree is impeccable, the premium undeniable. Clients will want her, she knows the market well enough to know that. They will find viewers for that package without a doubt and at a high premium.

Her name is Nina Hepworth and she gets the full four stars.

CHAPTER 34
JOON-GI

Strange things have been happening for some time at the house up on the cliff, Joon-gi knows that much. And when the new woman arrived, he knew for certain that they had not told him everything; he would have called the police but he has already tried that, so he left her the notes and waited to see what happened next.

A LOT HAS HAPPENED TO him since he was knocked out on the property three months ago.

When he woke up after cutting the power to the basement of the house, he found they had moved him to the gatehouse.

He stirred on the seat he was slumped in, slowly becoming aware that he was not alone. The atmosphere was strange, as the black-clad security guard offered him a plastic cup of water and watched him drink it thirstily. Then without a word the guard rose and slipped from the gatehouse, Joon-gi assumed, to inform someone else he was awake.

Joon-gi shifted in his seat, wondering if he should run, but he noted a camera mounted high in the corner of the gatehouse office and trained on him as he clutched his now empty, crumpled cup. There was little point in running.

He touched the back of his head gingerly. It hurt a lot; his fingers came away wet with red. His head throbbed and he felt strangely unreal. All of this did, because his life wasn't like this; things like this didn't happen to him.

He wondered if he should feel scared, because he oddly did not. They had knocked him out, yes, but they clearly meant him no immediate harm. And if he thought about it, weren't they well within their rights to have incapacitated him up on the property? Reality seemed to flood in around him. The truth was he had broken into private property and disabled a private security system. Joon-gi's slow seep of dread spread further through him; he was in a lot of trouble.

God knew what was going on up at the house, with that woman, but down here, in the cold light of day, it was none of his business and he had plain and simple broken the law.

He looked at the clock high on the wall behind him: he had been unconscious for over an hour. He wondered if the woman in the house was okay.

At that moment the uniformed security guard returned with another security guard. This one was in plainclothes, with the demeanor and authority of an overseeing officer. The uniformed guard took a seat behind Joon-gi. The other man remained standing and took in Joon-gi, then exhaled audibly through his nose.

Joon-gi opened his mouth to speak, but the broad-shouldered man lifted a hand to silence him.

"Save it. The police are on their way."

Joon-gi wondered if perhaps that was a good thing; he could explain to the police about the woman, the basement, his concerns for her safety. But as he ran through the scene in his head it began to sound more and more crazy even to him. Because he had no evidence of any of this. He had trespassed on private property and tampered with their security system, just because of a feeling, a gut instinct. He had broken the law on a hunch, like some kind of crazy vigilante.

The man in front of him seemed to sense the direction of Joon-gi's thoughts too. Perhaps Joon-gi was easy to read. Another worry to add to the rapidly increasing pile along with the police and his aching head. Miami and the idea of his beautiful apartment seemed to slip further away moment by moment.

"Here's what we're going to do," the man said. "Before they get here, we're going to have a quick chat because I think we both know you're in quite a bit of trouble. And while I'm sure you've got a great explanation for whatever the hell you were doing up there, I don't want to hear it. Okay?"

Joon-gi considered this then nodded. "Okay."

"Good. So here's how I see it. You were hired to fix an electrical issue. You signed an NDA before you entered the building. You met a female member of staff inside the property and then you decided to return a few days later and break into the property? Would that be an accurate description of what occurred?"

Joon-gi considered the form they had made him sign the first time he entered the gatehouse to collect his lanyard. That form meant he would not be able to tell the police what was in the house without being sued—the man was reminding him of this without saying it.

Joon-gi had a vague understanding of these contracts from other handymen on the islands; he knew that breaking NDAs meant incurring huge financial penalties. And it never would have occurred to him to do so until now. The only way you could legally break an NDA was if it stopped you from reporting a crime.

But what was the crime here?

Was that woman being held hostage? He had no evidence of that.

If he asked the police to go in the house and check, he would have to *disclose* why he thought what he thought and tell them about the locked basement, the rooms he knew were down there. And if the woman wasn't there, or if she was and it was all fine and he had imagined the whole thing, then they would sue him. He would lose everything, his savings, everything he had worked and sweat and bled so hard to accumulate.

His future gone in the blink of an eye.

Joon-gi licked his dry lips and answered.

"Yes, I think I made a mistake," he said carefully. The man in front of him seemed pleased about the direction this was going.

"I was concerned about—an electrical issue," Joon-gi continued, the words coming from some deep self-preserving well in his brain. "But I see now everything is fine. That's my problem, I think," he added, trying a careful smile now. "I am a very loyal employee and sometimes I can overfocus on a job well done. But what I did was not appropriate. I see that now."

Joon-gi looked at the man and the man held his gaze, looking for a crack in Joon-gi's poker face. He could not find one and seemed satisfied.

"I'm pleased to hear that, Joon-gi. I know the owners of the property were pleased with the work you carried out so I think on this occasion, given our understanding, we will not be pressing charges when the police arrive. A warning should be satisfactory, don't you think?"

Joon-gi nodded, but he could not help the panic rising inside him at the realization that a police caution would seriously impact his ability to gain more employment on the islands if word got out.

Again, the man in front of him seemed to read his thoughts.

"And as an article of faith we'd like to hold you on retainer. You can work for us, solely, going forward. We would of course pay you above your current freelance take-home. You would just need to be available as and when required. How would that sound?"

Joon-gi swallowed hard. "How long would the contract be?"

The man smiled. "How long would you like it to be, Joon-gi?"

THEY HAD EXPLAINED IT TO him over the next few weeks as they slowly gave him more and more access to service the house and the immaculate white rooms beneath it.

It was an experience. A sequence of rooms, escape rooms if you will, for the immensely rich.

Joon-gi himself had tried an escape room with an old college friend back in Miami. It had been fun, but it had been nothing like the rooms under that house. And at no point in Miami had Joon-gi ever felt his life hung in the balance. Why anyone would want to experience real fear was beyond Joon-gi, but then didn't the rich thrive on the edge of things—they were like sharks, if they stopped swimming they would die. They all did it in some way, flying planes, chartering submarines, hot-air balloons, rockets even, all to prove they were still alive. It made sense, just not to him.

But it appeared, if you had enough money and were bored of life you could buy this experience. The ultimate Ironman-style physical and psychological test.

It was dangerous, they explained to Joon-gi, but nothing in there could kill anyone. All the rooms were monitored, everything would cut off before a client was in serious danger. It gave only a very realistic sense of what it might be like to almost die and then not.

Joon-gi did his job. He tried not to ask questions. The pay was good and everything was going well until the new woman arrived.

She did not look rich, not in the way the rich out here looked. She looked classy, sure, well off maybe, but not *rich-rich*, not generationally wealthy. More important, she did not look like the kind of person who would pay for an experience like this.

Joon-gi tried to tell himself that she was playing along with the role. They had told him each client's experience was tailored specifically to their own requirements.

He had been required to change the sign on the house from CLIFF HILL to ANDERSSEN'S OPENING. He'd googled the name and learned that it was some obscure chess term, so he guessed the woman must love chess. But something about the way she was in the fleeting glimpses he'd seen of her gave him a strange feeling. The same feeling Maria had given him.

And that feeling has grown in strength until he cannot shift the idea that while this house might once have been an experience for rich, paying customers, it seems to be something else entirely now. The new woman did not seem to know she is taking part in an experience, but then what did he know about the kind of people who would do this kind of thing? Perhaps she is just incredibly invested in playing along with her own story, something about a dead father. Perhaps it's helping her in some way?

Joon-gi does not know. So he does what he's told, placing the handwritten signs where they tell him to, quietly doing his job. After all, he nearly has enough for that apartment. One more year of this and he will have enough.

It is so nearly over.

CHAPTER 35
NINA

The second room comes into view as Nina rounds the vestibule corner and when it does, she stops dead in her tracks, what she sees chilling her to the bone.

The room is large and white with a raised platform at its center. On that platform a six-foot-long glass box is laid out. A coffin.

Burial of the Dead.

She was right: the rooms will map the parts of her father and mother's favorite poem.

Why he did this, why anyone would do this she does not know, unless her father is still trying to tell her something. Though the thought of that seems to slip from her now that she attempts to grasp on to it, because why would he choose to tell her anything in this way? He was not like this, he was a good man, wasn't he?

Before her, in the center of the room, lies the immaculate glass coffin, its proportions slightly exaggerated. It's slightly wider and longer, its depth deeper, than the standard pine, mahogany, and oak coffins she was so recently shown back in England after her father's death.

Unlike any actual coffin she has seen this one is beautiful, incredibly beautiful, a sculpture almost; beautiful and terrifying.

It glints in the room's soft lighting, refracting twinkling beams across the ceiling as she approaches it.

There is something inside it.

At the head of it is a plate, and on the plate an apple, a slice of bread, and a hunk of hard cheese. Food. Beside it deep in the glass coffin sits a chilled metal tumbler of milk, beads of condensation clinging to its sides.

Nina looks around the space, one wall of the room a mirror; beyond it she is certain there will be more cameras. Or—she thinks with a shudder—actual people, because someone prepared this food. Someone is actually here watching this happen, right now, and not helping her.

Her stomach growls loudly but she ignores it and walks over to the mirrored wall, her own wild features reflecting back to her. When she reaches it she places both hands against its cool glass and tries to peer in, but of course the two-way glass does not permit that and all she sees are her own eyelashes and breath fogging the glass.

She pulls back. "I know you're in there. You made the food," she tells her reflection. "I don't know how you knew my father but he wouldn't have wanted this, I know that much. If he told you to do this then you have to tell me because I don't believe he was like this, that he would do this to me. Did he do it to other people? Did he?"

Nina looks at the silent glass, a wellspring of sadness bubbling up inside her. He is gone and she is here and perhaps this is what he wanted; perhaps she never meant anything to him?

Silent tears spill down her face. She watches them but no one speaks, no answers come. She sucks up the emotion and clears her throat.

"Okay, you want me to experience these rooms, okay. And what then? What if I get through every one of them? What then? You just let me go? Why should I carry on? Tell me that."

Nina jumps as Bathsheba's voice interjects loudly behind her.

"Please collect your rations from the plinth. You have sixty seconds."

Nina turns to the plinth, the coffin, and the food within. The food is right there, and unless someone comes in to take it away it will still be there after sixty seconds.

"Or what?" Nina retorts. "What, you come and get it? Good, I want to see your face. I want to see who you are."

Nina stops abruptly, a thought occurring with crystal clarity for the first time, an idea of who could be doing this to her. The inscribed book upstairs, the rooms themed after sections of that poem, the fact her father never married again or even considered meeting another woman, and this house out here.

Nina looks back at the glass, a cold terrifying calm settling into her.

"Mum?" she says to the glass. The glass remains silent.

Bathsheba speaks again behind her: "Thirty seconds remaining."

Nina turns to see that the glass coffin is now beginning to sink down into the plinth, the food with it.

Without a second thought she runs to it, leaping up onto the platform and jumping down into the retracting coffin. She quickly grabs as much of the food as she can and turns to jump out but to her absolute horror she can no longer reach up to the top lip of the coffin, it has sunk too low; she is trapped. She drops the food and tries to jump for the lip of the coffin above her but cannot reach. The coffin stops moving. She tries to wedge herself against the walls and shimmy up but the glass is too slippery against her wet clothes.

"Four minutes until game commencement. Please consume the rations provided," Bathsheba echoes above her.

AFTER NINA HAS RAILED AT the coffin walls, yelled and flailed in protest, after her energy finally flags, she sits down exhausted on the coffin floor and begins to eat her food.

WHEN THE FOUR MINUTES ARE up Bathsheba speaks again. "Please lie flat and prepare for the game commencement."

Nina swallows the chunk of cheese in her mouth hard and downs the last of her milk as she looks up at the coffin sides above her. She has no intention of lying down.

But as she watches, high above her a glass lid slowly begins to emerge from the lip of the platform and seal the coffin. Nina leaps to her feet ready for whatever might suddenly happen, visions of the coffin filling overtaking her thoughts.

But that does not happen. Instead the coffin floor begins to rise to meet the lid as it fully seals above her.

Through the sealed glass she hears a muffled Bathsheba: "Please lie flat and prepare for the game commencement."

The coffin ceiling is fast approaching. Nina is forced to kneel, then sit and quickly swivel down to lie flat, narrowly avoiding making contact with the thick glass above her.

Now lying flat in the coffin, Nina sees that she has risen back up onto the platform. A screen is visible on the floor to her side.

Welcome, Nina, to The Burial of the Dead.
Your task is simple: lower your heartrate to 70

beats per minute, or lower, for more than 10 seconds.

Nina blinks at the screen and rereads the task.

They can't be serious. This is easy, surely. She knows from her last health checkup that she has a resting heartbeat of sixty-two beats per minute. Seventy bpm would be a breeze. The situation is stressful, obviously, but she feels pretty calm.

Suddenly a pulsing number fills the screen and Nina's eyes flare. Her heart rate is 105 bpm. The shock of seeing it immediately sends it up further, to 109. Nina lets out a long, slow exhale, the glass above her fogging. It occurs to her that she is locked in a sealed glass box and her oxygen will eventually run out. The screen pulses up to 111 bpm.

Nina tries to forget what she has just realized. She lets her eyes blink shut and tries to loosen her muscles and sink into the coffin floor. She lies in the silent box and breathes.

After ten breaths she looks back at the screen. Seventy-one bpm. A warm smile blossoms across her face. She is doing it, she can do it, and with that realization the number drops again to sixty-nine.

Beneath it a countdown suddenly begins: *10, 9, 8, 7—*

Nina feels a tickling sensation down by her ankles and lifts her head incrementally to look. Sand is pouring into the glass coffin at various points: by her ankles, thighs, and elbows, and behind her head.

When she looks back at the screen the countdown has disappeared, her pulse now at eighty-two bpm.

Nina grimaces hard. She will have to ignore the sand, the limited oxygen supply, the enclosed space, and the fact that she will soon be buried alive if she cannot calm the fuck down. All she has to do is calm the fuck down.

Nina tries the breathing again but it only gets her so far,

hovering around seventy-four bpm. That's not good enough. She needs to calm mentally as well as physically.

The sand now hugging to the underside of her limbs and body is warm. She wonders if it came from outside, if it's from the beach, so close and yet so incredibly far from here.

She thinks of her feet sinking into that soft fine sand, the feel of it between her toes, the warm seep of sun on her skin. Through the coffin glass she sees her pulse drop to seventy-one. This is the answer.

She pushes away thoughts of the rising sand and fogging glass above her face and closes her eyes. The only way to win this is to forget she's even playing.

She imagines herself back there on the beach, her feet in the sand, the warm sun on her limbs, and a light sea breeze cooling her face. And suddenly she isn't on Gorda anymore, she's somewhere else in her mind—she is in Devon, England.

She's on the wide-open expanse of a quiet beach on the Devonshire coast. She's maybe eleven or twelve, she's sitting on the wet sand of the waterline in her bathing suit, a book in her hands as she reads and the waves crash over her feet, popping and hissing all the way to her thighs.

She looks up from the book back to the beach behind her. Under a beach umbrella two people sit. A man and a woman. The man is reading a large newspaper, the woman attempting a crossword, glasses on, pen in mouth. Her father and Maeve. A rare beach trip in her youth. She forgot they did this; she has forgotten this day.

He looks up then, her father looks up at her from his deck chair, from the past, and he smiles at her. He is a good man. She knows it in her heart, she knows it like she knows herself.

Nina's eyes jolt open as a loud bleeping sound abruptly snaps her back to reality. Time is up. Panic overtakes her as she becomes aware that the sand now covers her face and mouth, only her nose remaining free. And then even that is covered. Nina holds her breath. She tries to lift her face but the weight of the sand and the continuing flow of it makes it impossible. The panic crescendos inside her as the bleeping continues. She manages to stay calm long enough to free a hand and wriggle it through the weight of sand up to the coffin lid above. But to her horror she finds that there is no air left; the glass box is now entirely filled. The bleeping continues muffled now as she tries to remain calm, as she tries to think, but the truth is there is no way out. The warm sand embraces her and a strange instinct overcomes her, one she could never have anticipated. She lets herself drift back to that beach in Devon, the warmth of the full coffin becoming once more the warmth of the sun, and just like that, with a sudden shudder, the coffin floor shifts and the sand pours out through newly opened holes, cool air pouring in.

Nina gasps in a chest-aching breath, her eyes bursting open. She turns her head to take in the bleeping screen beside her. It's frozen on a heart rate of sixty-eight beats per minute, the time counter beneath it reading zero.

A surge of triumph forces its way through Nina unbidden as she coughs and splutters sand from her mouth and nose. She's done it. The sand continues to pour out from beneath her but she has done it.

The screen resets.

Congratulations, Nina!
You have completed The Burial of the Dead. Please proceed to the vestibule.

Above her the glass coffin lid begins to slide back and Nina rises from its confines gratefully. Up on the platform she stretches her cramped muscles, puts her head in her hands, and gives herself a moment to recalibrate.

She thinks, once more, of the beach in Devon. A memory buried so deep in her she cannot recall ever having stumbled on it before.

Her father was a good man, she knows that. And her mother is not alive. He would have found her, been with her if she had been. He missed her and they had been in love.

And for the first time it occurs to Nina that all of this, from the letter, from the very beginning, might have been a trick. That her father did not have a house in the Caribbean, that James does not work for a solicitor's firm, that there is no probate and the forms and documents she had been shown were just props. That the knickknacks upstairs, the few personal objects she found of her father's, were props stolen to get her down here. Props to make her play a game she would not otherwise have started. A game that has nothing to do with her or her family and everything to do with the fact that now she has no one back at home to miss her.

"Please proceed to the vestibule door," Bathsheba intones.

Nina looks at the new open doorway and the corridor beyond. At least now she has an idea of what might actually be going on here, she figures. And they're wrong, of course, because Joe knows she's here, and Oksana.

And perhaps Oksana is a lost cause, but Joe will come, Joe will come soon, if he isn't already here.

CHAPTER 36
LUCINDA

Lucinda watches Nina through the glass of the mirror.

She thinks of the day she went to visit Nina's father.

He had known, she was certain of it. He must have. He was brilliant. And yet . . .

Lucinda recalls it now. How she sat in her town car on John Hepworth's street in Highgate and watched Nina breezily leave the house, a tote bag of books and papers over her shoulder. She'd watched her slip into her own beat-up Ford Fiesta and drive off. Back to the university where she was scheduled to lecture twice that afternoon.

Lucinda had all the information at her fingertips.

In her hand she carried a copy of John Hepworth's lesser-known and only work of fiction, *Vauxhall Bridge in the Rain*, a postwar Graham Greene–style doomed-romance novella. A work his publisher had clearly felt obligated to print given his otherwise brilliant nonfiction output.

It wasn't that it was bad, Lucinda reasoned—having read

all 156 pages of it that morning after the courier had dropped it off—it was that it was too studied. There was no heart in it, as if the author had been too shy of showing any.

Lucinda grasped the book tight, told the driver to give her an hour, perhaps two, and slipped from the car, her well-chosen floral dress clinging to her, a cardigan covering her still-cable-tie-damaged wrists, makeup over her bruised temple.

Lucinda looked soft and kind as she headed toward the front door of John Stanley Hepworth, she looked friendly and easy to talk to and not dissimilar to his long-dead wife. Lucinda was good at this, which was why they paid her so incredibly well.

She knocked on the glossy red front door, catching sight of her medical alert band and hastily covering it. It was good to feel safe after what had happened, though Lucinda knew why she had really been chosen for her job—why she was the finder, why they actually paid her so much: because she had no one either. If she failed, there would be no loose ends. And she too was a very impressive young woman—she could very easily end up in that house.

Lucinda pushed the thought away as the door briskly opened in front of her and a spritely, kind-eyed old man gave her a surprised smile.

"Ah, I thought you might be my daughter—forgetting something. But clearly not," he said, taking her in, his surprise morphing into a mild confusion. "Now, do I know you? Are you a student? Have I done something awful that demands reprisal?" He chuckled.

His laugh caught her off guard. "No, God no," she said, smiling, a feeling like dread seeping into her bones at how personable this man was—at how lovely his daughter must be—but she pushed the thought away.

"No, sorry. My name is Lucinda and I heard that you lived

on this street and I'm being incredibly cheeky but I was wondering if you could sign my book? I'm a big fan. I would love it if you could."

John's eyebrows rose. He was an intelligent man, Lucinda knew that, that was sort of the point in all this, and he wasn't buying this for a second. And yet he considered the outstretched book for a moment before fully pulling open the door.

"Well now, I was about to make a fresh pot of tea. How does that sound to you, Lucinda? Do you have time to come in for tea?"

Lucinda felt a smile spread across her face. She knew who he was. He had designed the house. The original rooms. And she had reconfigured them. They were a good match—his ailing health only just allowing her to even enter the same arena.

She could tell he didn't buy it for a second but he was interested. And that was enough to get her in the house—which was more than she had bargained for.

The keys jangled in the front door as he closed it behind her and gestured for her to head into the kitchen.

It was warm and cozy and had the feel of a Cotswold cottage but in the heart of London. Books covered most surfaces. A battered armchair sat beside the Aga, and the scent of hot buttered toast seemed to pervade the house.

"Toasted crumpet? Biscuits?" he asked, gesturing for her to take a seat.

"Biscuits would be lovely," she answered as she perched on a straight-backed kitchen chair and watched him make the tea.

As the kettle simmered and popped, she asked, "So the daughter you mentioned. What does she do? Is she an academic too?"

John swiveled to take Lucinda in, still trying to make sense of the odd proposition that she was: a young woman not quite telling the truth in his kitchen. But he was willing to find out the old-fashioned way.

"She is, but far more competent than I. You see, that's the problem with trying a bit of everything—you never get the whole way through anything. She gets to the bottom of things, though. The dregs." As the kettle roared to boiling John asked Lucinda what she did. She found, had always found, that sticking as close to the truth as possible was the safest option.

"I'm a headhunter. For private investment clients," she told him.

He nodded, and several cogs clicked into place in his mind.

"And how are the super-rich these days?" he asked with a sly smile.

"As strange and hard to please as ever, I imagine," she answered.

"Yes, as it ever was. Well, rather you than me, I know that much."

He must have known who bought the house from the man he'd originally designed it for. He must have wondered.

Teapot steaming on a tray, biscuits arranged higgledy-piggledy on a bone china plate, John beckoned her to follow him into the sitting room.

They sat opposite each other, morning light filtering through soft linen curtains into the high-ceilinged Victorian sitting room, and they talked.

She asked him questions about his books, his life, and he answered. He told her about his youth, his lost wife, his daughter, his fears and hopes.

He must not have known what the house had become. He must not have realized.

She sailed as close to the wind of truth as she could get away with, because she knew he would sense a lie if it was offered.

He suggested another pot and she accepted. He rose to fetch it and told her to stay, to take a look at his books, to make herself at home. He turned to leave and then turned back to Lucinda.

"I suppose you're wondering why I'm telling you all this?" he said pointedly, then just as suddenly slipped into a world of his own thoughts. "You see, I've recently had a bit of bad news. Now, you're not far off my daughter's age, and I think I'd like your advice. She's a bit of a lone wolf as they say, an introvert; always has been. But we'll get to that. If you've got time for a few more biscuits?"

Lucinda shifted in her seat. John Stanley Hepworth might have worked out why she was here. She would do best not to drink any more tea.

"I can be bought with biscuits," she answered with a smile.

"Oh, I doubt that very much. I'm guessing these private investment clients don't pay you in biscuits, now, do they, Lucinda."

And with that he slipped from the room.

Lucinda stood and headed for his desk. She slipped the small desk clock, and a Montblanc pen, into her handbag. As the kettle flared up again in the kitchen, she gently tugged his central desk drawer open and slid out a thin copy of *The Waste Land* from its dark interior along with a small Moleskine journal.

The sound of a biscuit tin popping open in the kitchen sent Lucinda onward toward the bookshelves, where a dog-eared copy of the Alexandre Dumas classic *The Count of Monte Cristo* made it into her bag also alongside a small sterling-silver pig figurine.

Since the house had been repurposed clients no longer paid to experience the house themselves; they paid to watch others experience it. She had become very good at curating backstories to package participants for clients. Nina and her father were a fantastic backstory, on a par with Maria and her formative experiences at the Darién Gap. She would reconfigure the rooms to reflect their father–daughter story.

The rattle of a tray being carried back to her led Lucinda back to her seat, where she set down her laden bag with care.

She had enough already, though if she got his signature for use on documents she would have more than enough to tie this one up. But as he settled back in, more stories flowed. Stories about Nina and their shared past.

It was only as she was leaving that he let the veil slip. As he shook her hand in farewell, he palmed her the number. In case there was a recording, in case there was a camera.

She felt the sharp rasp of paper against her fingers as he held her eye. She understood. He knew who she was. And he was trying to tell her something.

"Take care, Lucinda," he told her, his hand still shaking hers. "If you ever run into my daughter, keep an eye out for her, would you. You seem like a nice girl." He released her with a warm smile and then chuckled lightheartedly. "You've just fallen in with the wrong crowd, I think. But money makes fools of us all. Who am I to judge."

As the door closed on her the wave of guilt threatened to overwhelm her and everything there had ever been.

She thought of Penny back home, of her soft shiny coat and her bouncy greetings and simple energy, and felt another wave of sadness.

But this was her last candidate. After this one she could stop. They had promised.

Back in the car she slowly unballed her fist. On the crumpled paper, a phone number. An escape route.

———

THE POWERS THAT BE HAD not been as good as their word. They did not create an exit strategy. They simply changed Lucinda's role and dragged her in further. Her responsibilities more profound. And the phone number Nina's father had given her became more and more enticing.

The house is fully automated now, so it requires only maintenance and one project manager on-site. Plus the single gatehouse guard who helped earlier with the local who'd arrived unexpectedly. Three of them in total, Lucinda, Joon-gi, and a carousel of nameless guards.

It's just her and the electrician up at the house when a package is in progress. It limits accountability and any room for human error.

The grounds are covered with more cameras than ever before, and she is under no illusions that they will come if they have to. The guard at the gatehouse will come, and more.

She looks down at the medical alert band on her thin wrist and knows they're watching. But the thing itself, the house, the experience, is now a closed system. She runs it on-site, the old man maintains its hardware.

She knows he's unaware of what exactly they're doing down there, that perhaps a part of him knows something is not quite right but that he needs or rather wants something else more than he cares about the truth. And she helps him with that. She helps keep up the lie.

The new system is working. They tightened everything up since the escape three months ago. It's impossible to exit the locked-down house now without clearance. Nina and whoever comes after will not get as far as Maria had.

Lucinda turns up the volume on her sound system so she can hear Nina's words through the glass; Nina is talking to her, or to the client, in a way, Lucinda supposes. Lucinda has no idea who the clients are, who any of them have been. They auctioned off each package to a few clients only, who then had access to the interactive viewing experience via encrypted servers.

Nina's package was subject to the usual bidding war, though her final fee had interestingly been slightly lower than Maria's; age and backstory, as always, affected that outcome.

"I know you're in there," she hears Nina say. "You made the food."

So she's talking to Lucinda after all. Lucinda preferred not to hear up until now but the way Nina is looking at her through the glass makes it impossible for her not to be at least a little curious.

Nina continues, "I don't know how you knew my father but he wouldn't have wanted this, I know that much. If he told you to do this then you have to tell me because I don't believe he was like this, that he would do this to me. Did he do it to other people? Did he?"

Lucinda thinks of Nina's wonderful father, then of her own parents, vague, disinterested shadows from her past; they visited less and less until she did not really have people anymore.

Nina's father was a truly loving and lovely man, though. He had cared for Nina so very much, and not once had Lucinda felt envy at that idea; only relief that such people existed. And yet, even so, she had done all this. She had continued to do her job. She had brought Nina here to the house.

Lucinda's guilt coils around her insides tightly.

Nina seems to look directly at her through the silent glass, and a wellspring of sadness bubbles up inside her. Lucinda's tears match Nina's.

After a moment between them, one that only Lucinda is aware of, Nina sucks up her emotion and clears her throat.

"Okay, you want me to experience these rooms, okay. And what then? What if I get through every single one of them? What then? You just let me go?"

Lucinda considers the answer to that but she does not like

the direction it takes her in. The protocol for house completion is not good. But no one has ever made it past the fifth room.

Lucinda simultaneously hopes Nina does and does not, kicking hope as far down the road as she dares.

Lucinda watches Nina get into the coffin, her attention drawn away suddenly by the sight of an intercom light flashing beside her.

The guard at the gatehouse. The man they took down there to recover must have woken up.

CHAPTER 37
JOE

Joe is coming around and he feels awful.

He's propped up in some kind of office chair and when he finally focuses, he sees that he's in the gatehouse that was locked when he arrived earlier and vaulted the gate. He checks his watch, frowns, then checks it again. He's lost over four hours.

A sound behind him makes him quickly swivel in his seat, to take in the black-uniformed security guard filling him a plastic cup full of water from the chilled watercooler.

Joe flinches as the man, substantially bigger than him and armed, approaches. The man gives him a tight smile and hands him the plastic cup.

Joe takes it carefully and nods thanks before greedily gulping it down. His head is hot and buzzing. Joe's eyes fall on the defense baton attached to the man's utility belt and makes a fair assumption that this is the cause of his throbbing skull.

Joe tries to talk but his voice catches. He clears it and tries again. "Any particular reason you thought it was necessary to knock me out?" he asks the guard.

The guard gives him a hard look and gestures for Joe to hand him the cup for a refill. Joe obliges.

"I've called down my boss," the guard tells him. "She'll be here soon. You can talk to her."

Joe frowns, then makes to rise. "The woman from before? I don't think I'll be hanging around for that. I think maybe I'll just give the cops a call and see what the hell they make of the random woman I met up at the house. She's not the owner. I know that much," Joe says, up now and heading to the door.

The security guard blocks his way, handing him his refilled water. "I'd sit down if I were you."

Joe gives a shaky laugh. "Oh, okay, I hadn't realized it was legal for private security firms to hold civilians against their will."

"Sit down, friend," the security guard tells him with a kind of warmth; the threat of Joe is clearly not a genuine concern to him. "I'm holding you here until the cops arrive. You were trespassing on private property talking about a person no one here has ever heard of. I'm not letting you go until I know someone's aware of you."

Joe's frown deepens. "What the hell are you talking about. Nina told me to come here. Nina lives here, her father died, she inherited the house. She asked me to come up here because she was getting weird notes and she was scared something was going to happen to her—"

Joe breaks off as the woman from earlier appears at the gatehouse window. He watches her type a code into the door and enter.

"Okay, try to relax and take a seat for me, okay?" the security guard asks Joe calmly, gesturing back to the seat. "Let's not do anything we'll regret here, okay?"

Joe considers the guard's words and the fact that police will be arriving soon and that he does in fact have priors on his record for minor trespassing offenses. This more than anything gets him.

"Fuck. Okay, okay, I'm sitting."

Lucinda gives the security guard a look, a nod, and then a "No, no. Please carry on," before she perches on the edge of a desk behind him and watches.

"Tell us about this woman," the guard says encouragingly, drawing Joe out.

Joe takes a deep breath and tells them everything.

Once Joe has finished the security guard blows out a hard breath and looks at the woman behind him. She nods him on and after a beat he says: "Okay, well, sir, it seems unlikely that you met Nina Hepworth today or that she called you from the house as Ms. Hepworth is an elderly woman in her eighties who lives in London and rents out this property to my boss here, whom you were just accosting up at the house. As you've just told us there appear to have been some previous mix-ups in your office over various Nina Hepworths already, is it possible that you have been the victim of a scam perhaps, sir?"

Joe stares at the man. "No."

"Really, you're sure of that? You're sure nothing was taken from your office today?"

Joe racks his brains. "She only took copies of the plans."

The guard shares a look with the woman, who remains impassive though Joe notices her fiddle nervously with the black band around her wrist.

"You say you let the woman today take copies? And the real Nina Hepworth had you sign an NDA to prevent you doing just that? Did you get a copy of this woman's ID at least?"

Joe tries to recall. Then remembers that Nina had held her passport out but did not hand it over. His father only briefly glanced at it.

"Oh fuck," Joe says simply. "Fucking fuck fuck. Son of a

bitch." For the first time in a long time Joe remembers how terrible he is with women. Just like his dad, he's too trusting. And he fell for the whole damsel-in-distress gambit again.

The guard pulls a tight grimace. "There it is. Okay, so I think we know what's happened here." The guard looks at his watch then back to the woman; she looks at him quickly.

"I think, if it's okay with you, Lucinda, we can let him go, right? I'll explain the situation to the cops when they get here. If you want to leave your address, we can pass it on to them. Obviously, we'll need to look into this incident a bit further if a random woman now has plans of the house but I'm not going to hold you here against your will, if you want to go?"

The guard pushes a pad and pen across to Joe. He scratches out his address. As the guard takes the pad back Joe looks up at the woman behind him, who is staring at Joe. She has a hand held tight over her watch as she holds his gaze and very slowly shakes her head.

The guard is not looking. She does it again.

Joe gives her an inquiring look; is she trying to tell him something? She points at the guard's back and shakes her head then swallows hard.

Suddenly Joe understands. He's walked straight into something very weird. Nina *is* real, she's in danger, and so too, in some way, is this woman.

Lucinda nods now, seeing understanding quickly dawn on Joe's features.

And in much the same way that Joe has walked into countless bad relationships he, without a further interrogating thought, grabs the guard's weapon from his belt and turns it on him.

CHAPTER 38
LUCINDA

The phone number on the paper John handed her was a trapdoor, an escape hatch. For use in case of emergencies.

As Lucinda bounds down the steps to the gatehouse, her watch beeping at the exertion, she depresses the exercise button as she now habitually does so that no one will rush to her aid. And as she does so the exact way this will all play out sets itself in concrete in her mind.

There will never be a way out of this unless she takes it herself. And she has an out. Nina's father saw all of this coming and laid a path of least resistance for her to tread.

He was a genius, but he didn't hold many cards. He just played the best hand he could and somehow suddenly he's winning. Things are aligning.

When she reaches the base of the hill, she disables the main CCTV surrounding the gate and gatehouse interior.

Then, after Joe has overpowered and incapacitated the guard, they lock him in the gatehouse outbuilding. And Lucinda sets about deactivating as many of the external cameras as she can from the gatehouse.

Lucinda doesn't know why she trusts Joe but she does. He has the same bright eyes as Penny and seems to genuinely care about Nina, perhaps as much as she now does.

She has a plan. She has of course thought through backup plans for months, since that meeting with John. Since she found out what the number on the piece of paper was for.

Lucinda pulls out her phone now and sends the encrypted message that she's been sitting on since the day John gave her that number, a message that offers her inside information on a specific type of people-trafficking now popular in certain echelons of the population. In exchange for that whistleblowing she will require protection and immunity from prosecution.

She might not get full immunity, she knows, but she is betting her life that they will keep her safe long enough to put the people involved on trial. And that seems like a surer prospect than her current chances.

As Joe and Lucinda race back up the hill, she thinks through their next moves. All Nina has to do is survive one more room and they'll be able to save her.

Back at the house, Lucinda disables the upstairs CCTV and explains to Joe that it isn't as simple as just storming downstairs into the basement rooms and grabbing Nina. The building is automated, and once the system is started it will not reopen until everything is completed, one way or another.

"The rooms down there, they're escape rooms. Very expensive, very dangerous escape rooms," she explains. "And you don't get out unless you solve them. The house used to be a challenge, for rich clients. Nina's father designed it. But as with everything, it adapted. It's been repurposed. Now the clients pay to watch other people try to survive it."

"And Nina's in it. Now?"

"Yes. But there is a way to stop the system—without completing it. It's a big move, though."

"Okay, let's do that then. Show me and we'll do it."

Lucinda shakes her head. "No. I need to ask someone else. Only they can do it. And I need you here. I need you to go down to the locked basement door and wait. Can you trust me? Can you do that?"

Joe looks at Lucinda afresh and notices her hands are shaking ever so slightly as they cling to her wrist band.

She's scared, and that seems like a good sign to him.

"Yes, I trust you," he says. "Go do what you have to do."

CHAPTER 39
NINA

The entire floor space of the third room is a chessboard.

Nina enters, cautiously, stepping from one large empty square to the next. Each lights up as her weight hits it.

This room is clearly A Game of Chess, though Nina doubts it will be like any she has played before.

"Take your position on a3. The game will commence shortly."

Nina looks across the room to the a3 square. This is Anderssen's Opening. They are going to ask her to play the Anderssen/Morphy game.

Nina stops in her tracks, a cold chill running through her, because she knows with absolute certainty that she does not remember the moves or script for that game. If making it out of this room relies on that knowledge, then Nina is as good as dead.

Across the room the entry door seals and the lighting state brightens.

"Welcome, Nina, to A Game of Chess. This game requires you to remain on Anderssen's Opening as long as possible. Stay on a3."

With that a low whirring sound begins to fill the room. At first Nina can't tell what exactly is happening, but as the first set of squares across the room loses their lights her eyes make sense of the scene. The opposite wall is moving toward her. The room is closing in.

Nina's eyes scan the room for a screen with more instructions, but there is none. There are no questions, there is no task to complete.

"Bathsheba," Nina calls, raising her voice above the hydraulic whir, "what am I supposed to do? What are the questions?"

Bathsheba's voice flickers back to life. "Stay on a3."

Nina looks down at her square, her mind rapidly scrolling through every possible meaning of that sentence. Is it a clue, a riddle, an anagram? She rearranges the words in her head quickly, watching as the wall approaches her, five squares away now and getting closer.

But nothing makes sense. The letters do not rearrange in any reasonable order. Stay on a3:

Y Sonata 3

3 Astony

Nasty an 3

It's not an anagram; it's simply an instruction.

But should she follow it or not, can she trust it or not?

At that moment another door opens opposite her at the other end of the board.

Again, Bathsheba reminds her, "Stay on a3."

But the wall is closing in. It's three squares away now and Nina has absolutely no idea what the trick of this room is yet—and time is very clearly running out.

She looks down at her lit square and the five squares surrounding it. She looks up at the open door and cautiously extends a foot forward toward the square in front of her.

"Do not advance. Stay on a3." Bathsheba's voice kicks in, causing her to jump.

Nina considers not moving but the wall is getting closer every second and if she doesn't move soon, she might not make it across the space in time to get to the door at all.

Slowly she lowers her foot onto the square in front of hers. And nothing happens. The square lights up and she gingerly shifts her weight onto it. Then she tries the next and the next and the next, growing in confidence with every jump, until the wall brushes her elbows as she leaps from the room and reaches the relative safety of the vestibule beyond.

Nina turns to look back into the room as her a3 square disappears and the moving wall meets the stationary one. If she had stayed, she would be dead now, dead or severely injured. She needs to remember that sometimes things really aren't that complex.

She watches and after a few seconds the wall begins to reset to its original position before the door closes behind her.

Chess is a game of strategy, but sometimes the best strategy is just to run.

CHAPTER 40
NINA

Nina hears the sound of orchestral music up ahead and follows it toward the next room.

Inside the white room stand three large tables, each with a small box placed on top of it. Nina walks toward them; the room seals behind her as she reaches the first of them.

"Welcome, Nina, to The Fire Sermon. The game will now commence."

A low hiss fills the room under the melody of the light classical music.

Gas; gas is being pumped in. Nina instinctually covers her nose and mouth but the sour, penetrating odor cuts through her clenched palm.

Nina spots the screen across the room and runs to it as words appear.

```
The gas you are now breathing is a nerve
agent.
```

> You have between 5 and 20 minutes before
> this fully takes effect.
>
> On the tables in this room there are three
> boxes, each containing an injection: a po-
> tential antidote.
>
> But only one of the syringes is live. The
> others are placebos. Choose wisely.

A timer replaces the text on the screen. One minute has already passed since the gas was administered.

Nina turns back to the tables and lifts each lid carefully, inside each nestles a loaded syringe. A small tag is attached to each. Nina reads then rereads them, her soul sinking inside her. Her father was a near clairvoyant at solving cryptic crossword clues, but she has never been as accomplished. She sounds them out loud.

The first reads: *"Unscramble this: O Nontheist."*

The second reads: *"English rock band; to well preserve."*

The third reads: *"Choose what is inside mothers."*

Nina coughs, her eyes suddenly itchy, her throat beginning to burn. It's happening. The gas is getting to her already, the hot scratch of it undeniable. The Fire Sermon.

Nina looks over at the screen. Two minutes have passed. The gas is potent and is beginning to hamper her.

She forces herself to focus.

Cryptic crossword clues have a strange system to them. She tries to remember it. They often contain the answer within the clue itself.

The first clue seems to suggest it's an anagram. *Unscramble* being the operative word. *"Unscramble this: O Nontheist."* Perhaps unscramble the words: *O nontheist.*

Nina squeezes her eyes shut and tries to concentrate, pushing away the burning itch of her eyes and throat, the letters of the clue scrambling around desperately in her mind, until they burst into order.

Not this one.

That's the answer. *Not this one.* That's what the letters spell out when rearranged; it is that simple if you know the rules. The answer is not in that syringe.

Emboldened, she turns to the next syringe. Three and a half minutes have passed.

The next clue looks to Nina likely to be a double-definition clue. Double-definition clues contain two different definitions of the word that is the answer.

"English rock band; to well preserve."

So what word is both the name of an English rock band and a way of preserving? *The Jam* immediately springs to Nina's mind.

But that doesn't make sense, does it? Jam?

Not this one is a pretty straightforward clue, but *Jam* means nothing to her.

No doubt it will make sense in light of the final clue, Nina tells herself. Because only one of the syringes is a real antidote. If she can work what two of the three clues are, the answer will present itself regardless.

The third syringe's tag reads: *"Choose what is inside mothers."*

The word *inside* gives the third clue away: this is a container clue.

Inside is the operative word: the answer will be literally *inside* the word *mothers*.

Mothers.

Others.

So, choose what is inside mothers. Others. *Choose others.*

The antidote is not in syringe three. Which means whatever *Jam* means it is the correct clue. Syringe two is the one she needs.

Nina picks up the syringe and looks at it.

"Bathsheba, how do I take it," she asks, her raised voice cracking and sending her into a sharply painful fit of coughing.

A diagram fills the screen across from her. She takes the syringe with her to the screen and watches as an illustrated figure slides their syringe into the skin of their upper thigh and depresses the plunger.

Nina winces at the image. A wave of faintness sweeps over her. She carefully sinks to the floor and places her head between her legs until it passes.

"Okay, okay," Nina tells herself as she pops off the syringe cap and sits up on the floor.

She takes a deep breath, the burning at the back of her throat intense now, then plunges the syringe into her upper thigh, administering the fluid within.

She sucks in a tight breath as she pulls it out, her skin snagging on the needle. Then as she waits for the medicine to take effect, she takes one last look at the tag before tossing it away.

She lets out a little chuckle as she reads the clue with fresh eyes. She finally has the answer.

It's not *The Jam*. It's *The Cure*.

CHAPTER 41
JOON-GI

Joon-gi is in his maintenance shed when she arrives.

He can tell there's something wrong just by looking at her as she catches her breath in the doorway. She is usually immaculate, one of those people who always seem like they've only just left the house. But of course he knows that's not the case, he sees her working here all day, or rather he sees her when she came up from the rooms.

But she's not immaculate now: her face is flushed, damp with sweat, her dress clinging to her abdomen and back, her hair askew; her breath is coming in tight gasps.

He rises from his workbench and opens his mouth to speak but she stops him.

"I need to talk to you. It's very important you know what is about to happen."

Joon-gi sits back down. "Okay. This is about the rooms, isn't it?"

The woman looks terrified, panicked. Something has gone

very wrong or is about to and he knows in that moment, in his bones, that what he has always suspected about the rooms must be true.

They are not exactly what they say they are.

Lucinda nods and closes the door behind her, locking it, her eyes scanning for the room's cameras and finding them. Their usually red lights are now dark, off. She sinks onto a seat by the door and leans forward to explain.

"The rooms used to be the experience. Clients *used* to come here. But now *civilians* come. It is . . . non-consensual." She reassesses then, desperately searching for the words—"I mean, there's a degree of choice factored into the experience but, I mean, they don't *know* what this place is when they enter. They don't know until it's too late. And then they're in there. There have been four participants already. None of them made it," she explains, then falters, because Maria *had* gotten out; Maria made it all the way into her kitchen back in London. Maria almost won a competition that wasn't supposed to be a competition anymore. And Lucinda watched her die.

To Lucinda's utter shame, it was only then, in that kitchen, that any of what she had been doing had actually seemed *real* to her. Seeing Maria in her home was the first moment in all of this that any of these people were real. Even hearing John talk about Nina, it all seemed like a story or an idea. But bruised and beaten in her own kitchen, the truth finally got her; they were hurting real, live people. And still, even after that, Lucinda continued. She quietly waited until the time was perfect to put her plan in motion; she brought Nina out here. Out of fear, out of self-preservation, out of weakness because she needed a distraction and she needed people to help her pull this off. This escape of her own.

She has a contact, a way out, and if she uses it right then she will get out of this with her life.

And if she saves Nina, if they all survive, her story is stronger, her bargaining chips bigger.

Joon-gi listens to Lucinda as she continues, her tone urgent. "The woman you left notes for, *Nina:* she is still down there and we need to get her out. Do you understand?"

Joon-gi nods, then a thought occurs. "The woman before. The nanny?"

Lucinda shakes her head quickly. "Her name was Maria. You helped her escape but she didn't make it."

Triumph and loss peak and crumple inside Joon-gi because he was right. He was right all along and he almost saved that woman. He wonders if she knew. He thinks of her face, her smile. She was so young.

"Since Maria the electrical inputs for the house have been changed, haven't they?" Lucinda asks, trying to refocus him. "You can't shut down the power to the rooms from the old substation anymore, can you?"

Joon-gi understands: they need to stop the rooms, to rescue the girl. He wonders if this is some elaborate trick. The last time he tried to do just that he was attacked. And yet looking at Lucinda's panicked face he doubts she is lying. She's scared and this is clearly an emergency.

But then he watches her depress a small button on her wrist band. "What are you doing," he blurts, pointing at the band. "Are you calling for backup, is security coming?"

She quickly shakes her head. "No, every time I press it they don't come, but they will come eventually. All the cameras are down. But help is on its way now too. I have a contact; the authorities are coming, but they'll be coming from the mainland. We need to do this ourselves as soon as we can. Or she'll die too."

Joon-gi straightens in his seat. "Am I going to jail? Are we both going to jail?"

Lucinda shakes her head. "No. I promise you. This is not your fault. It's mine and I will fix it. I'll tell them everything. I'll give them so many names that our names won't mean a thing. Okay?"

Joon-gi nods, then after a second he rises and grabs his bag. "The basement rooms' power runs off a generator now. I installed it, it's disaster-proof. Even if the whole island grid goes down that generator won't stop. If you want me to do this, I need to disable it," he explains.

"Is that hard?"

Joon-gi shakes his head. "Not hard, just far." He notes Lucinda's frown of concern. "I can get the whole thing powered down in ten, twenty minutes tops. Will she be okay in there for that long? Is it quick enough?"

He watches calculated thoughts whir across Lucinda's face, her jaw clenched tight. "Yes. Yes, she will."

And with that Lucinda leans forward and squeezes his hand, her eyes locking with his, a promise in them.

Joon-gi watches her set off across the lawns back to the main house. Then he hitches his bag onto his shoulders and begins to run as fast as his legs can pump down to the beach.

CHAPTER 42
NINA

After a few minutes Nina stands, but she is still dizzy, her eyes still itching, her throat still burning. She has no idea how long antidotes take to work or if it even has worked. Or perhaps certain damage has already been done. She has no way of knowing. All she knows is that she needs to keep moving. She needs to get to a hospital. She needs help. And she knows the only way out is through.

On the screen above her a new message has appeared.

```
Congratulations, Nina!
You have completed The Waste Land. Proceed
to the next room to begin the Four Quartets.
```

Nina cannot pull her blurry eyes from the screen, fear trickling through every vein of her body.

She had thought it was nearly over. She'd expected as many rooms as there are parts to the poem. But she has completed those parts and there is still more.

There can't be many more rooms down here, she tells herself, there simply can't unless the building goes farther down again.

The next room or the one after must be it. She'll be finished soon; it will be over soon.

She stretches her arms over her head and cricks her neck. Her body aches and throbs in so many ways, she can't focus on one particular sensation over another. The dizziness comes in waves that threaten to engulf her then subside. *It will all be over soon*, she tells herself, *it has to be*.

NINA WATCHES AS THE DOOR to the room opens, the vestibule beyond coming into view, curving around a corner, lit in that familiar pinkish tone.

She takes a burning breath and heads out.

As she turns the corner her blood runs cold: a white flight of stairs leads down.

The house does go on, how far she does not know. But there is a limit to the physics of any house, she tells herself, and reality is not elastic. Nina has been down here awhile now, though, and she doesn't quite believe the truth of that thought anymore.

She takes the stairs down. They lead directly into another room, the stairwell door sealing behind her.

THIS ROOM IS THE LARGEST yet. Nina takes it in, eyes stinging. Its massive floor is covered entirely with a thick layer of gray ash.

The door out of this room is different from all the others: it's a real door, a wooden one.

Half delirious, Nina wonders if it leads straight back outside. If beyond it lie the gardens and the beach and the sky. But of course she must be far underground now; there is no way that door leads out to the grass of the lawns. And yet she can't help thinking that a wooden door might signal an end to all this.

In some part of her exhausted mind, she wonders if she chose the correct syringe, if she should still feel this bad. But she pushes the thought away.

Nina steps forward onto the ash but quickly pulls her bare foot back to the safety of the doorway. The ash is hot. Really hot.

Nina sees the screen across the room fill with text. If she wants to find out how the hell to get out of here, she has to get to that screen. She takes a breath, braces herself, and runs as fast as she can across the hot ash.

She skids to a halt on the raised area beneath the screen. She's safe here. She shifts her weight quickly from one scalded foot to the other to ease the discomfort of the brief run.

Nina could have predicted the name of this room before she even looked up at the screen—and when she does, she sees she was right.

```
Welcome, Nina, to Burnt Norton.
The key to the door is all that's left here—
if you dance you can persevere.
```

"Find a key in here?" Nina exclaims, looking at the vast ash-filled room. "You have got to be fucking kidding me!"

She takes in the sheer square footage of the room, every bit of it covered in thickly packed ash except the raised area where she stands and the entrance and exit doorways. It will take her hours to search through all the dust—which wouldn't be a problem if the floor weren't burning hot. She has barely been able to stand on the floor for more than a few seconds.

The screen beside her updates, a temperature reading appearing where the text was. The floor is currently forty-five degrees Celsius.

As she watches, the screen clicks up to forty-six degrees. It's going to get hotter. It will just keep getting hotter and her prospects of getting out of here will fall exactly in line with that.

She needs to get in that ash now.

Another wave of dizziness floods her senses. Nina forces herself to focus, to remember the poem, the room's namesake. There will be a clue in all this, she's sure.

The poem is about the past and the future; about time. About the present and seizing it. Well, that sentiment is certainly relevant now.

She recalls that Eliot wrote the poem after visiting a manor house called Burnt Norton. It isn't actually about a burnt house, though the room clearly uses that symbolism. And in a way it's beyond apt, because God knows Nina wishes this whole house would burn to the ground or slip into the sea as James suggested the day she arrived.

James has not popped into her head for a while and as he does, she knows with certainty that he is a part of all this, to what degree unclear. But Nina knows he was aware that something wasn't right here when he left her that first day. She pushes the thought away. There is no time.

She needs to work out the room's riddle.

Nina racks her brains for lines from the poem and something pops out of the ether, a line instantly recalled, one of its most famous: *there the dance is, at the still point of the turning world.*

She looks out into the center of the room: *the still point of the turning world.*

She will have to go out there, right into the middle. And she will have to stay there awhile and dig in that hot ash.

The temperature readout beside her clicks up to forty-seven degrees Celsius. And without a second thought Nina runs straight into the middle of the room, dives down onto all fours, and begins searching in the burning ash for a key. Intense dizziness floods every part of her as she tries to push away the pain and find the one object that will save her.

CHAPTER 43
JOON-GI

Joon-gi's heart is thundering in his chest as he hits the edge of the beach, his sandals filled with warm sand as he swings around the final stair post and propels himself not toward the beach, but along the line of trees that back it.

The substation down here was built during construction of the house, so that the construction site could be powered while still off-grid.

The people running the house hadn't been aware of it until Joon-gi found the old cabling. They'd asked him to make the house impervious to power outages given the obvious problems blackout would cause, and he had fixed it.

It must be beyond irritating for them, he thinks, that the original programming on the rooms' safety doors is impossible to override; a built-in check and balance that they can't subvert. The house was built to challenge the participants but ultimately protect them from their own stupidity. While they were clearly able to change that programming on the limits of the challenges themselves, they could not rid themselves of the fact that technology requires power.

He flies through the tropical forest undergrowth, the sound of waves breaking through the woods just beyond him. And then the sound of something else.

Another noise catches Joon-gi's attention. The low hum of something. He pushes it away; whatever it is, it isn't an imminent threat.

He bundles through the branches and suddenly emerges in a small cleared area. A tiny brick outbuilding with a chipped light-blue door stands in front of him.

Though the door is old and made of beach-weathered wood, a brand-new keypad entry system sits on its frame.

They had insisted on it. He told them no one would come down here, and if they did they wouldn't even know what the building was. To put this kind of a lock on it singled it out as an outbuilding worth breaking into. They hadn't listened, of course.

But it doesn't matter. Joon-gi is the only person on-site with clearance to enter it.

He raises his palm to the panel and it blips.

Joon-gi frowns.

He tries again. The same blip. His clearance has been denied.

He pulls back from the door, and it is then that he notices the noise again. The hum is rhythmic and much louder now, almost like the sound of a chain saw or a propeller. Or a propeller motor.

Joon-gi's eyes fly through the trees to the beach. Through the gaps in the branches the sea is just visible, and there beating through the waves along the coast he sees it. A speedboat, on the prow the unmistakable sight of black uniforms.

Joon-gi turns back to the door. He sizes up the beach-weathered wood and makes a choice. It doesn't matter now if an alarm sounds, they're coming, and even if he isn't going to make it out of here alive this time, he is damn well going to save someone. And no one is going to take that away from him.

He hurls his weight against the chipped paint three times before it begins to give, then four sharp kicks to the splintered wood get him in.

He throws his bag in ahead of him, and right on cue the deafening alarm system begins to sound, first in the outbuilding, then as if in relay high above him in the distance back at the house.

Lucinda will know that he's in, and that it won't be long now.

He hopes the woman in the basement is still alive, that she is managing to avoid whatever strange torments they have sent her way.

Inside the outbuilding Joon-gi flips on his flashlight and inspects the generator, its hum now drowning out the sound of the boat approaching the beach outside. He looks at his hard work—the best work he has ever done—and wonders how he possibly could've not known all along that something bad was happening here. But in a sense, he did, didn't he? He just hasn't given his instincts the space they need to convert to action, he hasn't listened to that little feeling inside him and asked himself what it's saying. But perhaps his biggest crime is that he assumed the world was one way and it is not.

He looks at the power lever that connects the generator and stored energy to the house and without a second thought he heaves it back. The system lets out a cascading hum as it powers down. The rooms will shortly go dark in the basement, all power cut, in the same slow relay that the alarm took to kick in up there.

But turning the power off is not enough. Now that the generator's hum is silenced, he hears them on the beach, perhaps four of them. He isn't as young as he used to be, he doubts he could overpower even one of them. But he can run. He knows he should run, but then he looks back at the generator. If he runs, if he leaves the generator like this, they will come straight in here and flip the power lever back on and undo everything. The woman will die, he will die, Lucinda will die.

At speed Joon-gi bends to empty his equipment bag, tools rattling and clanging out onto the floor around him. He runs his hands quickly over them until he finds what he's looking for: the largest and heaviest of his tools, an adjustable wrench. He rises and hefts it in his hands then takes his first swing at the now silent generator.

By the time the first guard reaches him, drawn to the sounds, Joon-gi has done all he needs to do, the generator now unusable. And when the first bullet hits his upper thigh Joon-gi is surprised that it does not hurt as much as he had always imagined things like that might.

He looks down as the dark-red blood bubbles from him and looks back out at the young man now taking cover behind a tree. Joon-gi thinks it strange that he should hide, as if he believes Joon-gi might have a weapon of his own. Joon-gi looks at the wrench in his hand, almost surprised to see a weapon in his possession. He does have one after all. It's not ideal but it's something.

And with that thought he runs full pelt at the man with the gun.

The second bullet he *does* feel. He drops the wrench and the forest floor rises to meet him.

CHAPTER 44
NINA

The room flickers into darkness.

Nina blinks in the black that suddenly envelops her.

She isn't in the center of the room anymore. She tried her hardest. She stayed in the ash until the pain, like white-hot blindness, overcame her and she scrambled back onto the raised platform and rested.

The temperature readout has continued, unseen by her.

She stayed out there until it hit fifty-six. Her knees, hands, shins, and feet are mottled red and white, the pain excruciating.

She did her best but she could stay there no longer. She knows the key is in the center of the room but she hasn't covered enough of it yet. Her only hope is that the room will reach a certain temperature and then reset to forty once more. Though how long that might take and if she will stay conscious for that long, she does not know.

And now the room is in darkness.

Perhaps this is the end of the game, she muses, her breathing coming in slow deep pulls. Perhaps she will just be left in darkness. Across the space there comes a low hydraulic sound and then on her burnt legs the cool whisper of a breeze.

Nina looks up.

She tries to focus her eyes across the dark room, in the direction she entered. There's something different. She can't tell if it's a mirage brought on by her various, now severe injuries, or if it's real. But the darkness seems to lift ever so slightly at the other side of the room.

Nina stumbles up to standing and gently bends to hover a hand over the ash-covered floor. It reached as high as seventy-seven Celsius the last time she checked the screen.

She can still feel the radiating heat of it. She lowers her hand closer to its surface; it's hot, unbearably hot. She listens in the silence and thinks she can make out the distant sound of an alarm blaring.

Perhaps this is it, perhaps this is her being saved. But no one is here.

She might have only one shot.

Her mind weighs the choices and without missing a beat she flies across the burning-hot floor in great stumbling fluttering strides, plowing toward the open door that leads back up the stairs, her rasping breath tearing at her throat.

CHAPTER 45
JOE

Joe tries to ignore the alarm blaring around him. He tells himself to focus, to stay alert. In his hand is a mop, its head ripped off, the only weapon he's managed to find and fashion from the utility room beside the locked basement door.

He watches as the door slides open, bracing for whatever lies behind it to emerge.

When it's fully open, he steps forward to peer in. Inside is only darkness. He pulls out his mobile phone and turns on the light.

The space beyond the door is cavernous, an empty white room. Nina is not there. Then as his light swings across the back wall, he sees another doorway leading deeper into the house.

Joe looks behind him to the stairs, unsure what to do, but a certainty hits him: no one is coming to rescue him, or Nina. *He* is the rescue mission, he alone, and if Nina is going to get out of here he will have to go in and get her.

He licks his lips, his phone in one hand, his weapon in the other, and steps into the darkness.

CHAPTER 46
LUCINDA

When the alarm begins Lucinda stops what she is doing, the light on the flash drive pulsing red, downloading everything she can fit onto one after another drive from the house's hidden camera hard drives.

She will need a lot of bargaining chips. She will need a lot of leverage to get herself out of the hole she willingly jumped into. The cavalry is coming and if she doesn't want to go to jail for a very long time, she'll need to offer something in return.

But as she looks out across the lawns she feels the possibility of rescue slip away from her. A black-uniformed figure crests the summit of the beach staircase, and then another and another. House security guards, three of them, armed and sprinting flat-out toward the house.

She is not going to make it out of here. This information is not making it out of here. Nothing is.

She scrambles back to the house's hub screen and with shaking fingers initiates the external door locking system. The power might be cut to the rooms beneath them but it is not cut to the main building. And while the external security system is no match for the lockdown protocol downstairs, the shatterproof glass in the external doors will hold the men back for a few minutes at least.

Lucinda jumps as the first gunshot sings into the patio glass, turning it instantly milky, beyond their approaching bodies, now blurred. She cannot see them, but she knows what will come next. One by one the vast windows catch bullets and milk to opaque before her eyes.

She looks down at the four flash drives in her hand, the final one in the machine blinking and then flashing green. She has it all.

She removes the last drive, slips them all into her pocket, lifts the heavy bucket of water high over the hard drive unit, and pours. She leaps back as it fuses in a bright flash of white, crackling and fizzing as she flinches away.

The men behind the glass begin to pound on the weakened areas. They will be in soon. She doesn't have long.

She thinks about running, she thinks of every possible choice she could make, but instead she runs to the top of the basement stairs and calls out, "Is she alive?"

Because suddenly that feels like the most important thing in a world of incredibly important things.

And then in the silence that follows as she strains to listen, she hears the gentle, godlike *thud-thud-thud-thud* of helicopter rotor blades getting closer. The cavalry.

Behind her the sound of smashing suddenly stops and a flicker of hope flutters inside her.

CHAPTER 47
NINA

She was making good progress back through the rooms until she reached Burial of the Dead.

She hears the noises before she sees the light, the gunshots, blunt and unmistakable from the house above, the sound of something smashing into glass and then, in the room ahead, she sees a flashlight swinging wildly in the darkness.

She slips into the now defunct glass coffin and waits. There is only one flashlight, one person, but there are more upstairs and Nina is not going back down into the rooms. She is not going to die down here. The man who entered has a weapon as well as a flashlight, some kind of long baton.

The plate and cheese knife from the meal she ate hours ago lie in the coffin beside her. She feels for them in the darkness, her hand clenching quietly around the small bone handle. Then she waits until he has passed her and slipped into the next vestibule to rise from her hiding place and follow him into the corridor on silent feet.

She creeps toward his hunched, wary back, his eyes clearly not as adjusted to the darkness as hers.

She has almost made it to him when a call sounds back through the rooms, a woman calling someone. The man turns, his light shining directly into Nina's face, blinding her as he cries out in shock.

Nina braces for an impact. But the impact does not come. So she lunges, she lunges hard and fast for the phone, knocking it to the ground, and then she thrusts the knife harder into the unseen flesh of the figure in front of her.

His cry of pain echoes through the empty rooms as he sinks to the floor, dropping his stick. Nina kicks the phone away from him and moves to grab it.

But before she can swing the light back onto him, she hears a familiar voice come from the injured man: "Nina?"

It takes her addled mind a moment to make sense of it, of what is happening—then . . . "Joe?" her voice rattles in answer.

"What the hell did you do?" he asks, his voice strained. When he speaks again there is no mistaking the severity of his injury. "Oh Jesus Christ. I'm bleeding. I'm bleeding a lot. Fuck, I need a hospital, I need—"

Nina swings the light at him. He lies prone on the ground, a hand clutched hard to his stomach, his white shirt now dark, and that darkness still spreads across it as she watches.

"Oh fuck, Joe. Oh my God. Okay, don't worry, don't worry. I'll get you out of here. I'll get us both out of here." Nina cannot stop the surge of adrenaline that explodes inside her—and with it a resurgence of her lightheadedness, but she does not have the luxury of indulging it now.

Just before Joe loses consciousness, he feels her arms envelop him and begin to drag him out of the darkness.

The unmistakable sound of smashing glass reverberates from the house above them.

CHAPTER 48
NINA

Two years later

Nina looks out at the dark diner car park through the glass. The warm glow of humanity buzzes around her in the small-town establishment, a heated slice of cherry pie waiting untouched on the plate in front of her. The waitress has left two forks.

She needed to order something from the girl in the pale-pink uniform gliding among the busy tables, she hadn't considered that. And the pie looked nice, though right now, she can't risk pulling her eyes from the darkness outside.

She doesn't recognize the waitress; she doesn't recognize anyone here, which feels odd after two years of steering clear of strangers. They moved her to Charlotte, North Carolina—well, Belmont to be exact, a small town outside Charlotte—shortly before the first trial began.

She has been living under a new identity in sleepy Belmont for almost twenty-six months. She has friends there, a job in the local library, she volunteers with the historical society, her neighbors know her—she's made sure of it.

But no one knows her here in Davidson, the town three over. It isn't a huge misdirection, but she thought it best to meet here, just in case. Everything is always just in case these days.

She knows they aren't supposed to meet at all, even though the trials are over, even though everything is in the public domain now and she has told everything she knows many times over. They are theoretically safe by now, but they have been told they can never go back to their old lives, that they should never attempt to reconnect.

They could easily lead any leak right back to the other and after giving evidence, after being involved in bringing down a network that stretched across many continents perhaps, they were sensible to start over.

The American government has worked together with the UK's National Crime Agency to relocate and patriate her pretrial. They moved her twice in the early days to protect her. A brief stint in Pennsylvania, followed by even less time in Delaware, but fears over her safety were raised in both locations though she herself had noticed nothing. Perhaps that's the way bad things happen to you, they just do, and then that's it.

But she needs to see him and he has to see her; they can't just live their lives waiting for the worst to happen. Besides, she needs to apologize and to thank the man who tried to save her.

They emailed a few times since the last trial connected with the house on Gorda. There were other trials after theirs, there were other houses, but they were not required in those cases.

The flash drives Lucinda created containing information pulled from the house's hard drives enabled the FBI and the British National Crime Agency to track and locate several of the servers on which clients had watched the enslavement and murder of the four previous victims at the house on Gorda. And given them leads to other houses and connected networks.

Nina learned early in the case that while her father had built Anderssen's Opening, it had been repurposed after its sale to another buyer. Her father's house was just an elaborate parlor game, limits set that meant the homeowner could attempt to beat the odds without the fear of meeting their end. But part of her game had been to make her believe her father was responsible for the house as it was. She learned about the fabricated deeds, James's involvement, and Lucinda herself.

Nina still finds it hard to know what to think about Lucinda; what to make of her.

Nina saw her body as they were led from the house, crumpled and so seemingly innocent as she lay there, a pool of blood circling her.

He told her, after the fact, how Lucinda was really the one to save them. It was she who gathered the information needed to prosecute and end the activities at the house and others like it. Still, Nina can't feel grateful to her, not after what Lucinda had so willingly done. It sickens her to think of Lucinda, in her father's house, using up what precious moments of life he had left with her tainted presence.

She made her way into Nina's life and pried it apart. And yet Nina doesn't doubt that her father knew exactly what he was doing, her father read her and paved a way for everything that happened after.

He weighed the options and saw that kindness, sympathy, understanding—and tea and biscuits—might somehow save his only daughter down the road. He offered Lucinda an out. She doesn't doubt her father changed that woman from the inside out—good people can do that, a little kindness can do that; it has that power.

No, she can't think well of Lucinda no matter how hard she

tries, even though in a sense she knows she owes the woman her life.

The waitress in pink returns to her table and gestures to the untouched pie with genuine concern.

"No good?" she asks.

Nina gives her a smile. "I'm waiting for my friend. I think he deserves it more than me," she tells the waitress kindly.

"I'll get you a coffee refill, though," the waitress offers as she bustles off.

Nina checks the time. He's late.

Nerves shake her suddenly; she did not receive an email from him that morning and she wonders if something terrible might have happened, if this might all be an incredibly stupid idea. He might have been spooked; she might be a sitting duck.

Their correspondence needed to be vague over the past two years; they found they could share little of their lives with any safety, and since the trials ended the messages have dried up.

At least until he sent her the most recent one, on the day that the last of the convictions began. And they arranged to meet.

She does not know where he's traveling from, where they relocated him. She hopes it's nice. Bizarrely she feels responsible for all that has happened to him, and of course in a way she is responsible—after all he wouldn't have been there in the first place if it weren't for her.

She has to face the possibility that he isn't coming, and of course she can't blame him. If he doesn't believe it's safe, she can understand that. Even if the key players are now sentenced. Even if one of their number, the man she believed to be called James, already took his life in jail a year ago.

But rather than make her feel safe, facts like this make her *wonder* more than anything. They raise the possibility that "James"—or Nathan Cartwright as he turned out to be called—

was allowed to take his own life in prison because of the things he knew and the danger he posed to others involved. Facts and names that could cause important people important problems.

In spite of the National Crime Agency's and FBI's protestations, she is certain that there are still houses out there, that the key players have remained invisible—as they always are, until they aren't. Somewhere out there it is not over.

The truth of how those things were allowed to happen out there on Gorda and of the numbers of people involved undoubtedly stretches much further than the six convictions made. She knows it in her bones.

She looks at her watch again. If he doesn't come, she won't hold it against him. She understands the kind of fear that makes it hard to trust again because a part of her is still down in those rooms, and always will be.

She looks out of the darkened glass, her own reflection partially obscuring her vision as she watches the headlights of cars pass on the road beyond.

The waitress returns and refills her cup with that same sympathetic smile, steam rising as Nina imagines what the waitress sees: just another woman in her late thirties stood up, abandoned.

Nina smiles to herself. God, if only she had those problems; the problems she used to have; warm, cozy problems.

Sure, she's alone, but alone doesn't mean the same thing it used to. These days loneliness is an existential threat. Since the house, loneliness means you are a target, that you are not part of a pack.

Nina is always part of a pack these days. Everyone in Belmont knows Helen Fisher; she has made sure of it. She isn't lonely in that sense, but by God does she miss her father some days. The guilt she feels for doubting him is strongest at night, or when she wakes sweating in the early hours. They successfully turned her against her own father before unsuccessfully trying to kill her.

She misses him viscerally, and Maeve, and her old job back in innocent, self-important Cambridge with its old buildings and bloated ideas of itself. She misses it all.

A car pulls up across the lot from her window table and she straightens in her seat.

The driver cuts the engine and then after a minute emerges. It's him.

A man in his late fifties, smartly dressed in chinos and a sweater. He looks at the diner window from across the lot, spots Nina, and gives an almost apologetic wave.

He hasn't stood her up, he hasn't chickened out; Joon-gi has made it here after all.

CHAPTER 49
JOON-GI

Joon-gi came to on the prickly forest floor, the sharp pain in his collarbone from the second bullet intense but not fatal.

He rolled over carefully and touched the wound. The bleeding wasn't too bad; the bullet must have hit the bone of his clavicle and lodged, instead of penetrating his lung or heart.

He wondered fleetingly how rare that was, because he certainly knew how painful it was.

He lay there for a moment and listened to the sounds of the forest, and of the waves hitting the shore, and of the alarms blaring across the property. At a distance he heard the *pop-pop*s of gunshots.

He turned his head but the guard had long gone from behind the tree to his right.

He rose, the sound of a helicopter thundering overhead, and as he looked up, he could just make out the word on its underside. POLICE.

The pop of gunshots above ceased.

He wondered if they had made it out alive, Lucinda, the girl, and the local man.

He wondered what he should do now. How best to get the help he clearly needed. He listened to the sound of the helicopter landing high above on the cliff. He would need to make his way up there.

He looked down at his first gunshot wound. His thigh was still oozing blood into his cargo pants. He would need a doctor very soon; perhaps the others up there would too.

It was a long, hard, painful climb.

AND WHEN JOON-GI REACHED THE summit of the stairs, he saw the carnage.

The house's vast windows milked white by gunshots. Police officers spilling from the helicopter into the house. More gunfire.

He saw the British woman from the basement pulled out by the police, wailing, gesticulating frantically toward the local man, his body lifeless on the grass.

Joon-gi raised his hands high above his head in surrender as, knees buckling, he called out to get someone, anyone's attention—and the rest was history.

CHAPTER 50

When Joe returns from the diner restroom Nina is hugging Joon-gi.

He watches them for a moment, almost outside it all. It's strange that the worst moments of his life are now so fused with the best.

They were offered the chance to relocate together. To give it a shot and if being stabbed by your witness protection spouse and still wanting to be with her wasn't grounds enough for commitment then Joe isn't sure what could be.

Nina didn't want to be alone, and he didn't want to be without Nina. It was a simple choice. After all he'd already followed her into hell and back—what was moving to Charlotte?

Joon-gi catches Joe's eye and breaks away from Nina's embrace. He offers an outstretched hand to Joe, emotion thick in his eyes. The men shake hands and then Joe pulls him into a hug of his own. Nina tumbles in too, and then all three of the survivors are hugging, laughter coming in body-shuddering jolts among them.

They have made it, and they feel it to their very cores.

When the embrace subsides, they sit and talk, the waitress bringing a third fork and the hours rolling by.

IT'S ONLY ON THE DRIVE back to Charlotte that it hits Nina. As they roar down the highway, their smiles slip slowly from their quiet faces and Joe clasps his hand into hers almost subconsciously.

The game is over, the music has finally stopped, and this is where she landed.

The meaning of everything seemed so clear in the house: stay alive, don't die. It was easy in a sense.

Because now what is she supposed to do?

Outside the house the structure of things loosened, the rules were less obvious, life was opaque and uncharted territory. The clarity and importance of her every move seemed lessened, the point of it all ultimately unknowable.

Nina felt real life flooding back in, the everyday weight of it, the normality of it. And it scared her.

She watches the pavement blur past, and for the first time in her life she truly understands her father, the reason he worked so hard, kept so busy, built a house of escape rooms—because he understood how important distractions, complexity, challenge, and games were. To know the rules, to follow them and triumph. Life isn't like that.

He was left alone with a child, this brilliant man, his wife gone, and he could have sunk under the heft of that but he didn't; he swam, and he created, and he built a house that made life the ultimate prize. And though the original idea was warped by others, twisted into something else, Nina couldn't argue with the fact that she had never prized her own existence as highly as in that house. That house had made her fight for her life and every problem she had ever had before then or after would be nothing against that.

Nina turns to look at Joe, his handsome, kind face in profile, unknown thoughts at work behind his eyes.

Now the game is over and it's just them; them and their hard-won lives, their fledgling love, and a cozy two-bed in Charlotte.

And just as the terrifying fear of that floods into Nina a spike of adrenaline kicks it back and away.

Because—maybe normality is okay. Maybe it is enough.

Nina feels a bright twinkle of hope.

They are survivors, she knows that now, and if life isn't enough, they can always make it a game.

EPILOGUE

The superyacht sits 213 nautical miles off the Strait of Gibraltar, safely in international waters.

On board the 533-foot yacht, *Second Dawn,* a crew of over seventy busy themselves in preparation for dinner. The helicopter pads are now empty after the final arrivals, and all twenty-four cabins are filled with their requisite guests.

Drinks will be served shortly on the terrace deck.

In the master suite Oksana's maid helps zip up Oksana's dress before taking her laundry and exiting quietly.

Oksana sighs. She hates these dinners, but the guests traveled out to her so it seems the least she can do. A summit about pipelines. She cannot think of anything more boring, except perhaps the small talk she will need to involve herself in shortly. But she has people to assist with all of that, of course.

There are other things she would much rather be doing.

She perches on one of the suite's chairs and pours herself a short, cool glass of champagne. She sips it, then flicks on the large flatscreen above the suite's fireplace.

The interior of a slick, architectural house fills the screen, beyond the vast windows of the house the mountains of Japan are visible.

In the foreground of the scene on the screen a woman in her late twenties is reading a house manual intently, the sound of a door bleeping somewhere off-screen. The young woman stands, an alertness fizzling from her—she is beginning to panic.

Oksana pops a medjool date in her mouth and swigs another mouthful of champagne.

Oksana enjoyed attending dog races with her father as a child; he had taken her young. When she got older, he let her attend the dogfights with him too.

She was his only child and he wanted her to be as hard as any son. And she is. She is her father's daughter.

She enjoyed those days with him, before he was killed.

But dogs only hold so much amusement. After a while you just feel sorry for them. Not people, though.

Oksana has liked some of the participants, but they almost always disappoint her.

If she had to analyze why she bought the house, why she repurposed it, then perhaps she might alight on a core psychological need to see another woman beat the odds in the same way she did—through sheer bloody-mindedness and the remembered lessons of youth. But Oksana has always considered analysis and therapy an idiot's luxury, and she rarely indulges in that particular kind of narcissism.

She'd had such high hopes for Maria Yossarian, the survivor. But even Maria seemed to reach her limit eventually.

The young woman on the screen is now running with a raised metal chair at the huge glass doors with the serene mountain view. The chair makes contact, reverberating, causing no damage except to the woman herself. Oksana squints. This one will have to think more, panic less.

The young woman on the screen is an ex-Olympian who was kidnapped and held hostage for five months before escaping. But that was all two years back now. Oksana wonders if her pedigree will kick in soon. She hopes so.

Oksana was surprised by Nina's success if she is honest. And Oksana very much likes surprises. They happen rarely.

Nina's *pedigree* was excellent but she had no personal achievements of her own. And yet that didn't hold her back—after all she has been the only winner so far.

Oksana had wanted to get rid of that original house and the connection to the first designer anyway. After the repurposing all ties needed to be cut, for safety.

The game needed to move to new locations, expand, and Nina seemed a neat conclusion to that first house; to package her as its final guest seemed fitting. And there were eager buyers for the experience.

The girl on the screen now had a lot of interest from buyers too. Three separate viewers with view codes were watching in various locations around the world. She did not ask where. Other people dealt with logistics. They had shed a few low-level employees after Nina's escape, and the various consequences of that, but everyone who mattered was still intact.

Nina was their best participant to date, garnering five viewers. The most any guest had achieved.

One viewer required refunding after the game's unusual conclusion but the others were gratified by the ending. As was Oksana. Her *little red-faced friend* won. Oksana's father would have liked that. He would have laughed.

Everyone loves an underdog, a surprise, a romance, a happy ending. Don't they?

The girl on the screen is screaming now, tears streaming from her. Her mouth opening and closing in silence as beneath her on the screen an audio description scrolls on. Oksana winces. The girl is making threats; they often do. Coarse language. Sometimes it's best to watch on mute.

Oksana downs the last of her ice-cold champagne and shrugs on a cashmere shawl. Up on deck the temperature tends to drop.

She lifts the remote and pauses the screen: the girl freezes, her fists mid-pound on the glass.

Oksana doesn't want to miss her show.

She flicks off the lights to her suite and heads upstairs.

ACKNOWLEDGMENTS

Huge thanks to my wonderful editors: Kara Cesare and Jesse Shuman at Penguin Random House in the US and Stefanie Bierwerth at Quercus in the UK, and to the rest of the brilliant teams at Penguin Random House and Quercus.

Special thanks go, as always, to my brilliant agent, Camilla Bolton, at Darley Anderson. The best advocate an author could hope for—thank you for your continued support, dynamism, and knowledge of the industry.

Thank you, also, to the booksellers, reviewers, podcasters, and libraries for getting my books out there onto shelves and into people's hands.

And, of course, inordinate thanks to my husband, Ross, and our two daughters for everything else. . . .

LOOK
IN THE
MIRROR

CATHERINE STEADMAN

A Book Club Guide

A Q&A WITH THE AUTHOR

This is your fifth novel after *Something in the Water, Mr. Nobody, The Disappearing Act,* and *The Family Game.* What inspired *Look in the Mirror?*

I loved the idea of writing a very fast-paced action thriller and mixing that with T. S. Eliot and the themes of what it means to be a parent or a child. A lot of strong flavors there to dig into! I was also inspired by various other writers and their stories: the gothic governess tale of *The Turn of the Screw,* Angela Carter's brilliant Bluebeard story "The Bloody Chamber," Agatha Christie (of course), and screenwriter Hwang Dong-hyuk's brilliant thriller *Squid Game.*

You're known for your thrillers full of nonstop action, but also the way you explore the emotional lives of women and moral conundrums. *Look in the Mirror* wrestles with some big questions about family, trust, and the nature of survival. Why was this important for you to explore?

I was interested in looking at the idea that we are increasingly living in an age where there is a commodification of personal identity. Backstory, lived experience, and heritage can have the potential to pigeonhole us, almost setting us in aspic in terms of who we are and what should be expected of us in the future. The characters in *Look in the Mirror* have to fight through their pasts in order to make it out of the house alive—I thought that would be an interesting premise for a thriller.

What's one challenge you had while writing this book?

Knowing what level to set the room challenges at! I wanted the reader to be able to solve some rooms instantly and then wonder how to get through others . . . but it's important to remember that each game is tailored to the individual experiencing it. Your room would contain answers and challenges from your past!

Did you learn anything about yourself while writing?

I think I learned what both Maria and Nina learned—almost everything is solvable if you can just step back, take a breath, and reassess.

Both characters get out of tight situations this way, by not letting the import of the situation take control of them. But in the inverse, both have moments where they let their instincts, their primal impulses, take over—though they decide to do this, they do not let themselves be subsumed by the moment.

And for the final question, something just for fun! If *Look in the Mirror* were to become a movie, who would you want to see cast?

Oooo, this is an exciting question! Well, the first casting that immediately leaps to mind is the dad from the 2020 Oscar-winning Korean movie *Parasite*, Song Kang-ho, for Yang Joon-gi. That would be an incredible coup.

For Maria, I think Marisa Abela, the actress about to appear as Amy Winehouse in Sam Taylor-Johnson's *Back to Black*, would be perfect. She could definitely embody Maria's streetwise strength and fierce intelligence.

Nina could be played by either British actress Rebecca Hall or by *Normal People* and *Where the Crawdads Sing* actress Daisy Edgar-Jones.

And for Nina's father, perhaps Brian Cox on his softest setting! Or the lovely Vincent Price.

QUESTIONS AND TOPICS FOR DISCUSSION

1. What were your thoughts on the glamorous but deadly house, Anderssen's Opening? How does Catherine Steadman create a sense of claustrophobia and tension within the setting? How does the tension between the setting and what happens there contribute to the overall atmosphere of the story?

2. Nina is forced to question her past when she realizes that her father may not be who she believed him to be. How does her love for her father, and the memories they share, affect the choices Nina makes? Would you have made the same choices?

3. The book is structured with a dual timeline, two mysteries in one with layers of secrets to be revealed and revelations to be reached. What was a moment that truly surprised you? How did the author keep you guessing?

4. T. S. Eliot's landmark modernist poem *The Waste Land* plays a role in the story. Published in 1922, it is broken up into

five sections: "The Burial of the Dead," exploring disillusion-ment and despair; "A Game of Chess," which employs alter-nating narrations in which several characters discuss the fundamental emptiness of their lives; "The Fire Sermon," about self-denial and dissatisfaction; "Death by Water," a brief description of a drowned merchant; and "What the Thunder Said," a culmination of the poem's themes through the descrip-tion of a desert journey. Had you heard of this poem before reading *Look in the Mirror*? Why do you think the author chose it to inform and guide this novel?

5. Curiosity kills the cat. It certainly gets close to killing Nina, and of course, there's what happens to Maria. Why do you think curiosity often overwhelms our survival instincts? Has there ever been a time when your curiosity got the better of you?

6. What did you make of Lucinda? An efficient and ruthless character initially, she ends up having quite the redemptive arc. How did you interpret her change of heart? What moti-vates her? What do you think are your limits when it comes to sacrificing your moral code for money or power?

7. There are similarities between Nina and Maria, but there are also striking differences between the two women. Compare these two characters, and discuss how their ex-periences inform their means of survival. Did their resilience resonate with you? Did they provoke any reflection on your part?

8. Discuss the role of the secondary characters in *Look in the Mirror*. Who was your favorite? Which characters stood out to you, and why?

9. What do you think Steadman hoped to say with her cliffhanger ending, and the perpetuation of violence and the domination of the rich and powerful over the vulnerable?

10. Nina and John's memories together—though often reflective of a complicated relationship loaded with expectations—are crucial to Nina surviving the trials she faces. What is something a parent taught you that you carry with you? How has your past informed your present?

11. At the end of the novel, Nina remarks, "They are survivors, she knows that now, and if life isn't enough, they can always make it a game" (285). What do you take this to mean? How could one see life as a game?

12. Discuss each character's motivations for living and surviving. What motivates you?

13. After reading *Look in the Mirror*, are you motivated to try out an escape room . . . or will you want to avoid them forever?

14. "Chess is a game of strategy, but sometimes the best strategy is just to run" (250). Which is more important: brains or brawn?

ABOUT THE AUTHOR

CATHERINE STEADMAN is an author and screenwriter based in London. She grew up in the New Forest, Hampshire, and now lives in East London with her husband and two daughters. Catherine's first novel, *Something in the Water*, was a *New York Times* bestseller with rights sold in over thirty territories. She is also the author of *Mr. Nobody*, *The Disappearing Act*, and *The Family Game*, a *New York Times* Editors' Choice.

catherinesteadman.com
Instagram: @catsteadman
X: @CatSteadman

ABOUT THE TYPE

This book was set in a Monotype face called Bell. The Englishman John Bell (1745–1831) was responsible for the original cutting of this design. The vocations of Bell were many—bookseller, printer, publisher, typefounder, and journalist, among others. His types were considerably influenced by the delicacy and beauty of the French copperplate engravers. Monotype Bell might also be classified as a delicate and refined rendering of Scotch Roman.